WOLF'S MOUTH

a novel by **JOHN SMOLENS**

MICHIGAN STATE UNIVERSITY PRESS | *East Lansing*

Copyright © 2016 John Smolens

⊛ The paper used in this publication meets the minimum requirements of
ANSI/NISO Z39.48-1992 (R 1997) (Permanence of Paper).

Michigan State University Press
East Lansing, Michigan 48823-5245

Printed and bound in the United States of America.

26 25 24 23 22 21 20 19 18 17   1 2 3 4 5 6 7 8 9 10

LIBRARY OF CONGRESS CATALOGING-IN-PUBLICATION DATA
Smolens, John.
Wolf's mouth : a novel / by John Smolens.
pages ; cm
ISBN 978-1-61186-197-6 (hardcover : acid-free paper) – ISBN 978-1-60917-483-5 (pdf) –
ISBN 978-1-62895-258-2 (ebook) – ISBN 978-1-62896-258-1 (kindle)
I. Title.
PS3569.M646W65 2016
813'.54–dc23
2015018156

ISBN: 978-1-61186-270-6 (pbk.)

Book design by Charlie Sharp, Sharp Des!gns, East Lansing, Michigan
Cover design by David Drummond, Salamander Design, www.salamanderhill.com
Cover image is Grey Wolf Portrait (WV-9166) ©2014 Mark Graf and is used with
permission of the photographer (www.grafphoto.com). All rights reserved.

Michigan State University Press is a member of the Green Press Initiative and is committed to
developing and encouraging ecologically responsible publishing practices. For more information
about the Green Press Initiative and the use of recycled paper in book publishing, please visit
www.greenpressinitiative.org.

Visit Michigan State University Press at www.msupress.org

In Memory of

CARL EICHER

AMY ZEMMIN

■

For

ELLEN

Then & Now

■

I. 1944

1.

My mother often told the story about how I was born one afternoon in August 1919 in Macerata, a walled hill town that lies between the Sibillini Mountains and the Adriatic Sea. Usually she claimed that this sacred event occurred in the storeroom at the back of the family's shop, where cheese and sausages were kept cool, though sometimes she said it happened right on the stone floor behind the counter. Her telling likely included driving rain, thunder and lightning, and visions of angels and putti descending from the cathedral in nearby Loreto, though occasionally my father reminded her that the birth was brought on so swiftly because of the heat that often plagued Le Marche during the summer. The point was, always, that my mother worked every day in the shop while she was pregnant, which was intended to be instructive, if not inspirational, for she and my father both believed that one's life was measured by what one could endure, and how one could tolerate and adapt to any circumstance.

I was christened Francesco Giuseppe Verdi, in honor of our distant relative, the great composer, whose portrait hung next to the crucifix in our dining room. On my seventh birthday, we took the train north to visit Villa Verdi, which is outside of Busseto, near Parma. The mistress of the house was particular about the maestro's belongings; yet, because I had recently begun to study music, she allowed me to place my hands on the keys of one of the two pianos in his study. I played a chord, an A-minor, which resonated about us, causing her to daub her moist eyes and whisper, "So, Verdi lives." I believed that she was divulging a family secret, and for the rest of the day I wandered about the manor and its grounds, expecting to encounter the man whose portrait graced our dining room wall, his massive and intimidating white beard offset by humorous eyes illuminated by true genius.

Some dozen years later, it was apparent that I possessed none of the maestro's virtuosity for the piano or music composition. War was imminent and I was conscripted into the Italian army, and after several years of fighting in the *mezzogiorno*, the vast southern region of the Italian peninsula, my unit was shipped across the Mediterranean to fight with the German Afrika Korps. April 1943, we were captured by the Allies in Tangiers. After weeks of being confined to detention camps in the desert, we were marched to Casablanca and put aboard a ship bound for the United States. I was not seasick during the voyage, fortunately, but there were men who were ill for the duration of the three-week crossing. After we disembarked at the port city of Boston, we were sent west by train to Detroit, Michigan, and then north, to be ferried across the Mackinac Straits, and then taken on another train farther north and west, until we arrived in the spring of 1944 at Camp Au Train, which is outside the small town of Munising, on Lake Superior. There were a little over two hundred men imprisoned at this camp, which was one of five in the Upper Peninsula. As in all the camps, the majority of men held at Au Train were German soldiers, but there were also Austrians, Czechs, Poles, Hungarians, two Italians, and one Russian.

The journey from Boston to Michigan had been a revelation. It took longer than a train from Torino to Bari. American cities had not been bombed, as we had been told. There was an incredible amount of farmland, so much that the Po River valley would be lost in a state such as Michigan. I had never seen so many cars; they were substantial and well-made, but the remarkable thing was that most of them appeared to be owned by ordinary citizens. The architecture, however, was a disappointment. The houses were typically constructed of wood, and many were poorly maintained. Stone and brick were reserved for city buildings—town halls and post offices. These facilities lacked any sense of proportion and were uglier than anything Mussolini's architects had designed. At first this fact alone convinced me that though the Allies were going to win the war, America could not last because it was built out of wood.

But for the moment, our purpose was to cut down trees. The American military had so depleted the male labor force that prisoner-of-war camps had been established all over the country, housing more than 400,000 captured European soldiers. Some camps provided farm labor, while others, like ours, produced lumber. Toiling in Michigan's Upper Peninsula was healthy if tedious, but preferable to fighting in the African desert.

■　■　■

Geography had been a primary concern since we arrived at the camp, which was in the hills to the east of Au Train Lake, which fed Lake Superior a few miles to the north. Prisoners continued to attempt to escape, but their efforts routinely failed and only confirmed just how remote the camp was, there in the forest of Michigan's Upper Peninsula. Still, we were frequently drawing maps while planning to escape. The night before Corporal Gerhardt disappeared into the woods, Kommandant Vogel had instructed him to draw a map of the United States in the dirt with a stick. We were behind our bunkhouse, out of view of the guard towers, and about a dozen men stared down at the ground, speechless. Not simply because they couldn't comprehend what they were looking at, but because language was such a problem in the camp.

"It's not correct," I said. I was the highest-ranking member of the Italian army in the camp, a captain, and I spoke a fair amount of German, which naturally was the dominant language. Around me some of the other men whispered translations in Czech, Polish, and Hungarian.

"How can you say that?" Vogel demanded. He was a colonel. Because he was the ranking officer in the camp, he had assumed superiority over all of the prisoners, and we were required to address him as Kommandant. Among ourselves, we sometimes called him the Bird, which was what his name meant in German.

I took the stick from Gerhardt and pointed toward the map's east coast. "He forgot New York City, Kommandant."

"It's destroyed, completely," Vogel said.

I ignored this. "And San Francisco is not in Florida. And *this* is where Boston is—"

"What do you know of Boston?" the kommandant said.

"Our ship landed in Boston. I saw it on a map."

"Il Duce's soldiers can't read a map." Vogel looked around at the men and, after further translation, there was the obligatory laughter.

"*This* is Boston," I said, making an *x* with the stick. "And below that is New York, and down here is Washington, where President Roosevelt lives."

"Roosevelt?" Vogel said, folding his arms. "He's worse than Churchill: he's a drunk *and* a cripple. His ugly wife makes all the decisions."

"Maybe," I said. "But they live in the White House in Washington of the D.C., not—" and I pointed to the northwestern coast—"in Washington of the state, where George Washington was born." Though this too was translated, nobody dared laugh.

Behind me, Corporal Adino Agostino, the only other Italian in the camp, chuckled and said, "Gerhardt could walk to the White House. And Elena Roosevelt will fuck him many times, standing up, lying down, on her hands and knees, even sitting on top—and then she'll give him a souvenir, a signed photograph of President Roosevelt, and send him back to Germany."

"I don't want to go back to Germany," Gerhardt said. He did little work in the forest. He had proved most useful in the kitchen, peeling potatoes. I never knew how much Germans loved potatoes until I arrived at Camp Au Train. And beer. We could only get something called 3.2 beer, which meant that you had to drink many bottles to get a little drunk. It was preferable—more efficient—to buy the homemade potato mash from the Polish prisoners. There was no wine, ever.

"Where do you want to go, Gerhardt?" I asked.

"Milwaukee, Wisconsin," he said quietly. "A guard told me many Germans live there."

"I think it's down here," I said, pointing to the west side of Lake Michigan. "But it's hundreds of kilometers south. I think maybe Green Bay is closer."

"Are there many Germans in Green Bay?" Gerhardt asked.

I shook my head. "I'm not sure, but I may have cousins there." All the men looked at me in awe.

"Verdi means green," Adino explained. "So of course he has relatives there. And they are all related to the master who wrote *La Traviata*!" He began whistling "Libiamo Ne' Lieti Calici," and recognizing the melody to the "Drinking Song" the other men laughed.

Except Dimitri Sabaneyev, the Russian. He never laughed. He only stared fiercely at the rest of us as though he would kill us the first chance he got.

"When you get out of the woods," the kommandant said to Gerhardt, "you must do your duty. Kill Americans. Blow up trains. Destroy factories."

"And find an American girl with blond hair and a nice big bosom," Horst, one of the Czechs, said. "And destroy her with your thing."

"Whatever you do, Gerhardt," I said, rubbing out the map by dragging my boot across the dirt, "make sure you get back to camp before dark. Otherwise, you'll miss dinner."

.   ∎   ∎

Late the following afternoon we watched Gerhardt walk uphill across the clearing toward the line of uncut trees. He favored his right leg, which had been wounded in Africa. His timing was good because most of the POWs had already started down to the trucks that would return us to Camp Au Train, and the nearest guard was off somewhere in the bushes relieving himself. When Gerhardt reached the edge of the clearing, he was hard to see in the October twilight, which was hazy with sawdust from the day's cutting. He hesitated and looked back at Adino, me, and the German private who often worked with us, Wilhelm Ruup. Then Gerhardt walked off into the woods.

Adino blessed himself, saying, "I didn't think he'd really do it."

"At least he's walking in the right direction," I said. "South."

"He had no choice," Ruup said. "The kommandant ordered him to escape." He rested his shovel on his shoulder like a carbine, clicked the wood heels of his boots, and made a crisp military about-face. Like the other German prisoners, he wasn't allowed to wear the U.S. Army–issue boots with rubber heels, which were far more comfortable. Kommandant Vogel had ordered that all the Germans have wooden heels nailed to the soles of their own boots, so they could make a loud click when they came to attention.

I swung my axe up onto my shoulder and we walked down toward the trucks, dry leaves crackling beneath our feet. The guard emerged from the woods and followed us at a distance. His name was Shepherd, and we often referred to him as *the* Shepherd. This GI wasn't more than nineteen and he would never see combat—everyone knew the war wouldn't last another year.

"If Gerhardt doesn't return by dinner," Adino said, "a wolf might eat him."

"Coyotes," I said. "They're called coyotes."

"What's the difference?" Adino said. "You see them beyond the prison fence. They look hungry."

"One of the Americans told me that wolves are much bigger, and they're rare," I said. "But if Gerhardt did make it out of these woods, he might meet a woman."

Wilhelm looked back across the clearing. "What could Gerhardt do with a woman? He has only the one testicle left. I should follow him, in case he meets her and can't do it."

"Go then," I said. "Germany's virility is at stake." Wilhelm Ruup was a big man and he looked at me with hard eyes. He was often reminding us that because we were Italian we were naturally inferior. "Gerhardt will not find a woman," I said. "And he'll never make it to New York, or even Milwaukee."

"You heard the kommandant last night," Wilhelm said. "New York City has been destroyed."

"Vogel may believe such Nazi propaganda," Adino said, "but we know you don't."

Ruup said nothing—a good sign: he was learning to think for himself.

"Wilhelm," I said, "you saw the map last night. We are in the Upper Peninsula of Michigan. Gerhardt won't get out of these woods. He'll be back for dinner."

"What do you Italians know?"

"We live on a peninsula," I said. "It's hard to get off a peninsula covered with trees."

"The kommandant says it is our duty to try to escape."

"Then why has Kommandant Vogel never attempted to escape?" Adino asked.

"His men need him here," Ruup said.

"Or perhaps he needs the blankets," I said. "And the food that is plentiful."

"After the war they will shoot men like Vogel in Germany," Adino said.

"Do you really think so?" Ruup's voice began to quiver. The end of the war was a matter of great concern for the Germans. "He is a good soldier."

"He's a monster," I said. "And stop that. You always say it is the Italians who get emotional, but you find a reason to whimper every day."

"At least I don't cry over food, like Adino. Or that opera you listen to."

"Food and music are legitimate reasons to be sad," I said. "No race of men will be superior until they come to appreciate that fact."

"When I weep," Ruup said, "I weep for a woman."

"That, Wilhelm, is acceptable," I said. "There's hope for you yet."

Ahead we could see the other prisoners climbing into the trucks. I was twenty-four years old, and my muscles ached pleasantly from the day's labor of cutting wood. I had learned to try and not think too far beyond the next meal, which fortunately would be substantial. Even then, I had already come to understand that America was a great yet confusing country, but this was tempered by the fact that the food was ample.

■   ■   ■

Gerhardt didn't return in time for dinner. His absence seemed to quiet the entire camp, as though we were listening for him to come out of the woods, which this time of year smelled of dead leaves.

Au Train wasn't an ordinary prisoner-of-war camp. Before the war, it had existed for a number of years as a Civilian Conservation Corps camp, which had been built during the Depression, providing work for men who cultivated the forest and planted trees. The fact that Americans had stayed in these CCC camps was, to Vogel and his Nazi crowd, further evidence that the notion of democracy and freedom in the United States was another big lie. He was convinced that for years the American government had thrown its impoverished citizens into such camps, where they were worked to death, just as the Russians did in Siberia.

But the fact was, our camp was quite comfortable. Every one of the men staying there would admit that they were better housed and better fed than when they had been in the war. Even most of the Nazis, when they were out of Vogel's range, admitted this. The camp was a series of simple wooden buildings; there were latrines, a medical clinic, a large recreation area, and a central building designed for social functions. We held classes, performed music, produced plays and skits, and displayed arts and crafts. There was a canteen where a bottle of 3.2 beer could be purchased for ten cents. We were actually paid—eighty cents a day—to cut wood. There was a fence around the grounds, of course, and guard towers at each corner, but during the day the gates were often left open because work details came and went frequently. The gates were locked at night, but it would not have been difficult to get out—the lighting was poor, and there were many shadows along the perimeter.

The U.S. government made every attempt to adhere to the rules of the Geneva Convention regarding prisoners of war. Some believed this was because the

Americans were honest, decent people; others were convinced it was a matter of propaganda. It was both, really. Clearly, the U.S. government feared that to mistreat their prisoners would only encourage the Axis to do the same to American prisoners of war. We had heard that the Allies were air-dropping leaflets in Europe—leaflets signed by General Eisenhower himself—that promised excellent accommodations to German soldiers who surrendered. And conditions in the German army were such that more and more soldiers were giving up, approaching the Allies, waving leaflets. Such news infuriated Kommandant Vogel, and he liked to explain that in English "Allies" really meant "All lies."

We had sufficient access to news—newspapers, radio, movies—though Vogel was often trying to establish some kind of control over what we received. Some of the most reliable news arrived by the mail, both from our families in Europe and from relatives in other U.S. prisoner-of-war camps. The mail we received and sent out was censored by the Americans, and there were restrictions on how much we could send out: one letter and one postcard a week, and nothing over twenty-five lines. Adino, who was illiterate, asked me to write to his wife every week, until he learned to write well enough on his own in the Introduction to Italian class I was teaching two nights a week. He was remarkably proud of his first letter, which read: *Carissima Maria*, followed by *Ti amo* ("I love you"), written twenty-three times, followed by his name.

What we learned from other camps in the U.S. made most of us thankful that we were in Au Train. The Americans weren't the problem—it was the Nazis. They succeeded in taking over a camp, terrorizing any German prisoner who had been a Social Democrat before the war, or anyone who was not convincingly pro-Hitler. The only ones who were disturbed by the fact that we weren't under the same influence, naturally, were Vogel and his gang. Several of them were SS men, and they chafed at the fact that our camp operated so efficiently without being under complete Nazi control. So an incident such as Gerhardt not returning in time for dinner was for them a ray of hope. The men often sang while cutting down trees, believing that it would ward off an attack by wild animals, and I wondered if Gerhardt might actually be eaten by a bear or a wolf.

There were stories about other breaks that had occurred before I arrived at Au Train. Communication between the five camps in the Upper Peninsula of Michigan was frequent, particularly with Camp Evelyn, which was not far to the east. There were stories about men walking into nearby small towns. Evidently, many of the Americans living in the U.P. weren't even aware that prisoners of war were being held in camps out in the woods. So on several occasions, prisoners who entered a town were treated cordially, despite the fact that they were either wearing the military uniform of a foreign country, or wearing a prisoner's outfit, which included the letters *PW* on their shirts and trousers. In such cases, a member of the local law enforcement would be notified by the prison command, and soon the prisoners would be escorted back to camp, often to be greeted as though they'd been on a pleasant holiday.

But one break from a Michigan prison had been somewhat successful. Several prisoners escaped, and though most were quickly picked up, two of them were not. It soon became clear that they were on the run with one of the guards. Often when we were drawing maps in the dirt, there would be speculation about how these three might get out of the United States and return to Europe. Some, who paid little attention to maps, insisted that they could sail from San Francisco and cross the Atlantic. Adino suggested that they might swim to Cuba. I didn't understand why they would want to go back to Europe, at least until the war was over. But then I didn't have a wife and children, like many of the men, and my parents and sister, who wrote to me regularly, seemed safe in their villa in Macerata. I was most curious about whatever possessed the American guard who ran off with these two prisoners.

2.

In the morning we were awakened by machine gun fire echoing in the hills.

"That's about a half kilometer off in the woods," Adino said, climbing down from his bunk, which was above mine. He led me to the door, where we could look out across the yard. Nothing seemed out of the ordinary. It was dawn and the men were going about their morning routines. None of the guards in the towers and at the gates seemed unusually alert.

"It's dinner," I said. "They just shot dinner."

After breakfast, a group of us were taken in a truck out to a place where there were seven dead deer mowed down by machine gun fire. It was our morning's work to dress out the carcasses and bring the meat back to camp. Adino, who descended from generations of butchers in Naples, was expert at cutting meat. Because we arrived back in camp at noon, which was unusual for a weekday, we were fed lunch, a thick, salty soup of barley, carrots, onion, and chunks of venison. Afterwards we were given some free time, so Adino and I kicked the soccer ball around, discussing strategy for our upcoming match against Camp Evelyn. They were fielding an all-German team and had tied us, 2-2, a few weeks earlier. We agreed that the next time we needed to take advantage of our smaller size and use our speed.

When a truck stopped by the recreation field, the Shepherd, who was driving, told us to climb up in the bed. At first we thought he was going to take us out to where the other men were cutting wood, but the truck took a different route and soon we were on a paved road, the cold fall wind blasting our faces.

"We are going into the village!" Adino shouted, happy like a child.

"Just remember what your loving wife Maria said at the end of her last letter." He looked away in shame. "She said, 'When you go to bed at night, don't forget your prayers, and don't yank on your beloved thing so much because I want you to have plenty left when you come home.'" She only mentioned the prayers, of course. I added the rest because I was tired of waking up in the middle of the night with our bunk bed shaking to the point that it might collapse.

"I can't *help* it," Adino said, blessing himself. "When we go into town and see women..."

"Maybe I should blindfold you until we're safely back in camp. Or at night, tie your hands together in prayer. Or behind your back, like a prisoner."

"*Boh!*"

The truck entered Munising, a town that looked out on a spectacular harbor. All around us, steep wooded hills of red and orange foliage descended to a wide channel of blue water. Several miles out was an island, Grand Island, and in the distance beyond that we could see Lake Superior.

The Shepherd parked in front of a grocery store and we followed him inside, where there were sacks waiting to be loaded on the truck: potatoes, rice, carrots, onions, beans. Adino and I went back and forth, a sack on each shoulder.

"We will eat better than the pope," Adino said. "Except there's never any pasta. What kind of a country is this that's never heard of *farfalla* or *tagliatelle* or—"

"I made *tagliatelle* last night," a woman said from the next aisle—in Italian.

We went around to the next aisle. The woman was certainly over fifty years old and looked like she had spent her life in a medieval village. Her coat, dress, shoes, and scarf were black. She stared at the canned goods on the shelves with disdain.

"*Buongiorno, Signora,*" I said.

She continued to scrutinize the cans. "All this English, and I forgot my glasses. Can you read this?"

I looked at the label. "Whole tomatoes," I said. "*Pomodori.*"

She shrugged and dropped the can in her basket. "We moved here from the Soo and no one speaks Italian here."

"They speak Italian in the . . . Soo?" I asked.

"Sault Ste. Marie," she said. "Large Italian population there because of the plants and the mining." For the first time she looked me over, smiling at the sight of what remained of my uniform. "A couple of Mussolini's boys?"

"*No, Signora.*"

"The trains may run on time, but I will never go back. *Never.*"

She hobbled up the aisle to the counter, where there was a cash register. "Chiara!" she nearly shouted. "Come help me get these out to the car."

Adino tugged on my sleeve and I turned around. In the corner by the front window there was a red-and-white Coca-Cola machine. A girl with a mass of dark hair was leaning against it. She finished her Coke, slid the green bottle into the wood crate on the floor, and walked past us toward the counter. She might have been twenty and she wore a white sweater and blue jeans.

"Oh my God," Adino whispered.

"Shut up and keep your hands in your pockets."

Her blue jeans were rolled up so that we could see the lower half of her slender calves. Her thick hair was absolutely black and tumbled over her shoulders. She took a small package from the counter and again walked past us without acknowledging that we were standing there. The front door slammed behind her, and through the window we could see her climb behind the wheel of a gray Ford sedan.

Adino started toward the counter, but I caught his sleeve. "Remember, Maria's waiting." His face bunched with confusion. I went up to the counter and took both paper bags, and said to the woman, "*Posso, Signora?*"

She was counting out coins from a small purse—black, of course—and without looking at me said, "Put them in the back seat."

I walked to the door, which Adino rushed to open for me. Before I stepped outside, he reached up and brushed the hair back from my forehead. "Shut up," I said.

Out on the sidewalk, I leaned down to the open window on the driver's side of the car. "Your mother would like these on the back seat," I said.

She didn't seem to hear me as she stared out the front windshield. I had a difficult time opening the back door with both arms full, but I managed to set the bags on the seat.

"Put them on the floor," she said in English.

"*Mi perdoni?*"

"Put them on the *floor* so they don't spill over when I come to a *stop*."

"*Sì.*"

"And stop with the Italian. Where'd you get that accent?"

"Italy."

"Never been there."

"You should go someday," I said in English. "But I'd wait until the war's over."

For the first time she turned her head, her hair falling down across her breast. Glaring at me, she said, "*Perché?*"

"Because . . ." But I couldn't continue. She stared at me with her large, dark eyes as though I were hopeless, which was true.

Adino opened the door of the grocery store and helped the old woman down the steps, but she pulled her arm free of his grasp when she reached the sidewalk. I went around to the other side of the car and opened the door, but didn't dare touch her as she struggled to climb up onto the front seat. When I closed the door, she raised a hand and said impatiently, "*Andiamo.*" Chiara put the Ford in gear and pulled out into the street.

Adino came out on the sidewalk and we both watched the car in silence. When the Shepherd came out, we jumped up into the back of the truck. We kept our eyes on the Ford, which was a block ahead of us, until it slowed down and a long, slender arm came out the window. Chiara had pushed the sleeve of her white sweater up, and as she made the signal for a left turn I thought I'd never seen a more graceful hand and forearm. The car turned into the side street, and as we passed through the intersection we saw it pull into a driveway in front of an old house—an old house for America, something built maybe fifty years earlier, a wooden house painted white.

"Did you *see* her?" Adino said as the truck climbed the hill up out of Munising. "Did you see those calves? Did you see *those?*" He cupped his hands beneath imaginary breasts.

I had seen all of it. "Shut up," I said.

We didn't say another word during the trip back to camp. When we reached the gate, one of the guards, a tall one named Bobby, waved for the Shepherd to stop. Bobby got in the passenger seat and, to our surprise, the truck turned around rather than entering the prison yard. We drove through the woods for about twenty minutes, first taking several logging roads, and then turning down a two-track that ran through a dense stand of pines.

"We have never been out this way to cut wood," Adino said.

We came to a clearing where several other GIs were waiting. They had two dogs with them on leashes—German Shepherds, heeling next to the soldiers. One of the men waved with both arms, indicating that he wanted the truck to back down a path toward a stand of trees. It was dark in there and Adino and I had to duck and push branches out of our way, until we saw Gerhardt, hanging by the neck from the branch of a maple tree. It looked like he didn't have any bones left—his uniform and coat appeared to be in danger of sliding off his limp body. The Shepherd stopped the truck where Gerhardt was hanging above the sacks of potatoes.

Bobby climbed up into the truck bed, a long-bladed knife in hand. "Take hold."

Reluctantly, Adino and I stepped up to Gerhardt and put our arms around him. Adino looked at me with panic in his eyes, and I could smell it: shit. Bobby reached up and cut the rope just above the noose. All of Gerhardt's weight came down on us, and for a moment I thought we were going to lose our balance, but we managed to lay him down so that his back was on top of a sack of potatoes. I wanted to remove the noose from Gerhardt's neck, but I didn't dare touch him any more.

When Bobby got in the truck, the other GIs and the dogs jumped up into the bed. During the drive back to camp, Adino and I leaned against the back of the cab, and the two GIs sat on the tailgate with their legs dangling. No one spoke, but one of them offered us cigarettes, which we accepted. The dogs curled up by Gerhardt's feet and went to sleep.

∎　　∎　　∎

Like all prisoners of war, I arrived in the United States full of misconceptions. The most significant, perhaps, was that the Americans weren't who I thought they were—not in Michigan's Upper Peninsula, at least. I was exhausted and disoriented after the African campaign, and suddenly we were delivered to what seemed to be a forest as big as the desert. The Americans call it the forest primeval. The Americans we had contact with—people from surrounding towns that came and went from our camp, as well as the guards—I could not believe they were really Americans. Many of them were Finnish, or from another country in Scandinavia. Some were French Canadian or Indians. It was not uncommon to hear them speak languages other than English. At first I thought that they too were prisoners in this cold, isolated place. It wasn't the result of the war, however, but some other great, nameless tragedy that involved migration. An American diaspora.

My English was very limited when I first arrived at Camp Au Train, but at least I had some, and I was quickly identified as one who could be used for purposes of communication between the prisoners and the Americans. The result was that my English improved, and it wasn't long before I was giving evening classes in Italian and English conversation to the other prisoners. And because I spoke English, I was often thrust into situations that allowed me to talk with Americans. Soon I realized that the reason many of these people were in northern Michigan was because they were indeed immigrants, and their families had come from Europe to find work in mines throughout the region. Copper, iron ore, silver mines, which required men with strong backs. The other thing that became clear was that many of these Americans had lived in this remote forest for years, so long that there had been a great deal of intermarriage; thus they would often explain to me how they were one-half Finnish, one-quarter French, one-eighth Ojibwa, and the rest might consist of family lines of undetermined origin. I understood this to some degree because I had Austrian and Swiss ancestors on my mother's side, which was why, I had always been told, I had black hair and a Mediterranean complexion but light blue eyes.

But there was something else about these Americans that baffled me. They were not unhappy with their situation. They weren't overjoyed either, but most of them possessed a level of acceptance that I found truly remarkable. I was in northern Michigan because of the war; I had every hope that I would survive (like most other prisoners, I was pleased to be out of the fighting) and eventually return home. But these Americans seemed content to stay here. They worked—and worked hard constantly—they had homes, they married, they had children, and they had no desire or intention to ever leave. In fact, one of the guards, who was from Marquette, the largest town in the region, said he had never been south of the Mackinac Straits and vowed he never would be. This was an absolute revelation for me. It seemed that the rest of America, the place where there were enormous cities and vast farmlands, was vile and tainted as though harboring some sort of plague. By contrast, he viewed these north woods, frozen and barren much of the year, as a wholesome, pristine haven, where man, animal, and Nature, capital N, could thrive.

Our camp functioned well because the Germans, who constituted the majority of the inmates, actually ran the camp. Say what you will about Nazis, but they understood organization. They took great pride in being neater, more punctual and efficient than anyone else. They drove us crazy with their inspections, drills, codes, and regulations, but the camp was inhabitable largely because they made it so. The Americans often referred to Au Train as the "Fritz Ritz," and though our accommodations were quite Spartan, all of us came to realize that daily life in many other camps around the United States (even the ones in warm places such as Arizona) could be much worse.

I had arrived at Camp Au Train in May, when the ground under the shade of the trees was still covered with patches of snow—winter did not really end until June that year. The Allies had taken Rome that month, and then within days there was the assault on the coast of Normandy. We knew that it was only a matter of time before Italy would be liberated, and Hitler's Axis was going to lose the war. This gave hope to many of us who longed to return home. But for some it was extremely unsettling. The German prisoners could be broken into two categories: the Nazis, of course, and the Germans—men who had fought out of a sense of patriotism to their country, not to Adolf Hitler. And these two groups could be divided into two subcategories: officers and enlisted men. The rest of us—an assortment of Eastern Europeans, two Italians, and one Russian—were at best tolerated, at worst treated as an imposition.

In retrospect, it's easy to see things in a larger, historical context. But at the time, considering the fact that we were all tucked away in this northern outpost where our only real concern was survival against boredom and the elements, Vogel's response to world events was perplexing and increasingly threatening. When it was becoming clear that Germany was going to lose the war, it brought about a change in the kommandant—a tightening, an intensification like I have seen in no man before or since. He became more determined that here in Camp Au Train, Nazi ideals would prevail.

■   ■   ■

When we returned to camp with Gerhardt's body, it was early evening, and other prisoners gathered round the truck to see him draped across our foodstuffs, until Vogel gave the order to his men to push everyone back. Adino and I remained standing in the truck as Vogel alone approached the vehicle and inspected Gerhardt. The kommandant had a smooth-shaven jaw and a savage squint; though he wasn't yet forty, the skin around his eyes was dark, aged well beyond his years. Something in his stare was always searching for the flaw, the error, the weakness.

"I smell excrement," he said without looking at either of us. "He's lying on our potatoes in the last shit of his pathetic life. How are we to eat these potatoes?"

"It's still in his pants, Kommandant," I offered.

He raised his head and aimed his squint in my direction, as though he were surveying the atmosphere I inhabited. "Are you suggesting we eat this dead man's shit?"

"No, sir. But the potatoes can be washed, peeled, and boiled until they're clean."

The logic of this seemed to stun him for a moment. "*Clean?* And who will clean them?"

"Sir, they will be as clean as any potato you've ever eaten in Germany."

"They had better be," he said, stepping back from the truck. "You will both unload this truck, and you will prepare the potatoes tonight."

Adino looked at me quickly. "Sir," I said. "We are not on the schedule for kitchen duty tonight."

"You are now," he said. "And I will send an officer to inspect the potatoes." Vogel looked out at the men, who stood in a semicircle around the back of the truck, and they immediately snapped to attention, clicking their heels. "This man," the kommandant said, nodding toward Gerhardt's body, "could not fulfill his duty. He escaped, but he did not do his utmost to harass the enemy. So! He took the only other course of action: he killed himself. This is not an honorable act. It is not what we expect from German soldiers. This body will not be given a soldier's burial. But—but he was a German." He looked at two privates standing at one end of the group. "You men will take him and inter him before dinner." He started to move through the crowd, which parted for him.

Adino and I spent the next few hours washing, peeling, and boiling the potatoes, which the cooks then added to a stew consisting of venison, onions, and carrots. At dinner I stood between Wilhelm Ruup and Adino as we moved down the service line. "I don't understand why he would kill himself," Adino said.

"Perhaps he didn't," Ruup said.

"It is strange," I said. "He just stops suddenly in the woods and decides to hang himself." I took my bowl of stew from the counter and moved toward the bread.

Wilhelm stared at the bowl in his hand and said to the cook, "That's not enough. It's not as much as the others are getting."

The cook took the bowl from him and for a moment he looked like he was going to throw it in Wilhelm's face, but then he put it down on the counter and picked up another bowl. "Does this one look better?" he asked pleasantly. If anything, it had more stew than the others.

"Yes, better," Wilhelm said as he took the bowl.

We sat at our usual place, a long table near the south windows. Adino called it *Il Tavola di Calcio*, because it was where the members of the soccer team sat. As a captain in the Italian army, I was allowed to sit at the officer's table, which was on a small riser at the front of the hall, but as captain of the soccer team I preferred to sit by the windows, where we could discuss strategy. It was mostly German officers who sat up front anyway. At our table were sixteen men: several Czechs, Hungarians, and Poles; a Serb; a Croat; the Russian; and two Germans, Wilhelm Ruup and our goalie, Rudi Brandt. As captain and coach, I was largely responsible for assembling this squad. We had held tryouts, and these sixteen constituted the best talent the camp had to offer. Predictably, Vogel had questioned the fact that there were only two Germans on the team, and because of him the camp had come to refer to us as the League of Nations.

"Potatoes," Adino muttered, dipping his bread into his bowl. "After this war I will never eat a potato again."

The men at the table laughed.

Wilhelm said, "The venison, Adino, is cut to perfection."

"For generations we have been the best butchers in Naples. Here, one must know how to find and remove the bullets without causing too much damage to the meat. Bullets can be very bad for the teeth." He ate slowly, while Wilhelm, sitting across from us, was eating rapidly, as always. He was our biggest player, a defender, and often when he finished eating first, someone at the table would give him something from their plate. The portions were that large. Adino said, "What I would like—"

"Don't start," I said.

"What I would like is some oregano, and maybe a little fresh basil."

"Just eat," I said.

"Or pesto, with some garlic," he nearly sang. "Or a little pancetta, a couple of eggs, and a teaspoon of Parmesan cheese—*carbonara*."

Wilhelm stopped eating, and he looked curiously at both of us for a moment and then began chewing his food again, and slowly we witnessed a remarkable transformation. His method of chewing changed—he seemed to be trying to locate something in his mouth that tasted foul—and then his face began to contort as his eyes bulged. He wasn't chewing now, but trying to expel something from his mouth, and suddenly blood broke forth from his lips. Leaning over he choked and gagged as clumps of masticated food emptied into his bowl. The entire hall became silent. Wilhelm stood up and staggered toward the front door, but he collapsed on the floor, his mouth and chin covered in blood.

3.

Wilhelm spent the night in the infirmary and was tended to by the camp's medical staff. There was wild speculation in the barracks: the Americans were trying to poison us; it was a rare disease—influenza, or even the black plague—that would ravage the camp. No one got much sleep.

In the morning Adino complained about his breakfast. "I am eating this—Wheaties?" he asked, running his spoon through his bowl. "What is this 'Breakfast of *Campions*'?"

"Not *kaa*," I said. "*Chaa. Cha*mpions. Like *cena*."

"*Cena—chay-na*—is dinner," he said. It was bad enough that I was trying to teach him how to write in his native language; he couldn't accept that I was now telling him how to pronounce English. "This is . . . I don't know what this is."

"Adino, it says on the box: 'Corn flakes.'"

"What is 'flakes'? My mother never fed me *flakes*."

I pushed my bowl of Wheaties away and stood up. The other members of the soccer team gazed at me. "You know, Adino, you're absolutely right."

He put down his spoon. "I am?"

I left the mess hall and went to the commanding officer's headquarters. His assistant, Corporal Marks, was sitting in the outer office. He was nearly deaf due to an explosive device that had been detonated during a training exercise in boot camp. He put his newspaper down on his desk and shouted, "What?"

"I wish to speak to the commander," I said loudly. "It is about the food."

"*What?*"

There was a pad of paper on his desk. I picked up a pencil and wrote on the top sheet: WE WANT PASTA.

We were often told that Au Train was one of the smallest prisoner-of-war camps in the United States. This was their response any time we had a request or a complaint: Au Train was too small for special consideration. Corporal Marks looked at the pad of paper and nearly shouted. "What is 'pasta'?"

Slowly I said, "*Spa-ghet-ti.*"

The door beyond Marks's desk opened and Commander Donald Dalrymple peered out at us. He had a mustache that Americans called "pencil-thin." "Sir," I said, coming to attention.

"Yes, yes," Dalrymple said. He was not one for military etiquette. We were a small camp, so we told ourselves that Commander Dalrymple was what we got. The prisoners called him "Uncle Donald." He had also been reading the newspaper, which he still held in his hand. "What's this about spaghetti?" He had an accent unlike any of the other Americans at the camp; one of the guards told us that he'd been stationed up in Michigan as a reprimand, for what no one seemed to know, and no one knew where he was from—my English wasn't good enough to tell whether he was from the South, New England, or any of the other parts of the country where people have distinct accents.

"Commander Dalrymple," I said. "I wish to request that we have spaghetti for dinner. At least once a week. It is stated in the Geneva Convention rules that prisoners should be fed a diet they are accustomed to, and that means the Italian prisoners are entitled to eat pasta." I didn't know what the Geneva Convention said about food for prisoners, if it said anything at all, but we had learned soon after arriving in Au Train that the Americans were petrified at the thought of not complying with these regulations. "It's in Article 32, sir."

Marks had been leaning toward me, trying to read my lips, but now he turned toward the commander and shouted, "He's complaining about the *food*, sir."

Dalrymple's face went blank, and Marks seemed to understand that his assistance wasn't necessary. The commander then smiled at me as he folded his newspaper under his arm. He came over to Marks's desk and rested one haunch on the corner. This was part of his uncle routine; he was going be straight with me, as he liked to say. "I'll be straight with you, Captain Verdi. Ours isn't a very big prisoner-of-war camp and the government, well, it doesn't give us everything we ask for. I am aware that they make spaghetti at some of the other camps. But there is a war going on and, as you know, there are shortages. The reason you men are up here is because there's a shortage of manpower. Pulp wood is necessary to the war effort."

"Sir," I said. "As you know, nearly every day we eat venison, carrots, potatoes—a great amount of potatoes. It is not what we eat in the Italian army."

"Captain, you're just upset because that soldier took ill at dinner last night."

"I am making a formal request, sir," I said.

"Based on the Geneva Convention—I believe it was, what, Article 32?" The ends of the commander's pencil-thin mustache lifted slightly. He thought he was humoring me. The commander did so—he called it giving me "the time of day"—because I was useful: I acted as a translator and, more important, I was captain and coach of the camp's soccer team. "And if I deny your request?" the commander asked.

"I will make a request in writing," I said loudly. "And I will send it to Mrs. Roosevelt."

Marks coughed. The commander almost lifted his haunch off the corner of the desk, but then, as if to restrain himself, he unfolded his arms, causing the newspaper to fall to the floor with a slap.

"Captain," the commander said, "we provide you with a nutritional diet, one that's far better than what I'm sure you got when you were in combat—I know it's better than what our own troops are eating, and even better than what many American citizens are eating. In fact, I was just reading a column in the newspaper accusing the government of 'coddling' you prisoners of war. Your English is quite good—you used the word 'entitled' correctly. Do you know what 'coddling' means, Captain?"

"Is it something you eat, a kind of baby fish?"

He shook his head. "Coddling is somewhat like entitlement. It means giving prisoners anything they want, like spoiled babies. It's upsetting to Americans who have sons overseas eating K-rations. My God, last week we managed to get in a shipment of pork chops and pickled herring!"

"Sir," I said. "In my letter to your First Lady I will mention the Geneva Convention, and the venison."

"What about the venison?"

"They're hunted illegally, sir. We often see hunters in the woods—they all have licenses pinned on their hats or jackets. Your guards shoot the deer with machine guns, and I don't see any licenses on their uniforms."

"Well, at least they're not breaking the Geneva Convention regulations." The commander smiled, but when he saw that I wouldn't, he held out both hands, pleading. "Captain Verdi, where am I going to find spaghetti up here?"

"In Munising, sir."

"In Munising?"

"Yes, sir. There's an Italian woman—I don't know her name, but I know where she lives. When we were getting supplies yesterday she told me that she made pasta in her home."

The commander raised both hands as though he was going to lift the air off his shoulders, but then he grabbed his head. His short gray hair bristled between his fingers. "Captain, I can't ask some woman in Munising to make pasta for over two hundred men."

"Two men, sir. For myself and Private Adino Agostino."

The commander sighed and then stood up. This was to indicate that he was a reasonable man and that he had come to a decision. Looking at his assistant, he said loudly, "All right, Marks. You have to take that German soldier to the doctor this morning anyway. And you take Captain Verdi along with you and"—he picked up his newspaper and started back toward his office—"see that this man gets his spaghetti."

"Sir," I said, and the commander stopped at his door and looked at me. "Wilhelm Ruup needs to go to the doctor?"

"Yes, Captain. We only have your medical officers who were trained for combat duty on duty here. And, as you know, there are the regular visits from the Red Cross. But we do provide proper medical attention—in accordance with the Geneva Convention—and so we are sending Ruup to see a doctor in Munising."

"What's wrong with him, sir?" I asked. "Was there a bullet in the meat?"

"Bullet?" The commander ran a finger along one side of his mustache as he studied me, trying to determine whether I could be trusted with highly sensitive information. "No, terrible accident," he said finally. "Apparently, the man ingested glass."

"Ingested?" I said. "I'm sorry, sir, I do not understand this word."

"He ate crushed glass, Captain."

. . .

I helped Marks get Wilhelm into the commander's Jeep, which had a white star in a circle painted on the hood. Wilhelm sat in the back seat, his head wrapped in a towel. He had the eyes of a man in considerable pain. As we drove out of the woods, the Jeep bucked over the corrugated two-track lane, but Corporal Marks whistled loudly, completely off-key. Each time I turned around, Ruup looked worse, and finally I touched Marks's sleeve and said, "Could you stop that whistling, please?" He did, and when I glanced back at Ruup he nodded carefully in gratitude.

The doctor's house had a view of the vast harbor in Munising. It was the first time I'd been in an American home, and the waiting room had comfortable sofas and chairs, and copies of *Life*, *Look*, and *National Geographic* were laid out on a coffee table. Marks quickly leafed through the *National Geographic*, pausing at photographs of dark-skinned bare-breasted women. From the front windows of the waiting room I could see down the main street to the intersection where Chiara and her mother had turned left in their Ford. For some reason, the image of her languid forearm and hand making the turn signal was more vivid than anything else. Through much of the night I had tried to recall her fine ankles, her slender calves, her breasts beneath the white sweater, her black hair cascading down her back, but it was the image of that arm that tormented me.

"Corporal Marks," I said, and waited for him to look up and stare at my mouth. I nodded toward the office door. "This could take a while, particularly if Ruup has ingested much glass."

"Are you in a hurry to get back to work?" Marks asked pleasantly.

"No." I smiled. "When I was impatient as a boy, my father always used to say, 'No one is following you.'"

"Right. My father used to say, 'What, are your pants on fire?'"

"While we wait," I said slowly, "I could go to request the pasta." I pointed out the window. "The Italian woman's house is just down the street there."

"You want to go over and ask while I wait here?"

I nodded, and to my surprise he shrugged.

"Are you sure?"

"Do I trust you?" Marks almost shouted. And then he laughed. "You really don't have any idea how far you are from anyplace else, do you. I'll pick you up."

"*Molto grazie, Signore.*"

Though I knew he couldn't read my lips, Marks nodded his head.

There was the clearest blue sky overhead, and a gusting north wind came off Lake Superior, swirling leaves up into little tornadoes that scuttled down the empty street. Some say you can only smell oceans, but that day I could smell the lake; it didn't smell like anything else, just a great big lake with deep water that remained cold year-round. I knew that the water we drank at the camp came from the lake and it was the best water I had ever tasted. Walking by myself down that blustery street I felt like lake water—nothing but water, clear through.

This may seem strange, a man wearing a prison uniform with *PW* stenciled in large letters on his clothes, walking alone down the main street of an American town. But no one seemed to notice. Only a few cars passed by and none of them stopped or slowed down. I was just a man on the street, and I had not felt so liberated since before I entered the Italian army and this God-awful war. I was also nervous with anticipation, and despite the chilly air, I was sweating beneath my shirt. After crossing the intersection, I walked up the street to the white clapboard house with the Ford parked in the driveway. At the front door I saw that a piece of paper had been taped above the doorbell: *Frangiapani.* In a country where many people have short, blunt names—Jim, Bill, Ann, Beth—I was relieved to be standing in front of a house occupied by someone named Frangiapani. As soon as I pressed the doorbell I heard voices inside, and then footsteps, and after a moment the door was yanked open. There was a storm door between us, and the way Chiara gazed through the glass you'd think she had never seen a man before—she seemed frozen in the moment, and I too could do nothing but stare back at her.

Then her mother pushed her aside and opened the door. "At last," she said in Italian. "You have finally escaped from that prison out in the woods."

"No, Signora Frangiapani, really I haven't—"

"Come in," she urged. "We will hide you in the attic."

"Signora—" I began, but she took me by the sleeve, pulled me into the house, and slammed the door shut. "Really, I'm not—"

"In the last war," she said to her daughter, "we hid many boys. Italians, Austrians, a Serb who was wounded and died slowly. That's how I met your father, you know."

Chiara sighed, and said in English, "Yes, Mother, I know. He spent months on your farm until the war ended, and you were married in the spring."

Her mother looked up at me sadly. "Her father, Renaldo, was an officer. Older than the other soldiers, but he was a man, a fine man. I bore him two children. Shortly after we came to America the oldest, young Renaldo, died of influenza. This broke his father's aging heart, and my husband died less than a year later. So this one I have raised by myself."

Chiara was nearly beside herself with embarrassment, and her dark eyes were angry.

"Signora Frangiapani, please," I said. "I only come to make a small request."

But the old woman took Chiara by the arm—today the girl was wearing a purple short-sleeve blouse and she had the finest black hair on her forearms. "Chiara, we must get blankets for him, and candles—but," she said, turning to me, "you *must* be careful about light at night. A light in the attic will surely give you away."

And then Chiara lost it. She pulled her arm free from her mother's grip and both women began shouting at each other, the daughter in English and her mother in Italian. They were so vehement, I was tempted to slip out the front door and run away, but I couldn't take my eyes off Chiara.

"*Abbastanza,*" I said politely, but their arguing only became even more vehement. Finally, I took both of them by the wrist and shouted, "*Basta!*"

They both fell silent and stared at me.

"Now," I said in English. "I have come only to ask if I could buy some pasta."

Chiara, who calmly removed my hand from her wrist, said, "You want *what?*"

"The food at the camp, it's—you said you made pasta. Could I buy some for myself and Adino, the other Italian prisoner?" I put my hand in my trousers pocket and pulled out a small wad of paper. "I have no money. They don't pay us in real money, but they give us these coupons that we can use at the PX and the canteen. When the American corporal comes to pick me up, I will ask him to trade some U.S. money for these coupons, which he can use at the canteen. And if this is not enough, I would be glad to trade something else with him. The guards, they like souvenirs—buttons, hats, anything from our military uniforms. It's like currency to them."

First, Chiara revealed *un sorriso*—a hint of a smile—and then she laughed. It was the first time I'd seen and heard her do so, and it was like bathing in one of the gorgeous arias written by the great Verdi. Her mother, however, went over to the living room couch and sat down heavily. "You have not escaped from prison?"

"No, Signora. I gave the corporal my word that I would not run away."

Chiara stopped laughing. "And where would you go?"

I nodded.

"*I* can't get away from here," she said, "and I am free to go where I please."

She folded her arms and looked toward the picture window in an effort, I believe, to conceal her face from me. I looked at her long, black hair against the back of her blouse, trying to lock that image in my mind, but then through the picture window I saw the commander's Jeep pull up in front of the house.

"I wouldn't take your money, or coupons, or your buttons for a little pasta," Signora Frangiapani said. She pushed herself up out of the sofa and shuffled into the kitchen.

I went to the picture window and waved to Corporal Marks, indicating that I would be out in a minute. Ruup sat in the back seat, the lower part of his head now wrapped in a bandage, with only a small hole over the mouth.

"What's the matter with him?" Chiara asked.

"He had an accident."

She looked at me. "You don't sound like you believe what you say."

This took me by surprise—she had never spoken to me this way before. "No, actually, I don't—it wasn't an accident. Somebody didn't break some glass, sweep it up, and mistakenly put it in his bowl of stew."

Chiara leaned back from me slightly. "It was intentional?"

"The glass was ground up very small, so it wouldn't be detected."

In dismay, she put a hand to her chin and ran her forefinger over her lips, and I knew that this was the image that I would recall later. Her mouth was full and wide; it seemed to possess its own language, neither English nor Italian.

Her mother came back into the living room, a brown paper bag in her hand. "I don't have much left. We will have to make more after Mass on Sunday."

She handed the bag to me, and inside, the hard coils of uncooked fettuccine resembled pale bird nests. "Signora, I must pay you—"

She shook her head. "Not one word, please."

I went to the door and opened it, but as I had my hand on the knob of the storm door I turned around. Signora Frangiapani looked at me sorrowfully, and then she blessed herself and began whispering a prayer in Latin. Her daughter folded her arms and studied me as though trying to determine if I was real, or something that she was imagining. Behind me, Corporal Marks's whistle was impatient and off-key.

4.

That night Wilhelm rested in his bunk, while in the mess hall the men inspected their food carefully. Everyone knew that the doctor had pumped out Ruup's stomach, and that forceps had been used to remove the larger slivers of glass embedded inside his cheeks and tongue.

At the soccer table other members of the team dissected their venison pot pie as though they were performing a delicate surgical operation, and they watched with grave apprehension as Adino and I ate our fettuccine. We had gone into the kitchen early, commandeered one of the stoves, and boiled a large pot of water. In a skillet, we had no choice but to prepare a simple sauce: butter (when we asked one of the cooks if they had olive oil, he offered us Crisco), salt, pepper, onion, one dried-up clove of garlic, and some grated cheese from Wisconsin. At the dinner table, we ignored our teammates as we leaned over our plates, twirled with our forks, and ate without pausing. Adino kept shaking his head as he sucked long strands of pasta into his mouth, and at one point I thought he was going to cry.

After dinner, one of the officers tapped his fork against a metal water pitcher, indicating that Kommandant Vogel would address the men. As Vogel stood up on the platform, it occurred to me that his head resembled a fist. That squint, combined with his bunched eyebrows, his pinched mouth, even his blunt nose, all suggested tight knuckles. "Today is a day," he began, "that we need to give thanks to our Führer because without his guidance and inspiration . . ."

Adino snorted, causing a couple of Germans at the next table to glare at him. What this little speech meant was that certain instructions would soon be conveyed through the ranks—not here, where there were several GI guards present, but later, when officers would visit the barracks. The kommandant went on for several minutes, spitting out the usual platitudes about the Fatherland (never once in these inspirational homilies would he acknowledge that some of us were not German), and when he was through, he snapped to attention. Over two hundred men in the hall bolted to their feet, heels were clicked, arms were raised, and there came a resounding *"Heil Hitler!"* All of us, regardless of what country we were from, went along with this because if we didn't, one of the Nazis would take notice. Adino made a clicking sound with his mouth.

There was a half hour of free time until evening classes began. I went back to my bunk to collect my books. One of the remarkable benefits of being a POW in the United States was that it was possible to take university courses. For months I had been enrolled in a correspondence program with Wayne University in Detroit. Regularly I received packets in the mail from Assistant Professor June Stillman; they included grammar, vocabulary, readings, and essay assignments. She had also sent a textbook that contained a series of lesson plans for my Introduction to English Conversation course.

Before returning to the hall where classes were held, I walked to the far end of our barracks to see how Ruup was doing. He was lying on his side in the lower bunk, sipping salted water through a straw. Outside, members of the team were kicking the soccer ball around.

"Wilhelm, I think we're going to have to keep you out of the match on Sunday."

He sat up and motioned with his hands, indicating that he wanted my notebook. With my pencil he scribbled on a blank page: *You know how this happened?*

I looked down the long aisle that ran between the bunks. There were other men in the barracks, so I took the notebook back from him, and we wrote the following exchange:

Do you think it was an accident?

No. The doctor couldn't understand how the glass was crushed up so small. It was on Vogel's orders.

I think so too.

Gerhardt—he wasn't a good Nazi. They gave him two choices. Break out and kill Americans. Or kill himself. He couldn't kill anyone, even if he got out of these woods.

How did they convince him to do that?

Threaten his family in Germany. To do this from here they use code in their mail.

Why you?

I'm the next example. Not a "good Nazi." My parents, my two brothers are all dead. I have no family—so I get the glass. I am a German. *Not good enough for them.*

Wilhelm handed me the pencil and notebook, and then he took my forearm and held it firmly. We sat for a moment, and then I said, "We'll get you back on the pitch soon."

■　　■　　■

Shortly before lights were out at ten, Kommandant Vogel came to our barracks. He spoke quietly, in a swift, precise voice. "I am ordering a work slowdown beginning tomorrow."

After a moment, I said, "Kommandant, you haven't been here as long as some of us. We have done this before. Once we even had a strike. The first time, the Americans marched us many miles through the woods, making men exhausted and sick. The next time, their response was 'no work, no food,' and they cut back what we got a little more each day. It went on for a week. Again, it only resulted in men becoming sick and exhausted."

A hanging light above Vogel's head cast long shadows down his face and darkened the hollows of his eyes. "We are doing too much to aid the enemy in their war effort. Thus I am ordering this action."

"Kommandant," I said. "Are you aware that the German government has expressly stated that we should perform the duties given us while in captivity? The Americans have, too. It's the same on both sides. They are doing so to protect their men who are being held in prison camps."

Vogel ignored this and said, "Furthermore, the kommandant and his officers have devised a new plan for a mass escape. The details are being worked out now." And then he looked at me. "Captain Verdi, you are aware that it is the duty of every prisoner to try and escape?"

"Yes, it's stated in the Geneva Convention."

There were snickers, which quickly stopped as Vogel looked around at the men.

"You are not only expected to attempt to escape," he said, "but when you do get out, you are to perform acts of sabotage and murder—*any*thing that will aid the war effort."

I was about to speak, when Adino said, "Kommandant, couldn't we take a vote on this?"

There were murmurs of agreement from some of the others.

"What do you think this is?" As Vogel straightened up, the light above him shifted and I could see the fury in his eyes. "You think this camp is America? You think this is some democracy?"

"You know what the vote would be," Adino said. "You might get 15 percent."

Vogel inhaled deeply and then walked over to Adino. He was several inches taller, but Adino didn't move. "There will be no vote," Vogel said. "There *will* be a work slowdown. Tomorrow." He turned on his heels and went out the door, followed by his group.

"Whenever Nazis leave the room," Adino said, "the relief is like a good fart."

Some of the others laughed, until I said, "Adino, shut up."

．　　　．　　　．

When we were in the war, there was never any question about what we should do. You simply did what you were told by your superior officers. If you didn't, you could be shot. What to do, what not to do as prisoners of war had been a great dilemma. After being captured in North Africa, there was overwhelming uncertainty and exhaustion, complicated by a sense of relief: the war was over for me. When I was with the army in Italy, even though I was in unfamiliar territory, I seldom felt that the end of the war was near for me. I was not close to the front, but helping to organize sending supplies and men forward. I understood that in those rugged hills of the *mezzogiorno*, it has always been hard to see one's enemies, and this somehow protected me. But when we were shipped across the Mediterranean to Africa, the landscape changed and the war became something utterly foreign. In Africa, even Dante would be struck dumb by the horrors we witnessed. The land was essentially flat, lifeless; sand was everywhere and got into everything. Field Marshal Rommel's cunning had elevated him to mythic proportions, but it was only a matter of time before the Allies would turn it all around. I was convinced that I would not leave Africa alive.

Since arriving at Camp Au Train, most of the prisoners (not Vogel and his

Nazis, of course) had come to some difficult realizations. The war was truly over for us—that was not difficult to accept. What would come after the war was impossible to predict, and it was too distant to contemplate, other than knowing that the world as we knew it would no longer exist. The hard thing, the unexpected revelation, was that the Americans were not what we had thought they would be—we had been told that despite their smiling faces they were inherently evil, and if they won the war, everything that we knew and believed in would be swept away. If we survived such a loss, we wouldn't know who we were: our history, our traditions, our beliefs, all crushed and forgotten. There was no option but to fight to the death. Instead, we had been captured, and to our surprise—even to our horror—most Americans treated us with decency and fairness.

In the morning the camp trucks took us several miles into the woods to a new site. As usual, we were met by American civilians, men who drove the trucks for the Bay de Noc Lumber Company. The drivers operated the skids and the equipment that loaded the logs onto the long flatbed trucks. They were earnest, hard-working men and we got along well with them. It was not uncommon for us to share a cigarette during breaks, and some of their wives had them bring us tins of cookies or brownies, or something I'd never had before arriving in the United States, sugar doughnuts.

When we climbed out of the transport trucks, we went to the tool van, which was hitched to the back of an army Jeep. The Shepherd unlocked the doors, stepped back, and we began to distribute axes, bow saws, and shovels. I took an axe and followed Adino up the hill. We usually worked in threes, but Wilhelm had remained behind in the barracks, so today Adino and I would do the job ourselves. He had a shovel over one shoulder, the four-foot saw over the other.

"Wait," I said, gesturing toward his saw. "Let me see that."

We inspected the long row of teeth on the blade and found that they'd been twisted and bent out of line. I took the axe off my shoulder, and as I lowered it to the ground the head fell off. Looking at the top end of the wooden handle, we could see that the metal wedge that held the head firmly in place had been removed. Next we examined the shovel: the shaft had been sawn halfway through. We started down the hill and saw that the other men were making similar discoveries.

Officers only performed manual labor if they wanted to, but they did supervise. As a captain, I chose to cut wood simply because there were only two Italian prisoners and I couldn't bear to sit around and "supervise" Adino all day, and without the work the days would seem interminably long. Kommandant Vogel, who had never had a blister or a splinter in his hands, stood in front of the tool van, explaining to the Shepherd that the men would not work without properly maintained equipment. The Shepherd looked cornered.

"Until this problem is resolved," Vogel told him, "we should return to camp."

"How'd you get into the van?"

Vogel turned to me, mildly surprised that I would have the insolence to question him.

"The Shepherd has a key," I said. "There must be others."

Now the Shepherd seemed not only confused but scared. "I don't know," he said.

Vogel folded his arms. "What are you saying, Captain Verdi?"

"You know what I'm saying. How'd your men get into the van overnight?"

Vogel raised his chin, insulted, and then said to the Shepherd, "I demand that my men be placed back on the truck and returned to the camp."

The Shepherd looked at the other guards, who were all younger and duller than he was, while the American drivers leaned against their trucks, smoking cigarettes.

"All right," Vogel said loudly. "Everybody back in the trucks!"

There were about thirty prisoners in this detail. As usual a small group of them—I counted seven—stood around Vogel, staring back at the rest of us. Even though the Nazis were outnumbered, a few of the men began to move toward the transport trucks. But then they stopped at the sound of crackling branches. We all turned and saw that Adino was working his way up the hill, pulling brush out of the ground.

"May I suggest, sir," I said to Vogel, "that we all clear this area—it will have to be done anyway before the logging trucks can get up the hill, and in the meantime the van can go back to camp for more tools."

Vogel said, "Are you suggesting that our men use their bare hands?"

I reached into my back pocket, pulled out my work gloves, and held them up. "No, sir, I'm just saying we can work productively until replacement tools arrive." Vogel continued to stare at me, his arms folded, so I pulled on my gloves and walked away. Moving up the hill, I took hold of a bush and gave it a good yank. Though several branches broke off in my hands, the roots were firmly planted in the soil. I pulled several times more, and then one of the other men, the Russian,

Dimitri Sabaneyev, fell to his knees and began digging at the earth around the base of the bush. Using the head of an axe, he cut through larger roots, and the bush began to work free of the soil. When we had the bush out, I looked up and saw that most of the men were also clearing brush.

"*Halt!*" Vogel shouted.

I dropped the bush and looked downhill.

"*Halt immediately!*" he yelled.

The other men had stopped and they were staring at each other uncertainly.

Vogel made a sweeping motion with his arm, and the seven men standing behind him began to walk slowly up the hill. Some of them had picked up tools, while others had sticks, which they held before them like clubs. One had a rock in each hand. As they advanced, the first men they encountered on the hill backed away, their hands raised in an effort to indicate that they did not want trouble. The Nazis continued up the hill toward the rest of us. To my left I saw Adino break a good-sized branch off of a bush—it was the length of a baseball bat and he raised it up above one shoulder. Several others also quickly found weapons.

The Nazis stopped a few steps below us on the hill and no one moved. I had seen that stare so many times; it was something fierce, unwavering, and committed to one purpose: victory. But now these stares were directed at me, and they were only too happy to kill anyone who stood in their way. One of the Nazis, a private named Beutel, threw a rock, which glanced off the left side of my neck. Adino lunged forward, swinging his long stick, which made a loud *whop* when it struck Beutel's shoulder. The two groups came together, hurling rocks, swinging sticks and fists. I took blows on my head, arms, and thighs. Adino was attacked by two men, and I saw all of them tumble down the hill together.

The fighting stopped at the sound of a rapid series of gunshots. At the foot of the hill, the Shepherd fired another burst into the air. The shots echoed off the surrounding hills, and then there was stillness. I turned and looked farther up the hill. A number of men—at least a dozen—stood about twenty yards away. They had opted to stay out of the fight, leaving the rest of us to the Nazis, who had done their damage quickly and well. Men were bloodied; they held arms and hands in pain; they breathed heavily, spewing vapor into the chill morning air. Kommandant Vogel stood by the tool van, his hands clasped behind his back, clearly pleased with the result.

■   ■   ■

The guards put us on the trucks and drove back to Camp Au Train. Several men required medical attention at the infirmary. Others treated each other as best they could. I had a gash over my left eyebrow, and Adino wrapped my forehead in a strip of cloth torn from the end of my bed sheet. His shoulder had been injured, and we fashioned a sling for his arm. We slept through much of the afternoon, and when we went to dinner we both limped badly. As the prisoners gathered in the mess hall, it was clear that the Nazis had taken their lumps as well, but they had gotten the better of us. The reason was because so many men had refused to enter the fight, and that was the Nazis' real victory.

The doors to the kitchen were closed, which was no surprise. The guards instructed us to stand at our tables. Some of them had the German Shepherds on leashes, heeling at their sides. The dogs were always a presence around the camp; they often accompanied guards as they patrolled outside the fence, but seldom had it been deemed necessary to bring them inside the grounds, and never before into the mess hall.

When we were in our places, Kommandant Vogel sat at the officers' table up on the riser and scrutinized the men. He appeared pleased because so many of them had worn their Wehrmacht uniforms. Camp rules regarding dress required men to wear their prison fatigues during the day when they were on work detail; but otherwise, they could wear whatever they wanted. Ordinarily, the majority of the German prisoners came to dinner in their PWs, as they were called. Only a small number, less than 20 percent, donned their military uniforms. Vogel could, of course, order them to do so, and did on special occasions. But now he looked out at the prisoners and at least half were in uniform. The fight on the hillside hadn't suddenly converted many of these men into Nazi fanatics, but it had convinced them to go along.

As Vogel pushed back his chair and stood, the hall became absolutely silent. "This afternoon I met with Commander Dalrymple and discussed this morning's events. It appears that there was a work slowdown, or complete stoppage, in every work detail that left camp. There was, as you know, an altercation in one detail. The American commander has expressed deep concern regarding these events, and he has determined the following." The kommandant took a sheet of paper from inside his jacket, unfolded it, and read, "One: damaged and destroyed equipment will be replaced or repaired by the day after tomorrow. The cost of this will be deducted from our daily pay and our general fund. Two: all prisoners will be placed on reduced rations for two days. Three: the canteen will be closed until Sunday. Four: prisoners who were involved in the altercation will receive individual review by the German command, as well as by the American command. Further reprimand will be determined on an individual basis." Vogel folded up the sheet, and then he nodded his head once. The other officers at the table got to their feet and stood at attention.

"Dear God," Adino whispered. "Not this."

Vogel produced a pitch pipe and blew into it, sounding a single, clear note; then he counted off, one-two-three, and most of the men began singing the Horst Wessel Song. Those of us at the soccer table who were not German listened. The American guards didn't move, nor did their dogs—except one, which tilted its head incredulously.

When the song was concluded, the kitchen doors opened, and the cooks emerged with dinner: two loaves of bread and four pitchers of water for each table.

5.

In the morning we learned that during the night Wilhelm had collapsed in the latrine after shitting blood. Guards had taken him to the infirmary. After breakfast—bread and water again—I received instructions to report to the commander's office.

Corporal Marks had an open box of doughnuts on his desk. He was finishing a doughnut, and powdered sugar was caked in the corners of his mouth. "Sorry, I'd offer you one," he said loudly, "but rules is rules. Now, we have to take Ruup back to the doctor's, though I don't know what he can do about glass up the ass."

He sorted through the box, selecting a doughnut that had chocolate on top, and led me outside. We got the commander's Jeep, picked up Ruup at the infirmary, and drove out of camp. Marks left the doughnut untouched, lying on a paper napkin on the seat between us. I tried not to look at it.

Instead, I turned around. Wilhelm lay curled up in the small back seat, his eyes closed. The bandage that had been wrapped around the lower half of his face had been removed.

"Don't ask," he muttered. "You have no idea."

I faced forward and looked out at the road. None of us spoke, all the way into Munising. The doctor's waiting room was crowded with old people, and one young woman with a little white dog that yapped constantly. Marks, of course, didn't seem to mind, and soon he was mesmerized by another issue of *National Geographic*.

When it was Ruup's turn to see the doctor, he walked with deliberate care into the examination room, and we remained in the waiting room for perhaps half an hour. I kept looking out the window toward the Frangiapanis' roof, beyond the trees, which had now lost most of their leaves.

"You're not going anywhere this time." Marks spoke loudly, and the others in the waiting room watched us with curiosity, if not alarm. "You get no spaghetti, just bread and water like everyone else. Sorry, pal. Besides, I didn't understand the doctor so good the last time, so he'll have to talk to you."

One of the old women leaned over and whispered to her husband, who then said to Marks, "Shouldn't he have handcuffs or something?"

When Marks continued to leaf through his magazine, I nudged him, and he looked up. "He's deaf," I said to the old man.

The woman looked away from us in disgust.

"*What?*" Marks asked.

"Never mind," I told him.

The nurse opened the door and motioned to us. We followed her down a corridor and entered a small examination room, where Ruup was on a table covered with paper. He lay on his side with a white sheet draped over him, and he looked like he was about to scream. The smell in the room was worse than the latrine on a hot day.

"I don't know if this enema is going to work," the doctor said to Marks. "I would suggest that you get permission to take him to the hospital in Marquette."

Marks looked at me and said, "What about Marquette?"

"Ruup should go to the hospital," I said.

"You can call the commander from my office," the doctor said. "You should get this man to Marquette immediately."

Beyond the doctor I could see out the window. A column of smoke was drifting into the sky above the Frangiapanis' house. It seemed too large, too dark to be burning leaves, and it certainly wasn't coming from a chimney. I turned and opened the door, walked quickly down the hall to the waiting room and out the front door. Marks called after me, but as soon as I got down the steps I broke into a full run. Instead of going up to the intersection and turning left, I ran through several yards and leaped over one fence. It wasn't until I was across the street from the Frangiapanis' that I realized that the smoke wasn't coming from their house, but from somewhere beyond. I sprinted around the side of the house and saw gray smoke pouring from the first-floor windows of the house directly behind the Frangiapanis', and there was a young woman lying in the backyard, coughing. She wore a frilly apron and her hair was wrapped in a red bandanna.

When I reached her, she wheezed, "*My . . . baby! I couldn't . . . get . . . upstairs!*"

I ran toward the side door, which was partially opened. Before entering the house, I took the bandage off my head and held it over my nose and mouth. In the kitchen the stove and the wall above it were on fire. The smoke was incredible. I went into the dining room, then turned right and saw the stairs in the living room. Taking the steps two at a time, I reached the second floor, where the smoke wasn't too bad. I could hear sirens in the distance.

There was a crib in the bedroom at the end of the hall. The baby was asleep on its back. It couldn't have been more than a few months old. I went into the room, picked up the baby, wrapped it in its blanket, and to my surprise it remained asleep. It had fine dark hair and remarkably tiny hands. I couldn't get over the small, perfectly shaped fingernails.

Turning around, I saw that the smoke was coming up the stairway. I went to the window in the bedroom, but it was a sheer drop to the concrete driveway. The smoke was getting worse, and I could hear the crackle and pop of fire down on the first floor. I held the blanket over the baby's face and ran down the hall, into the smoke. It was difficult to see going down the stairs, but in the living room, light came through the three diagonal windows in the front door, which I opened. I went out on the front steps and was surprised to see so many people in front of the house—neighbors, policemen, firemen rolling hoses out from their truck. When they saw me and the baby, there were shrieks and cries of joy. The mother, her hair now free of the bandanna, came across the yard, her arms outstretched. I handed the baby to her, and the child began to cry. Out by the curb, an elderly woman was on her knees, praying with a set of rosary beads dangling from her clasped hands.

My throat and sinuses were full of smoke and I leaned over and began coughing. Then there were people around me, touching me, patting my back. A woman kissed my cheek; a man shook my hand. Someone was taking photographs. Marks was there, too, shouting things like "*Verdi, you did it! You saved the baby!*"

At the back of the crowd that had gathered around me, I saw Chiara and her mother looking on. Chiara was in a yellow bathrobe, and her hair was piled on top of her head. Though she held the lapels together against her throat, I could see her graceful, slender neck.

Then I must have passed out for a moment, because I suddenly found myself sitting on the front fender of the commander's Jeep, sipping from a green bottle of Coca-Cola.

· · ·

I spent the night in the camp's infirmary. My breathing was very shallow. In the morning I was offered a bowl of oatmeal, but because the other men would be on bread and water for another day I refused it. The two medical officers looked at each other, and I told them that I wouldn't say anything if they wanted to share the oatmeal. They didn't bother with the spoon but simply used their fingers.

That night I was released from the infirmary. Adino and many of the other men cheered when I returned to our barracks. Pinned on the announcement board by the door was the front page of the local newspaper, which was accompanied by two photographs: one of the house with smoke pouring from the windows, and another of me clutching the baby to my chest. The headline read: "POW Saves Baby from Inferno!"

Adino insisted I translate the article into Italian. When I read the headline, he folded his hands over his heart and moaned, "*Sei Dante!*"

I slapped him gently on the side of the head, saying, "I'm not Dante." When he responded with those big, soft eyes I began to read the article, but stopped after a few paragraphs. "It says I'm a member of the German Afrika Korps," I said. "There's no mention that I'm Italian."

"Americans," Adino said in disgust. "We're all 'krauts' to them. It's because of the bread, I tell you. They eat this white bread that's like cake, and they don't know one damned thing."

6.

We had new or repaired tools the following day and, after being served a breakfast of eggs, bacon, rolls, and coffee, we returned to lumbering in the forest. We didn't work too hard that first day because we were all so weak, but after several days it was clear that many of the men were following Vogel's orders regarding work. Our progress was sporadic, and there were frequent problems with equipment.

One evening after dinner, I was summoned to the officers' barracks, escorted by two of the kommandant's men. At night these men had taken to patrolling the grounds until lights out at ten o'clock. They wore the gray uniforms of the Afrika Korps. Vogel's "office" was an area at the back of the barracks where blankets had been hung from the rafters to create a small, private cubicle. Drawings of Hitler, Himmler, and Rommel were pinned to these "walls." He sat behind a "desk" that was made from boards laid across stacked produce crates.

"Captain Verdi, I wanted to give you the good news personally," he said. "The officers have discussed your situation and decided not to court-martial you."

"Court-martial? What would the charges have been?"

Vogel stroked his smooth cheek a moment as he squinted up at me. "Oh, any number of things. Striking a German soldier. Insubordination. Perhaps even treason."

"That's nonsense, Kommandant."

Vogel took a book off of a stack of papers on his desk and picked up a folded sheet of newspaper. It was the front-page article about the house fire in Munising. "These people may consider you a 'hero,' but this—*this* is sufficient evidence that you have committed treason."

"I carried a baby out of a burning house."

"You escaped from your captors, which is to be lauded, as it is every prisoner's duty to do so. But instead of using your freedom to harass the enemy, you save the life of this child—who may one day grow up and join the American armed forces."

"Certainly, Kommandant, the Third Reich plans to win the war before that happens."

Vogel leaned back in his chair; he seemed to be attempting a smile. "You *do* believe that, Captain Verdi: that we are going to win the war?"

"The bulletins and reports your officers issue always contain positive news from the front, so why would I think we might lose?"

"Precisely," Vogel said. "And I have more good news for you, regarding Lieutenant Wilhelm Ruup. His treatment at the hospital has been somewhat successful, but it has been determined that he will be sent home." The kommandant's finger tapped a sheet of paper on his desk. "He has agreed to memorize this list and take it back to the authorities in Berlin." Now he attempted to smile again, which meant he looked like he was in excruciating pain. "You are not on this list because you are a member of the Italian army."

"Who is on it?"

Vogel shrugged. "German soldiers whose behavior has been suspicious or unsatisfactory. The Third Reich needs to know that they have not been doing their duty while in captivity. They are too willing to work for the benefit of the enemy. Some of them, we have noted, have attended religious services on Sundays when ministers come out from the village. It is one thing for you and the other Italian prisoner to attend Mass when the priest comes to camp, but the authorities will want to contact the families of these men. Such primitive religious ceremonies are no longer necessary in Germany."

"And Ruup is going to convey this information to Berlin?"

"Yes," Vogel said. "It is not uncommon that messages be sent home through ill and wounded soldiers. It's an excellent form of communication, one the Americans can do nothing about."

"And in exchange for his services Ruup might be protecting his own family—but he told me his parents and his brothers were all dead."

"The wages of war," Vogel said. "Very unfortunate."

"So who's he protecting?"

"He writes to a girl in Leipzig. He never mentioned her?"

I shook my head. "But your men know about her because they inspect everything before it goes out in the mail."

Vogel didn't bother to confirm this; he got up and came around the makeshift desk, his hands clasped behind him. "Captain," he said quietly. "I also wish to talk with you about another important matter: the football team. As captain and coach of the team, you will have to replace Ruup in the match on Sunday."

"That's right."

"Who will you use?"

"I haven't decided yet."

"I would like to make a suggestion," Vogel said. "Gunnar Staudt."

"He's not even on the team."

"There is now only one German, your goalie, Rudi Brandt. I fear that he might feel alone, playing for a team comprised of Czechs and Hungarians and Poles and Italians—and even one Russian."

"Kommandant, we have the best men playing on this team. I made that clear when I agreed to coach the squad. There would be tryouts, and players would be selected strictly for their ability on the pitch."

"How democratic of you."

"Au Train is a small camp," I said, "yet we are still undefeated."

"I know. Quite remarkable. But we are playing this other small camp, from a place called Germfask. Brandt has requested that we give some other men an opportunity to play. Saturday afternoon the Red Cross inspectors will be here. It only makes sense that a camp that is comprised of nearly 90 percent Germans should field a team that is more representative. It would be the democratic thing to do, no?"

"Football, Kommandant Vogel, is not democratic."

■   ■   ■

One afternoon during that week, Adino and I were cutting brush so that the other men could get farther up the hill to a fresh stand of trees. As we climbed higher, clearing a path, the sound of the men and their saws below became faint, absorbed by the woods. It was very peaceful up there, and at one point we paused to rest. Adino went over behind a bush, unbuckling his belt and pulling a wad of toilet paper from his pocket. While he was gone I stood and looked about; it was very quiet, the air still—so still it didn't seem to exist. There was a stand of birch with luminescent white bark curling in places away from the trunk, and black knots that made me think of eyes, the kohl-painted eyes of Egyptian queens. We would divert the path, though it probably wouldn't save the birches. So I studied those trees as though they were beautiful women I would see naked only this one time, or like the great works of art in museums and galleries in Italy. The birches were more beautiful because I knew they couldn't be saved. Little in this war could be saved, even a stand of birch trees.

Then something changed; a greater quiet seemed to come over the woods. A powerful quiet that I didn't understand. It made me alert, and I picked up my axe, which I had leaned against the trunk of a maple sapling. From higher up the hill there came a rustling of leaves and the sound of something running fast, crashing through the brush. Though I couldn't see anything, I could follow the sound as it moved through the woods, until it stopped abruptly. There was a high, piercing cry, and then it was quiet again.

Adino came out from behind the bush, fastening his belt. He'd heard it, too. He didn't say anything and he looked startled. I began climbing the hill—it was so steep in places I had to claw my way up, grabbing at roots with my free hand. Adino followed, until we reached an outcropping of rock. We stood on the ledge, scanning the hill above us.

And then I saw it. I wasn't sure at first, the way it blended in with the ground cover about twenty yards away, but when I nudged Adino's shoulder he saw it too and took a step backward—I grabbed his sleeve before he fell off the ledge. We remained absolutely still then, my hand clutching his jacket, looking up into the woods where a wolf was eating a small animal. A hare, I thought. The wolf was completely preoccupied, tearing and pulling with its teeth. Its snout was bloodied and there was fur hanging from one corner of its mouth.

The wolf looked up, its eyes fiercely curious. There are moments in life when you look into the eyes of another living being, a parent, a lover, or perhaps someone who is a threat, some opponent, and in that moment you not only see their eyes, but you are looking right into them—you are staring into their very being, and you're convinced that they are doing the same. It is a disquieting moment. You are not yourself, and yet you are, and you feel utterly exposed. Everything is revealed: the truth about you, about what you are and what you aren't, it's all there to be witnessed by the eyes that are locked upon yours. To do this with another person is one thing, a most rare thing. It often reveals love, or at least some deep understanding and caring for the other. But it can also expose a pure desire. Once, when I was in Africa, I came upon a soldier who had been wounded. There had been shelling, and a piece of steel protruded from his bloody chest. He was German and he was lying on the side of the road as vehicles passed—we were withdrawing. But when I heard him speak, I stopped and knelt down beside him. I couldn't understand what he said, so I opened my canteen and gave him a sip of water, most of which ran down his chin. I thought I should try again, try to get some water down his throat, but then I looked in his eyes. They were pleading with me, and at first I didn't know what he wanted, but then I realized that his entire body had gone rigid, that he was dying, and his eyes were saying to me that he wanted to live, he only wanted to live. And then his eyes changed, they turned hard and unseeing, and his body seemed to lose its tension.

But now I was looking into the eyes of an animal—a wolf, I knew it was a wolf. There was a clarity and intelligence in its stare that I couldn't comprehend. Its stare was unlike anything I'd ever experienced before. There wasn't exactly an emotion in its eyes, but there was an awareness, of me, of itself, of this moment that we shared. It was the only moment, a moment that ruled out every other moment. I didn't feel anything. Not fear, certainly, though perhaps there was curiosity. The fact was, though I was aware that Adino and I might be in danger, I didn't want the moment to end.

Calmly, the wolf lowered its head, picked up its quarry in its mouth, and bounded off into the woods. We listened to the leaves rustle as the wolf climbed the hill, and then there was silence again.

"That's not like the other coyotes," Adino whispered. "I wanted to sing but I couldn't."

We saw coyotes frequently, particularly outside the camp fences, where they were always looking to scavenge for food. "I don't think so," I said. "Much too big. It was beautiful."

"And so alone. Solitary." Then he laughed nervously. "With blood on its snout."

That night in the mess hall, we told the other members of the football team about what we had seen, and they didn't believe us. Of course, it was only a coyote. There were no more wolves in these woods. They now were nothing more than a mythical presence.

After dinner, while we were out in the yard smoking, Adino and I approached one of the older guards, a man named Walter. He was related in some way to the Shepherd, and it was clear that he was knowledgeable about hunting. More than once he had expressed disgust at the practice of shooting deer with machine guns—not because he didn't believe in killing deer, but because doing so with a machine gun was an insult to the animal. We told Walter what we had seen, and he questioned us about the height and length of the animal, the size of its paws. Adino and I both were certain that this animal was easily twice the size of a coyote. Walter had a deeply lined face and sad eyes, and he often looked at us with a kind of sympathy that the other guards lacked—they usually didn't really seem to see us. He had smoked yet another cigarette down until it was a stub pinched between his yellowed fingers, and then, dropping it on the ground, he said, "You saw a wolf. Most of us roam these woods all our lives and we don't get to see one."

"But they're no more," I said. "Ex . . . extinguished, no?"

"Extinct," Walter said. "No, the wolf is still out there. I've never seen one, but I've seen signs. Tracks in mud. We've about killed 'em off. One day there'll be packs of wolves in these woods again."

"You really believe that?" I asked.

Walter nodded as he left us. "But I won't live to see it."

.   .   .

The routine of the days and nights made time an adversary. Americans call it *doing time.* But I didn't look at it that way. Time in Au Train was a wheel driven by hunger, thirst, physical exertion, weariness. Time moved forward, but I remained stationary—it was the train, and I was standing on the platform unable to board because the locomotive, though it might slow down, never stopped. Sleep and monotony were strange bedfellows. I had dreams that caused me to awaken, startled, confused, soaked in sweat. They would fade within seconds, and during my waking hours I'd try to recall something from them, but they fled, went wherever dreams disappear to, leaving me feeling deceived and abandoned because I suspected that somewhere in my dreams I experienced a sense of freedom that I never had when I was awake. Days were interminably long, yet weeks seemed to evaporate. Months didn't just pass, they vanished, and you wondered if you'd even lived them. Summer was brief and fall soon gave way to winter. December first we had about eight inches of snow on the ground. The temperature often dropped below zero at night, and we were issued heavy wool coats for our days in the woods. Though some men made an attempt at wreaths and decorating trees, there was no real sense that Christmas was approaching.

News from the outside world, news of the war, was sporadic, contradictory. We were never sure what to believe. A headline, glimpsed in a newspaper, would bolster or destroy the day. As we approached Christmas, Faenza fell under siege as the Allies moved north, but then their advance stalled when torrential rains caused flooding in the Lamone River. Within days the headlines in the *Marquette Mining Journal* shifted from joyous optimism to horrified despair. The war, which some had believed would be over by Christmas, suddenly seemed destined to continue as the Germans mounted a counteroffensive, reportedly moving old men and boys to the front lines. When speaking to the men in the mess hall, Vogel never mentioned this fact, but he often said that this war of attrition would allow Germany time to finish the development of a new weapon, the V-2 rocket, which would certainly lift the Reich to victory.

Il calcio—football, or, here in the States, soccer—kept Adino and me sane. Every day while lumbering, every night while lying awake in our bunks, we talked about the team, its strengths and weaknesses, the various plays and strategies we could try. Practice provided a sense of release from the oppression of being a prisoner, and the games often resulted in a most welcome sense of exhaustion, as well as the exhilaration of victory. Adino believed that the two most important things in life were sex and football. He often said that without *il calcio* his longing for his wife Maria would overwhelm him and he would kill himself. Had he lived in peacetime, I'm sure he would have been an outstanding player for one of the great Italian teams, Juventus, or one of the clubs in Milan, A.C. or Inter. I had never seen someone use the entire foot the way he did; had never seen such accurate backward passes with the heel. There were times when he would approach you and his legwork would seem to make the ball disappear momentarily. It was on his left, his right, between his feet; he appeared to overrun it, and then, miraculously, it was back in front of him, and he was poised to strike. He was not a tall man, no more than five-foot-six, but he had broad shoulders and sinuous, muscular legs, Michelangelo legs. There was both power and lightness to his movement, and nothing ever seemed predictable. Our offensive philosophy was built upon one concept: get the ball to Adino.

Our last match of the season took place on Christmas Eve. In order for the game to be played, the members of the team had to clear the snow off the field. Previously, our opponents had been teams from other prisoner-of-war camps in the Upper Peninsula or northern Wisconsin; but this time we faced Americans. They were prisoners in their own country, and they wore red jerseys with *CO Bombers* hand-painted in white letters on the front. Some of my teammates didn't understand what the *CO* stood for, and I tried to explain the concept of a "conscientious objector," but they just stared at me in disbelief.

Marek Haltof, our steadfast Polish midfielder, said, "They didn't want to fight, so the American government put them in their own special work camp up here?"

"Their refusal is based on religious or moral beliefs," I offered.

The Hungarian forward, Victor Skowalski, said, "They don't just shoot them?"

The others nodded in agreement, and I said, "Let's just concentrate on the match."

When we took the field, the other Au Train prisoners, standing along snow-banks on the east sideline, were unusually restrained. In fact, what little applause came from them quickly subsided, and it was clear that they were following the example set by Vogel and his men, who surveyed the field impassively, their arms folded. Equally curious was the reaction from the other side of the field. Ordinarily, a small crowd of Americans came out from the surrounding villages to watch the matches through the high barbed-wire fence. They were always quiet, but this time there was enthusiastic applause as we took our positions.

Adino looked over at me and, placing his hand on his heart, said, "Dante! Our hero!"

"Shut up." But I scanned the group of Americans and realized it was true: the Americans were applauding me. Except Chiara. She was there with several other girls and boys, leaning on the hood of a yellow convertible. When I noticed her, she looked away from me. Her hair was tied back in what Americans call a ponytail, which allowed me to see more of her face, the graceful line of her jaw, her full mouth. Suddenly everything was changed: I was accustomed to playing these matches for the pure sake of the game, but now I was keenly aware of

Chiara's presence. I wanted to play well for her, which only made my movements seem self-conscious and awkward.

The game began, and the CO Bombers proved to be unlike any other team we had faced. We were accustomed to playing teams that were physically equal or even superior to us, but they were invariably disorganized. Quickly our positional play, passing, and speed would allow us to take control of the game. The Americans were not particularly strong (though we understood that they too spent their days cutting down trees, several looked like they wouldn't last two minutes wielding an axe), and they were remarkably slow. But they understood positional play, and only a few minutes into the match it was clear that they had managed to establish an excruciatingly deliberate pace to the contest. We could barely connect a pass, and seldom penetrated beyond midfield for any sustained period of time. And there was something else disconcerting about this team: many of the players didn't look like Americans. They wore unkempt beards and mustaches, and when they spoke to each other they used English words I'd never heard before. I quickly realized that they were well educated, and that we were in trouble.

Then they scored on a long, lazy shot, which bounced once before it reached the crease—our goalie, Rudi Brandt, dove to his right and got both hands on the ball, but it rolled past him and into the goal. He was usually reliable; it was a bad goal. But even more curious was that the American spectators began to boo. They were booing the COs, while across the field the prisoners looked on quietly.

The game built in intensity. We began to move the ball better, connecting passes and getting some shots on their goalie, who looked like he was about seven feet tall. He had good reflexes and twice stopped Adino cold. About a half hour into the match, they scored again. This time the ball went between Rudi's legs. Adino went to him, swearing in Italian and gesturing. I quickly separated them, pushing Rudi back toward the goal.

"What's the *matter* with him?" Adino shouted as I escorted him up the field. He had to shout because the Americans were booing even louder now. Some threw things over the fence at the COs, and one of their forwards was hit on the shoulder with a ripe tomato. "*What is going on?*" Adino screamed.

"Just play." On the east sideline, Vogel beamed with satisfaction. I signaled to the Shepherd, the referee, that I wished to make a substitution. At the sideline I said to Dimitri Sabaneyev, "You play goal." The Russian didn't move—he'd never played that position before. "Just get *in* there!" I yelled. After Dimitri ran out to our goal, Rudi came off the field reluctantly, glaring at me.

Several minutes later, we scored on a corner kick. I arched the ball toward the crease, and Adino headed it into the goal—a beautiful play.

During halftime we gathered around the large rock at one end of the field, where we always rested and drank water. Usually the players sprawled on the ground while I sat on the rock, discussing strategy. But this time I said nothing. We just rested and watched what was going on down the field. The Americans beyond the fence were taunting the COs, calling them "conchies," chickens, and faggots. The COs ignored this, and some seemed even to enjoy the attention, smiling and waving back at their countrymen.

The second half was excellent football, a pure defensive battle. And the crowd on both sides of the field was into it now—the Americans cheering for us, and the prisoners cheering for the COs. Once, when the ball rolled out of bounds on the west side, I went to the fence to retrieve it, and stood within five yards of Chiara. She was leaning against the car, her arms folded, as she had been throughout the match. Unlike the other Americans, she had remained quiet. As she stared back at me, the breeze tossed her ponytail over her shoulder. Then the Shepherd blew his whistle and I walked over to the sideline, raised the ball over my head with both hands, and threw it back into play.

Unlike American football, soccer has no visible clock. The referee keeps time on a watch. Players on the field only know approximately how much time remains. In the last couple of minutes, with the CO Bombers still ahead, 2-1, play turned furious. We knew time was running out, but we didn't know exactly when that would happen, so our playmaking was desperate, intense, and quite brilliant. We managed two shots on the CO goalkeeper, which he deflected away with his long arms. Finally, there was a moment when Adino had the ball. He was about twenty yards from their goal and surrounded by opponents. But his legs performed magic and suddenly he broke away from them, sprinted toward the crease, and curled the ball into the far corner of the goal.

The match ended in a 2-2 tie, but my teammates piled on each other at midfield as though we had won a championship. The American spectators hurled more produce—very ripe tomatoes and a few large heads of cabbage—over the fence at the COs. Vogel gave the order and the German prisoners marched in formation back to the barracks. When I looked toward the yellow convertible, I saw it bouncing down the dirt road toward the prison gate. Chiara was sitting in back, in what Americans call the rumble seat, and I watched her ponytail snap behind her head until the car disappeared into the woods.

■　　■　　■

As we were walking off the field, Commander Dalrymple waved to me. He was standing next to a black sedan. I went over, and Father Ignacio, who sat behind the wheel of the car, greeted me in Italian. Usually, he came out on Sundays to say Mass for the Catholics in camp. "Tomorrow," Father Ignacio said, "we are going to celebrate a special Mass of thanks for the life of the child you saved." He was an old priest with kind eyes and a nose full of burst blood vessels. "The Imlachs and their neighbors would be honored if you would attend the service in Munising. One of my curates will come out to say Christmas Mass for the other prisoners."

I looked at Commander Dalrymple, who said, "This is a rare request and you may attend, if you like, Captain Verdi. Merry Christmas."

7.

E ven though the match had ended in a tie, our squad celebrated the fact that we were still undefeated. We traded cigarettes and canteen coupons for a bottle of moonshine (made in the barracks that housed most of the Poles). Rudi Brandt wasn't part of it. We hadn't seen him since the end of the match, and we all agreed that on Vogel's orders he had tried to throw the game. On an uncharacteristically democratic impulse, we voted him off the team. After that we drank and danced and sang in our barracks well past lights out, and it being Christmas Eve, the guards didn't bother us.

The following morning I had a brutal hangover as Corporal Marks drove me into Munising. Adino and I had been able to put together the semblance of a dress uniform, though on me his jacket was too broad in the shoulders and too short in the sleeves. When I got out of the commander's car, Marks said that someone from the village would return me to camp. I watched him drive off, and then climbed the steps and entered the church, which was packed with town folk. As I walked up the center aisle, everyone stood up. At first they were silent, but then someone began to clap, and in a few moments applause resounded through the church. I was offered a seat in the front pew with the Imlach family, who had been burned out of their house. For the most part, Mass was a blur. During the sermon, I was nodding off when Father Ignacio mentioned my name, startling me awake. He was recounting my act of heroism—a word he used several times—and explaining that such bravery knew no nationality, race, or creed.

After Mass there was a lunch in the parish hall. I endured bone-crushing handshakes from men, hugs from women wearing perfume so strong I thought I might faint. The Imlach family—George, his wife Dorothy, their grandparents, aunts, uncles, cousins, nephews, and nieces—all crowded around me for more photographs for the newspaper. Finally, the hall began to clear, and eventually I was left seated with Father Ignacio, Mrs. Frangiapani, and Chiara, who had agreed to drive me back to the camp. My hangover was fading at last and everyone at the table spoke Italian. Chiara, seated directly across from me, wore a blue-and-yellow print dress, and her attitude toward me seemed more receptive, even though she hardly said a word.

When we arose from the table, I offered to get Mrs. Frangiapani's and Father Ignacio's coats and started for the cloakroom at the back of the hall. Chiara followed me, saying she would get her own. When we entered the cloakroom, she pushed me back against the coat rack, put her arms around my neck, and kissed me. Empty wood hangers clacked about our heads, but her kiss became fiercely ardent—and then it was over. She released me, took her overcoat off a hanger, and fled the cloakroom.

On the way back to camp, Chiara drove, and I sat next to her while her mother occupied a corner of the back seat. "If they really want to show their appreciation," Mrs. Frangiapani bellowed, "they'd let you go free."

"Momma," Chiara said. "They do not send war prisoners home for heroism."

"Nonsense. All it would take is for Father Ignacio to write a letter to the Vatican, and then the pope would tell President Roosevelt to let him go home!"

Chiara laughed, and she almost drove off the winding dirt road, but I grabbed hold of the steering wheel with my left hand. "We are at war, Momma." Chiara took my hand off the steering wheel and held it on the seat between us.

"With the Germans," her mother insisted. "The Italians are another story."

"But Mussolini has allied us with Hitler," I said.

"Il Duce's just confused," Mrs. Frangiapani said. "Men like him are always confused."

Chiara's fingers stroked the palm of my hand.

"The war will come to an end," I said weakly. "Maybe in a year?"

"You can wait that long?" Chiara asked.

"I don't know," I said. "It's getting more difficult in there every day."

Then I felt Chiara's hand leave mine, and I watched it reach across the seat, until it rested on my upper thigh. I feared that our silence would give us away, so I said the first thing that came to mind. "I'm not sure I would want to go home if the war ended."

"What?" Mrs. Frangiapani shouted from the back seat.

I turned slightly, so that I could look back at the old woman, which only allowed Chiara to get a better hold on me. "Oh, I'd go back to visit, to see that my family was all right," I said. "But I would stay in America if I could."

"I'm not sorry we left Calabria," her mother said wearily. "Except sometimes when it seems it will never stop snowing here."

Chiara turned the car off the road and we passed through the camp gate, where the guards merely waved at us. When she stopped the car, she said, "It's really bad in here, isn't it?"

"You've just made it a lot worse. You both have given me a taste of freedom. *Grazie.*"

Mrs. Frangiapani looked like she was about to cry, but then she spoke harshly to her daughter. "Well, go on. Give it to him."

Chiara opened her door, and as she swung her legs out from beneath the steering wheel I caught the briefest glimpse of the top of her stockings. I got out on the passenger side and went to the back of the car, where she lifted the trunk. "This ought to hold you and your friend Adino for a while. *Buon Natale, Francesco.*"

It was the first time she'd ever called me by my name. I picked up the paper bag in the trunk and glanced inside: *farfalle.*

I went to the rear door and leaned down to the open window. "*Molto grazie, Signora.*"

"And there's a jar of pesto at the bottom of the bag." Mrs. Frangiapani was daubing her eyes with a handkerchief. "I will pray for you."

∎   ∎   ∎

That night the others at the football table watched in awe as Adino and I ate *farfalle*, which we explained meant butterflies in Italian. A few tasted it, but didn't like it. They were put off by the green color of pesto.

It was a quiet evening, like all Sundays. There was a hollow feeling, and we seemed most aware of how far we were from home. In our barracks men played cards and chess, wrote letters, read, or just smoked and talked. The following morning we would be driven out into the woods to resume the tedious work cutting down trees. No one knew how long we would be kept in this limbo. As usual, I worked on the English lessons sent to me from Wayne University in Detroit.

A little after nine, men started to go out to the latrine before lockdown at ten. I was completing a vocabulary quiz when we heard the screams. We went outside and one of the prisoners waved us toward the back of the mess hall. It was quite dark behind the building, but I could see that it was Adino, writhing on the ground, making horrible grunts and groans.

Two of the guards arrived right after us and they trained their flashlights on Adino. There was blood in the dirt under his feet, and at first it was difficult to see what had happened. The Shepherd knelt down and held his light close, and said, "He's been cut, back here—I forget what you call this."

"*Tendine.*" I could only think of the Italian word. Then I said, "Achilles."

"Right," the Shepherd said. "Both of them are cut."

.   .   .

Though the other prisoners were soon told to return to the barracks, I was allowed to stay because the guards thought I might be needed as a translator. Adino was carried on a stretcher to the infirmary, and it was determined that he would have to be taken to the hospital in Marquette, an hour away. Adino was in agonizing pain, and the two medical officers—both Germans—gave him only an aspirin. When Commander Dalrymple finally arrived, I tried to convince him to let me go to the hospital with Adino, but I was sent back to my barracks.

I lay in my bunk for hours, unable to sleep. I hadn't felt such terror since Africa. In Camp Au Train you thought you were removed from the war. As dull and tedious as life in those north woods was, it seemed safe. You came to believe that you could survive it. The enemy here wasn't out to kill you; in fact, they housed you and fed you better than your own army had done before you were captured. But now it was clear that the enemy wasn't the Americans.

We had heard about these things happening in other camps. There were Gestapo and SS; there were midnight tribunals. Men who were easily labeled as traitors to the Führer were killed or, often, given the option to commit suicide.

The Americans wouldn't or couldn't do anything about it. Ironically, they had posted a bulletin in each barracks urging any prisoner to report incidents that made him feel he was unsafe. The Nazis would immediately deem such an act as collaborating with the enemy. We'd heard about one prisoner in Arizona who had been tried and found guilty of conspiracy against the Third Reich because he liked jazz. His ears were cut off. Now many of the men in Au Train, particularly the Germans, were changing their behavior. They were even wary of talking with those of us who were not German.

I knew Vogel's men would come for me soon. When I was in southern Italy and Africa, the dead and wounded were everywhere. My hope was that when I died it would be sudden and immediate. A bullet in the brain. A direct bomb hit. A mortar shell. I feared the slow death: the shrapnel in the intestines. The faces of those men carried their agony into death. And perhaps most, I feared being maimed: life without a leg, an arm, a penis.

It was clear that Vogel believed in forms of punishment that he deemed suited to the crime.

■　　■　　■

In the morning I was put to work with two new men, the Russian Dimitri Sabaneyev, and a German named Otto Werner. We hardly spoke. A few times Sabaneyev caught my eye, and I realized that he too had suffered a long, sleepless night. Werner had complete disdain for the notion that he was expected to work with either of us. When we asked him to help, he ignored us, believing that he was doing his job, slowing down our efforts to help the enemy.

Before dinner that evening, I went to speak to the commander. Corporal Marks stepped into Dalrymple's office, and after a moment I was admitted—a bad sign because previously the commander always came out of his office to speak to me. Marks closed the door behind me, and Dalrymple gestured toward the chair in front of his desk. I remained standing. "I would like to know how Corporal Agostino is doing, sir."

The commander nodded but avoided looking me in the eye. He wasn't going to give it to me straight.

"You have heard from the doctors, Commander?"

"It's not good, Captain Verdi. His Achilles tendons were completely severed. The doctors suggest that he be moved to a hospital in Detroit, where they're better able to deal with such situations." The commander stared at me for the first time. "They aren't sure if your countryman will walk again."

I sat down in the chair.

The commander opened a lower drawer and placed two glasses and a bottle of liquor on the desk. He poured two shots and put one on the outer edge of the desk. "I suppose you'd prefer a little wine, Captain, but this is all I've got."

I picked up the glass and held it up to my nose.

"It's Kentucky bourbon."

I didn't like the smell, but it seemed less vile than what the Poles made from potatoes. The commander drank down his bourbon and placed his glass on the desk. "Captain," he said, and I could tell by the resolve in his voice that he was now determined to be straight with me. "Something is going on in this camp."

"Yes."

"There's a loss of discipline," he said. "Fights, escape attempts, suicides—and this terrible thing that has happened to Agostino."

"Yes, sir."

"I've had a talk with Kommandant Vogel about it."

I drank my bourbon, which burned my throat and sinuses. "You have?" I wheezed.

"Indeed, he shares our concern. We agree that there's a lack of discipline, that certain elements in the camp are bent on creating pure chaos."

I put the empty glass back on the desk and said, "Elements?"

"As much as I detest the Third Reich and many of the things Hitler stands for, as a military man I wouldn't be honest if I didn't acknowledge that there is much to be admired in the way his army conducts itself. Particularly the Afrika Korps. They are first-rate. But here we simply don't have enough of them to keep the other troops in order. Vogel, oh, he's trying, but what can one officer do? This thing they are up against is evil; it's as bad as anything the Führer can do, maybe even worse."

"What thing, sir?"

"Communism."

I wanted to stand up, but my legs wouldn't move.

Dalrymple leaned on his desk and said, "Captain, I mean no disrespect. You are clearly a man of honor and dignity. You speak several languages and have been of great assistance to this camp as a translator. I understand that you're furthering your education through a correspondence course. Your act of heroism in that burning house speaks for itself." He sat back in his chair, exhausted. "But Agostino is different. He has little education and he comes from the peasant class, is that not true?"

"His father is a butcher, Commander. My family owns a shop where cheese and meat are sold, and we have an olive grove."

"Yes, you are landowners."

"What are you saying, Commander?"

"Captain Verdi, you know very well that when the war is ended we will face a potentially greater danger. And you know that countries like Italy are full of people who are waiting for fascism to fail."

"You think Adino is a communist?"

"Captain, it is a terrible thing that happened to him, but you must see that this is all part of a pattern. I can't say with absolute certainty anything about him—perhaps he has resisted the influences of communism and was punished because of it. Kommandant Vogel has suggested this as a possibility. It's the way the Commies are, of course; they cut you at the first sign of resistance, and—"

I stood up then, the legs of the chair scraping loudly on the wood floor. "Sir, Adino Agostino is not a communist. He was not cut by any communists. There is no communist organization here."

Dalrymple looked disappointed, but with patience he said, "You see, Captain, that's exactly why they're so . . . insidious—do you know that word?" I merely stared at him. "They're all around you, like snakes in the grass, and you don't even see them. Even *here*, in the United States of America."

I went to the door, but when I had my hand on the knob, the commander said, "I'm afraid, Captain Verdi, that I must take steps before this gets out of control." I looked back at him as he splashed more Kentucky bourbon in his glass. "I'm sorry, but one of the first things I must do is put an end to this soccer team."

"For the winter, yes, but certainly in the spring we will schedule matches with—"

"Captain," he said without looking up at me, "there is no more soccer team."

8.

ecember 29, word went around the camp that Glenn Miller was missing. He'd been in England for much of the past year, giving concerts for the military. News reports were vague: he'd told his wife, who was in the States, that he was about to travel to France, and then there was no word of his whereabouts. I'd never seen the guards and American staff so distraught. It was as though they'd lost a member of their family.

That morning as Otto Werner, the young German who had replaced Adino in our work detail, wandered off to defecate behind some bushes, Dimitri Sabaneyev took something from his pocket and held it out to me in his massive, calloused hand.

"Bones?" I said in Polish. "Chicken bones."

We could only communicate in short bursts of Polish and German, or the two languages cobbled together. "I find under pillow," Sabaneyev said. "Means I die." It was a cold, raw morning, and white plumes of vapor poured from our noses and mouths. "Today Werner smile at me. He knows." He tossed the bones to the ground. "This war. I am forced into Russian army and made to work. I am captured by Germans and I am made to work. I am captured by Americans and I tell them I am Russian, an ally. But I have no papers. Americans do not know what I am and they send me here and I am made to work. Here I die? No." He spit on the ground where the bones lay. "Here I leave."

"Where will you go? Back to Russia?"

"To Stalin? To work and die?" Sabaneyev grinned at my stupidity. "I live in America."

"Far, Dimitri. You don't know how far it is to America. Many *versts*."

Werner came out from behind the bushes. I picked up the saw, but as I turned to the tree we had felled, Sabaneyev put his hand on my sleeve. "You must to go, too. Here you die. You know that."

I pulled my arm away from his grip and began sawing a limb of the tree. "I know."

Sabaneyev glanced at Werner, who was buckling his belt. "We talk tonight. Go soon."

■ ■ ■

Getting out of Au Train Camp wasn't the problem. It was staying out. Transferred prisoners brought word about escapes from other camps. Most escapees were caught within hours; few remained at large for more than a day. ("At large": a colloquialism I love—when I first heard it I thought that being a prisoner made me "at small.") The methods of escape were not as unusual as the reaction of Americans when they encountered a prisoner on the loose. He would be a man with a strange accent and poor command of English (if any), wearing a prison outfit, yet it often wouldn't dawn on them that they were dealing with an escapee. Sometimes they would take these men in and offer them coffee or a meal. In one instance the police chief in a small town gave a prisoner a lift. Even when Americans understood that they were dealing with an escaped prisoner of war, they were seldom alarmed. A number of prisoners were harbored by women—in one case, a mother in her mid-forties fell in love with a prisoner half her age. One of the most famous stories was about the Luftwaffe pilot, Hans Peter Krug, who escaped from prison in Ontario and rowed a stolen boat from Windsor to Detroit, where he was given shelter by an American named Gordie Stephan. Eventually, Krug made his way to Chicago and down to the Southwest, with the intention of entering Mexico, but he was captured in San Antonio. Stephan was the first American tried for aiding an escaped prisoner; he was found guilty of treason and sentenced to hang (though later the sentence was commuted to life imprisonment).

That night Otto Werner came to my barracks and handed me a note. "This is an order from Kommandant Vogel. Don't be late," he said.

I sat on my bunk and opened the note, which read: *Officers' Barracks, midnight tonight.*

The note meant a tribunal. Vogel and the others expected me to sneak over to their barracks and stand before the German officers and listen to them try me. Sabaneyev, a Russian captured by the Germans, could simply be given a small pile of bones and killed. As a captain in the Italian army I was being granted the privilege of a trial where evidence would be offered and I would be allowed to speak in my defense. Most likely they would build their case around my work as a translator and a teacher of English as evidence of my willingness to assist the enemy. After the discussion with Dalrymple, I had no doubt they would also use my handling of the football team, particularly the fact that we made certain decisions by taking a vote to remove our German goalie from the team. To close their case, they would argue that I was in collusion with a known communist, Adino, who was unable to be present to refute such claims. No matter how flimsy or circumstantial the evidence, no matter how strong my defense, the verdict was predetermined. They put on this charade not for the accused, but for the accusers; it was essential that they act according to what they perceived to be strict military justice. I would be punished immediately. In other camps, convicted "traitors" were often beaten badly, and it would take several days for them to die.

As I tucked the note in my shirt pocket, I looked down the length of the barracks. The other men seemed preoccupied—except Sabaneyev, who was lying in his top bunk facing me while he smoked a cigarette. When I nodded once, he rolled onto his back and stared at the ceiling above him.

·   ·   ·

In the morning a cold wind swept through the hills above Lake Au Train as we climbed off the trucks, gathered our tools, and spread out in the woods. It was Friday, the last day we'd work before the New Year arrived Monday, which would be a holiday. As usual, the Americans who drove the lumber trucks had already marked the trees they wanted cut. Sabaneyev and I walked among the trees, until we found a pine with a white tag nailed to it.

Otto Werner followed us, empty-handed. "You did not appear at the trial, Herr Verdi." He had the high, cracking voice of a teenager who has recently entered puberty. "Kommandant Vogel and the officers were greatly insulted. I am to inform you that you were tried in absentia and found guilty. It was a unanimous decision."

"They took a vote?"

"The trial was flawlessly executed," he said.

"I have no doubt," I said. "You are all masters of execution."

I nodded to Sabaneyev. We set the blade against the bark, fell into the push-and-pull rhythm of sawing, and quickly cut into the trunk. Pale sawdust showered my arms as the damp air became thick with the smell of pine sap.

"Your punishment will be announced after mess tonight," Werner chortled.

We ignored him and only stopped sawing when we heard the wood crack. I put both hands on the tree bark and pushed; the tree leaned over but wouldn't fall. We resumed cutting, until the trunk began to tilt, then we stepped well away because sometimes the bottom would kick back off the stump unpredictably. Several prisoners had been injured because they had stood too close to a falling tree trunk. The tree crashed down to the forest floor and we looked at it for a moment as though expecting it to move. All around us there was nothing but the sound of other men cutting trees—the rhythm of saws and the knock of axes, which reverberated off the surrounding hills. Some men sang, believing that doing so would ward off an attack by wild animals. Adino and I sometimes used to sing arias by Verdi or Puccini, much to the annoyance of Wilhelm Ruup.

Sabaneyev picked up his axe and began to trim the lower branches from the felled trunk. He picked up several and tossed them at Werner's feet. "Do something."

"Why?" Werner said.

"To live you must work," Sabaneyev said.

"Pile the branches over there," I said.

Werner merely stared at us. He was a tall boy, perhaps not even twenty. Years earlier I had learned to see the war in a man's face—not the war, but his war. In a man like Sabaneyev, you could see that he'd been captured, that he'd been worked like a slave, and that he'd only survived this long because he was strong and determined. In Werner's pale face and his light blue eyes you could see that he hadn't had much of the war. He had been captured too soon, before he'd seen enough. If anything, you could see that he was disappointed that he would miss the rest of the war. This was what he tried to hide with that confident smile.

"Stack branches," Sabaneyev said.

Werner shook his head.

Sabaneyev leaned his axe against the tree trunk and went over to Werner. They stared at each other, and then Sabaneyev bent over and gathered up several branches. He walked around Werner, who folded his arms and looked pleased with himself. After dropping the branches on the ground, Sabaneyev sorted through them and selected a branch that was about three feet long.

I started to turn back to the trunk, but then said to Werner, "What was I charged with? Treason? Aiding the enemy?"

Werner nodded.

"Communism, did they work that in, too?"

"Yes," Werner said. "Both you Italians are communists. And the Russian, too."

Sabaneyev walked back toward us, raised the branch with both hands, and swung it like an American baseball player hitting a home run. The stick passed through the air with a *whoosh*, causing Werner to turn so that he was struck on the side of the head. Fortunately, he didn't cry out. His body pitched forward, and he didn't even break his fall as he landed face down in the snow and mud. His cap had been knocked off and blood soaked his blond hair.

"Communist?" Sabaneyev dropped the stick and began walking into the woods.

I looked around but couldn't see any of the other men. The sound of their tools and their voices—some of them were singing—was muffled. I had come to like working out here in the woods. It was simple but purposeful labor, dull, repetitive, and safe. Though in prison, we were protected by the forest. But as I followed Sabaneyev up the hill, I was afraid, and after only a few steps I realized that I had no choice, that it was impossible for me to go back.

■   ■   ■

Soon we came to a logging road that ran along a ridge above Au Train Lake. We could still hear the faint sound of saws and axes in the distance, which meant they hadn't discovered that we were missing yet.

Sabaneyev said, "We split up."

"Yes."

He pointed down the two-track road. "South."

The wind, which was at our backs, was coming from the north. "I think so."

"I want south. America."

"Long way. Good luck."

Sabaneyev extended his arm and we shook hands quickly. His palm was enormous.

I headed north along the road. It was easier walking in the tracks made by lumber trucks. Soon I reentered the woods—eventually, the guards would drive the logging roads searching for us—and moved through the snowbound forest, keeping the wind on my left so I was heading east in the direction of Munising. I followed high ground, avoiding frozen swamplands down below, and when I came to a clearing, I would break into a run, and walk when I reached the woods again. I could hear nothing but the wind in the trees. Around the middle of the day, it began to snow.

Several times during the afternoon I would stop when I heard vehicles on a road somewhere downhill from me. The woods seemed endless, eternal; but at dusk, I came to a vacant brick building and I rested in a doorway to get out of the wind and the snow. There was a road leading away from the building, which I followed once it was dark.

When I began to see lights ahead of me, I abandoned the road and worked my way down through the woods. Branches whipped my face and I had to walk with my arms held up to protect my head, until I came to the edge of the woods, where through the snow I could see a street lined with houses. Some had Christmas lights in the windows. I walked through backyards and alleys and found my way to the main street in Munising. The snow was steady and I saw no one, occasionally hearing a dog barking in the distance.

I came to the Imlachs' house. Portions of the roof were gone. I walked around to the backyard, the ground strewn with wood and debris. Through the snow I could see the lights of the Frangiapani house. I went back to the Imlachs' and found that the kitchen door was unlocked. Inside it was nearly pitch dark and smelled of charred wood. I made my way through the kitchen and into the dining room, which had a window that looked out on the backyard. From there I could see the Frangiapanis' house, thirty yards away. I sat on the floor with my back against the wall, pulling my wet coat tightly about me.

II. **1945**

9.

was awakened by a sound—a car door slamming. I got to my knees on the dining room floor so I could just see over the windowsill. In the backyard chickadees pecked at the ground, their shadows cast long by the early morning sun, and a police car was parked in the Frangiapanis' driveway.

I crawled to the corner of the room and stood up so I couldn't be seen through the window. I was stiff and sore from the long trek through the woods, and I was hungry. Keeping close to the wall, I moved into the kitchen, which was completely burned out. There was a door, half opened, which led to the basement. I went downstairs and saw shelves stacked with canned goods, a workbench with tools—none of it damaged by fire. I gathered several cans in my arms—peas, wax beans, corned beef—and spilled them on the work bench. My hands shook as I picked up a hammer and started to drive a nail into the can of peas, until packing juice squirted my face, and then I saw that the corned beef had a small metal key attached to the bottom of its oblong can. After opening one end of the can, I worked the meat out with my fingers. The corned beef was salty, greasy, coated with a brown, gelatinous glaze, and I ate all of it in seconds.

I returned to the dining room and peeked out the window. The police car was still there. As I leaned back against the wall, I noticed a mirror across the room above a small hutch. In the mirror I saw a man, his gaunt, unshaven face and clothes covered in black soot, his hair matted to his skull. Out the window beside him, I could see a policeman step out the side door of the Frangiapanis' house. He paused in the driveway a moment, speaking to someone holding the door open. When he got in the patrol car and backed out of the driveway, the storm door to the house swung closed. Exhausted, I lay down on the floor.

■   ■   ■

When I awoke, tree shadows lay across both backyards and another vehicle was in the Frangiapanis' driveway: the commander's Jeep.

At least a half hour passed before Corporal Marks and Commander Dalrymple stepped out into the driveway. This time there was no pausing; the storm door to the house closed immediately, and the two men got in the Jeep and left. After a few minutes, I was considering returning to the basement to get something else to eat, when the Frangiapanis' side door opened again. Chiara came outside, wearing an overcoat and heavy boots, and she carried a wicker laundry basket tilted against her hip. She walked along a path in the snow into the backyard and began to hang bed sheets on the clothesline. There was no other movement anywhere—the houses to either side of the Frangiapanis' were partially obscured by bushes and trees.

I rapped my knuckles on the window glass. I could only see Chiara's boots below the hanging linen, and her hands paused above the clothesline. I knocked once more. She stepped around the linen, a clothespin in her mouth, and peered toward the burned house. I turned around and stepped sideways so that she could see me through the window. When she raised a hand to her throat, I moved back out of sight. In the mirror, I could see the confusion on her face. She took the clothespin out of her mouth, and after a moment of indecision hastily continued to hang the laundry. When she was finished, she dared look around the last sheet once, and then took the empty basket inside.

I went into the basement, where I found a canned Virginia ham on the shelf. I suspected that Virginia was in the southern part of the United States but wasn't sure. Wherever it was, I was thankful that they raised hogs there, and that they also attached a small key to the tin.

■   ■   ■

It was dark when I heard footsteps in the backyard. I looked toward the dining room window and saw Chiara standing with her face right up to the glass, her hands cupped around her eyes. I got up off the floor, went into the kitchen, and opened the back door slightly. She came inside and I shut the door.

"They said they thought you'd come to our house," she whispered. "I told them you weren't that stupid." She was absurdly bigger than I remembered—she wore a bulky man's red-and-black checked jacket. "You must be starved," she said, unbuttoning the jacket and producing a loaf of bread. She handed it to me, and then took a paper bag out of a pocket. "We only had some cheese in the house—but it's a pretty good provolone. Tomorrow I'll get some meat." From another pocket, she produced a bottle. "And water—you must be thirsty."

"No, I'm not hungry," I said, taking the bottle. "But water I can use." I unscrewed the cap on the quart bottle, splashed some water in my other hand, and rubbed it on my face. I could taste charcoal, but my skin felt good just to be wet.

"You're not hungry?"

"No, there's plenty of food in the basement. I have some ham left over—"

"Ham?"

"What makes the ham from Virginia so special? Is Virginia south, or west?"

She sighed in exasperation, and then began to remove the baggy corduroy pants she was wearing. She had difficulty getting them over her shoes, but after a moment of hopping around the kitchen she got them off. She was wearing another pair of pants. "These were my father's," she said, handing me the corduroys. "I think they'll fit."

"I must wash before I put anything on."

"Then get out of those dirty things."

She gave me the wool jacket and hat, and then tugged a sweater over her head; beneath that she wore a heavy flannel shirt, which she unbuttoned. "I have been imagining this for days, undoing some buttons with you, but I didn't think it would be . . . in a burned-out kitchen." She removed the shirt and underneath she was wearing another sweater. She took the pile of clothes from my arms and turned around. "Go on, if you're so shy. I won't peek."

I took off my prison uniform—everything except my socks—and washed myself as best I could with the quart of cold water.

"Does your mother know?" I asked.

"No. If she did, she'd insist I bring you to the house so we could hide you in the attic. She told you about how she met my father in the last war and hid him on their farm in Italy? She tells everyone, and I was half expecting her to tell these soldiers when they came looking for you today. But she kept her wits about her, though I thought she might take a bite out of that commander."

"Dalrymple—did he say anything about the other escaped prisoner?"

"There's another one?"

"We split up in the woods."

Though I was still wet, I pulled the corduroy pants and flannel shirt on, and said, "Okay, I'm decent."

She turned around and shook her head. "You in flannel, I don't know. Just don't open your mouth because that accent will give you away." She stepped closer and helped me pull on the jacket. "What are you going to do?"

"Anything but return to that camp. I go back, they'll kill me."

"This Commander Dalrymple said you could be shot if they find you're on the run, but if you give yourself up you'll come to no harm." She pulled the collar of the jacket tight around my neck. "We don't kill prisoners, he said."

"They don't have any idea what goes on in that place. It's the Germans. They've already tried and sentenced me to death."

■   ■   ■

Chiara could not stay long but promised to come back soon. The next morning I looked through the basement and found a folding lounge chair and some wool blankets that would be more comfortable to sleep on than the dining room floor. There was also a box of candles. I covered up the one small window in the stone foundation so that I might have some light. It was safer, I decided, to stay in the basement.

Late afternoon I was sorting through the tools when a car pulled into the driveway. I took a crowbar off the pegboard and hid in the darkest corner, behind the water heater. Overhead I heard two car doors slam, and then footsteps as they entered the house. It was two men, and though I couldn't understand everything they said, I soon realized that it was some kind of town official—perhaps a fire inspector—and an insurance agent. They spent a good deal of time in the kitchen and determined that the fire had started on the stove.

When the basement door swung open, an oblong of light illuminated the stairs and I could see the shadow of one of the men in the doorway. "What they ought to do with this place is knock it down," he said. "Looks like the basement wasn't harmed. They can build a new house on the old foundation."

The other man, who from the sound of his footsteps was the heavier of the two, came over to the basement door. He was shorter, fatter, and he wore a fedora. "The home office isn't going to like that, Lou, us paying these folks to build a brand new house in place of this dump."

"You're telling me the Imlachs' insurance wasn't paid up?"

"No, they're covered." The man in the fedora paused to light a cigarette. "We got to pay them something, but we don't want to lose our shirts in the deal. Next thing you know, other folks are getting ideas about burning down their houses."

"Most people up here aren't like that, Charlie."

Charlie moved away from the basement door, the kitchen floor creaking beneath his weight. "To knock this place down and build new would cost five, maybe even six thousand. I'd like to see us settle with them to rebuild this place, come in at two or three, tops. It just takes a little persuasion, Lou."

"And my cut?"

"Oh, 10 percent."

Lou turned in the doorway but didn't say anything.

"All I got to do is toy around with the stove here," Charlie said. "Make it look like it might have been intentional. That's all it'll take to convince 'em to settle. Keeps it quiet. The Imlachs don't want people thinking they're trying to pull some insurance scam."

"Seven hundred," Lou said.

"That's a little steep—I'll have to talk with my boss."

"You do that then." Lou walked across the kitchen and opened the door to the driveway. "And you do what you have to do later, when I'm not around. Then after New Year's we have a little talk with the Imlachs and tie this thing up."

Lou left the house, but Charlie remained in the kitchen a moment longer. He drew the smoke deep into his lungs a few times, until he dropped the cigarette on the floor and crushed it out with his shoe. I was tempted to shout up the stairs, *Why bother?*

■　　■　　■

After dark Chiara returned with a pail of water, which we brought down to the basement. She unzipped her coat and from inside removed a bottle of Chianti. "It's New Year's Eve," she said, taking a corkscrew from her pocket. "I should only stay for a few minutes. Our neighbors are coming over to listen to Jack Benny."

As I opened the bottle, I said, "Any word about Glenn Miller?"

"No. Apparently, he was flying to France where his band was going to give a concert for the troops. They believe his plane might have gone down in the English Channel, but they're not sure, or they're not saying. Planes go missing and then show up."

I filled a coffee cup I had found on the workbench and handed it to her. "Here's to men that go missing."

We drank from the same cup—Chianti, good, warm Chianti—until she put her arms around my shoulders and buried her face in my neck. "Candlelight, wine. I'll have to try and steal away long enough to—" She kissed me, and this time it wasn't rushed like in the cloakroom at the parish hall. Everything was slow, and we held each other tighter, until finally I pulled away.

"Listen, Chiara."

Again, she pressed her face into my neck. "Don't say it. Don't say anything."

"I'm an escaped prisoner. Of war. You offering me any assistance, it's—do you know who Gordie Stephan is?" She shook her head, her cheek warm against my skin. "He's an American. Lived in Detroit. He aided a POW and they convicted him of treason."

She pulled her head away. I looked at her face in the glow of the single candle, and I knew she had already been thinking about the consequences of what we were doing. "I don't know what has happened to me. I move to this sleepy little town with my mother because a friend of my mother's has a house we can have cheap, and I make the best of it. One day I'm in the grocery store and I see this man wearing this tattered uniform, and for some reason it frightens me. But I keep thinking about him, and I don't know why, though it occurs to me that it has something to do with the fact that he is off-limits—inaccessible, forbidden." She stepped away from me and picked up the coffee cup of wine, which was sitting on the workbench. "And then this strange thing happens—our neighbor's house goes up in flames. And he comes running out of the house, carrying that baby in his arms."

"We're at war, Chiara."

"*We* are not at war," she said, coming toward me again. "Do you understand what I'm saying?"

I nodded.

"It doesn't matter. If this is treason, hang me."

She kissed me then, our mouths tasting of warm Chianti.

■　　■　　■

I was sound asleep when I heard the kitchen door open. It was the middle of the night, and I remained still under the blankets on the lounge chair in the basement. No car had pulled into the driveway this time, but I was certain that it was Charlie's heavy step overhead. He had a flashlight, and its beam sent a shifting oblong of light down the basement stairs. There was the sound of metal, and then a scraping on the floor as he moved the stove. The silence that followed was occasionally broken by a tiny snapping noise as wires were being cut. It took a few minutes, and then Charlie got to his feet, shoved the stove back in place, and left the house.

10.

In the morning I found a road atlas with a map of Michigan. Detroit was more than five hundred miles away. In order to get there, you had to drive east, cross the Straits of Mackinac at a place called St. Ignace, and then go south to the base of the palm of the Lower Peninsula. I considered going west and then south through Wisconsin to Chicago, but I decided I should stay in Michigan for what I realized were irrational reasons: it was peninsulas, two of them, and there were villages named after saints. I had at least seen Detroit, if only briefly from a train, and I knew someone there.

I couldn't stay in that house another day. There was plenty of food, and I had even located the water main—but I was afraid to turn it on, fearing that somehow the authorities would discover that the water line had been tampered with, leading them to investigate the house. I needed to keep moving. It would be better for Chiara if I just disappeared. I told myself that eventually I would write and tell her that I had left because I loved her, and hoped that someday we would be together again. But I didn't believe that would happen. I didn't really expect to get out of the Upper Peninsula of Michigan, let alone to Detroit.

After dark, she didn't come to the house. I was distraught, but also relieved.

I suspected that she had come to her senses, or that her mother had got the truth out of her, and she, too, realized how dangerous it was to be involved with me. I imagined that the police, or even Commander Dalrymple, had returned and brutally interrogated Chiara—and that at any moment a team of prison guards would break into the house and haul me back to Camp Au Train. So I kept telling myself it was time to leave. I should walk out of the house while it was dark, go a few blocks down to the main street, and stick my thumb out. Get a lift from a salesman or a truck driver. Somehow get to Detroit. Five hundred miles. I wasn't sure exactly what a mile was—only that it was longer than a kilometer. The idea of America, of its size, was much too big for me to comprehend. The entire Italian peninsula would fit in the state of Michigan. It seemed unfair.

Instead of leaving, I finished the bottle of Chianti and fell asleep.

■   ■   ■

Until I heard shuffling footsteps overhead. I could also hear rain and wind against the foundation of the house. From the top of the basement stairs, Mrs. Frangiapani said, *"Dov 'è sei?"*

"Yes, down here," I said.

"Well, you don't expect me to climb those stairs, do you? Come up here." She called me *ragazzino*—little boy. I got out of the folding lounge chair and went to the bottom of the stairs. There was daylight behind her, so I couldn't see her face very clearly. Her black raincoat was drenched. "Hurry," she said angrily.

I started up the stairs, but then heard the sound of a car pull into the driveway, and I stopped. "That's the fire inspector," I said. "He and the insurance man have done something to the stove. They're going to accuse the Imlachs of starting the fire."

"On purpose?"

"Yes. Then to keep it all quiet, they'll offer them less money to rebuild the house. The fire inspector gets a payoff, and the insurance company—"

Outside a car door slammed, and then another. Mrs. Frangiapani raised her hand, made a pushing motion toward me, and I went back down into the basement and stepped out of view from the top of the stairs. I didn't bother hiding behind the hot water heater as before, because if anyone came down into the basement they would immediately see that someone had been living there.

The kitchen door opened and George Imlach said, "Mrs. Frangiapani?"

The fire inspector, Lou, said, "Ma'am, this house is unsafe and you're not supposed—"

"She's our neighbor," George said. He couldn't have been much older than me, mid-twenties. His voice was soft, timid, and he'd never see through Charlie and Lou's scheme. I remembered him at the church, taking instructions from his wife Dorothy, holding the baby during the Mass. I remember envying him, his freedom, his family—but not envying the fact that his life seemed so predetermined.

"It's really not safe for you to be here, Ma'am," Lou said. "And I'm going to have to ask you to leave the premises."

"I know what you're up to," she said. "George, he's going to tell you about the stove—"

"We are here on official business," Lou said. "I'm asking you to leave at once."

"Or what?" she said. He didn't answer.

"What about the stove?" George asked.

"This fire inspector and your insurance man," she said, "they're in it together."

"Now that's enough," Lou said.

"In what together?" George asked.

"All right," Lou said, nearly shouting. "Let's go. I'm getting the police over here."

"You do that," Mrs. Frangiapani said. "Show them the stove. George, they did something to the stove so it looks like *you* started the fire on purpose."

"How could you possibly know that?" Lou said. "You don't know anything."

"I don't understand," George said. "Why would I do that?"

I went to the bottom of the stairs and said, "The wiring, George. They did something to the wiring on that stove."

As I climbed the stairs, Mrs. Frangiapani swore repeatedly in Italian. Lou and George watched me step into the kitchen, stunned.

"They're going to make you take a lower settlement," I said to George. "Two or three thousand instead of the six it would take to build a new house. They worked it out here in the kitchen, and your insurance man came over in the middle of the night and—"

"You're that prisoner," Lou said. "The one that they haven't caught."

He had the delight of a child on his face. He was incredulous, overcome with excitement. And then George punched him, his fist landing square on his jaw, and he dropped to the floor on his side. He didn't move.

Now it was George who seemed incredulous, and he whispered, "I can't believe I—"

Mrs. Frangiapani slapped his shoulder and shouted, "*Bravo!*"

George looked at me helplessly. I ignored him, and asked Mrs. Frangiapani in Italian, "They captured the other prisoner, the Russian?"

"Yes," she said. "We heard about it last night from our neighbor who makes deliveries out there. He was brought back to camp, but then he had to be taken to the hospital in Marquette. He was beaten up—so bad they weren't sure he was alive when they put him in the ambulance."

"It wasn't the guards," I said.

"That's what Chiara told me," she said, and then she wagged a finger at me. "That girl can't keep the truth from her mother. When she said that, I knew something was up, and I got it out of her."

"What's going to happen?" George asked.

"I don't know," Mrs. Frangiapani said. "But there's hope for you yet." Taking me by the sleeve she pushed me toward the kitchen door. "Now *you*, you have to get a move on."

George still seemed befuddled as he walked over to the stove. "They were going to cheat us? But I paid my insurance premiums on time."

"You just stay, George," Mrs. Frangiapani said. "You just keep him here a little while. I'll be back, and we'll make sure Lou understands a thing or two about you and your premiums." She opened the door and pushed me outside. "*Andiamo!*"

It was snowing, quite heavily. We started across the backyard toward her house, but then I stopped and ran back to the fire inspector's car. I opened the driver's side door, reached around the steering column, and found that the keys were in the ignition. I took them out, threw them in the bushes along the side of the house, and then ran across the yard after Mrs. Frangiapani. When we reached the driveway, Chiara opened the side door. We went into the kitchen, snow melting on the linoleum floor.

Chiara grabbed me by the front of my sweater. "What happened?"

Her mother was peeling off her wet overcoat. "You must go, quickly," she said. "You take our car. You might have an hour's head start."

"Go?" Chiara said. "Go where?"

"Detroit," I said.

"Detroit?" Mrs. Frangiapani said. "In this weather, you probably won't make it to St. Ignace." She sat down at the kitchen table, weary. "But you have to try.

Steal another car, if you can." Then she looked up at me. "Good God, you don't even know the roads."

"I studied at a map."

Chiara went over to her mother and sat next to her. "I'm going with him."

"No," I said.

They stared at each other a long moment. Two women, mother and daughter. I wasn't in the room.

"No, Chiara," I said. "You're in enough trouble as it is."

"I'm going," she said to her mother. "You know I have to." Mrs. Frangiapani looked away from her daughter, and for the first time I thought I saw fear in her eyes. "You and Papa did. You hid him and then you ran. Momma, you couldn't help it either."

"We ran—we ran all the way here, to the United States," Mrs. Frangiapani whispered.

Chiara stood up. "If I go we can make it to Detroit."

"*Signora, per favore,*" I said. "Don't let her do this. I should just give myself up."

The old woman got to her feet slowly. She came across the kitchen and stared up at me. "I will go back to the Imlachs, and I will tell this fire inspector what he and this insurance man are in for. I don't know if it'll keep him from going to the police, but if he does, George and I'll see that he loses his job. You will take the Ford. We just filled the gas tank today." She turned to Chiara and said, "You would not believe George. He will make a good husband yet." Raising her fist and gently tapping my jaw, she said, "One punch!"

There was a moment then, the three of us standing in the kitchen and nothing happening. It seemed nothing could ever happen, and I wished that time would stop. The three of us there, listening to the snow pelt the kitchen windows.

■   ■   ■

It was the one thing we had in our favor, the snow. At times it was so heavy that there were few cars and trucks on the roads. We drove on through the snow, and at times we couldn't do better than twenty miles an hour. Little was said those first hours. We were hypnotized by the rhythm of the windshield wipers, and we were both in shock over what we had done.

I had never been in love before, not like this. I wondered if all of this would be happening if I hadn't fallen in love with Chiara. Escaping from Camp Au Train was a matter of survival, but I had found my way through the woods to Munising because of Chiara. At moments in those first few hours of freedom, it occurred to me that I wouldn't live long, that what I was doing would certainly end in death. I would either be killed by a bullet from some American law officer or, if I were returned to the camp, I'd be beaten to death by Vogel's goons. I hoped it would be the former—a clean shot and immediate death. But the belief that my life was about to end drove this other thing, this desire to love, which was as strong as the desire to survive. Perhaps it was even stronger, I don't know.

And here we were: I drove while Chiara navigated, the road map spread across her lap. We headed east toward Newberry, until we turned south and reached the shore of Lake Michigan, and heading east again we passed through small towns with names like Engadine and Brevort. We didn't steal another car, as her mother had suggested, although we stopped when we saw several cars that had been left to rust out in a field. Some had license plates, and I removed a pair and put them on her mother's Ford.

"I guess what surprises me most," I said as we got back on the road, "is your mother."

"No, not at all," Chiara said. We'd hardly spoken for some time, but it was as though we were in the middle of a long conversation. "All my life my mother has talked about my father, hiding him during the last war, running away with him. Ordinarily a woman like my mother would protect me against someone like you, but she *knows* what is happening. She never regretted doing what she did with my father, except for one thing."

"That she could never go home."

"Yes. She often says she'd never go back to Italy, but she thinks about it all the time."

Chiara looked down at the simple gold wedding ring on her left hand. We had been hastily pulling on coats when Mrs. Frangiapani left the kitchen. She seemed to be muttering to herself as she went into the room at the back of the first floor that she used as her bedroom. A few minutes later she came out with a silk purse and a tiny gray box. At the sink she soaped up her left hand and removed her wedding ring. After drying it off with a towel, she placed it and the box on the kitchen table.

"You'll need those," she said. "I always planned on giving them to you before your wedding, but you'll need them now."

Chiara picked up the ring and slipped it on her left hand. She wept then, and her mother pulled a tissue from the cuff of her black sweater and gave it to her daughter.

"This was my husband's," Mrs. Frangiapani said. She opened the gray box and removed a wedding ring. "He would want you to have it."

I hesitated, but then I took the ring and put it on. "Of course it fits," I said.

"I haven't much." Mrs. Frangiapani unsnapped the silk purse and removed a small wad of bills. "But this should get you to Detroit." She counted out six twenties, a ten, and then she added three ones. "I would go to the bank but there isn't time." She handed the money to Chiara, and looked at me. "I always held the money—so will she."

This made Chiara smile as she wiped the tears off her cheeks with the palm of her hand.

"She could never bear the thought of being considered a 'dishonest woman,'" Chiara now said, looking up from the map. "She and my father wore these rings before they actually could get married. She said they were married the moment they put them on."

"That's true," I said. "It was true then. It's true now."

11.

We drove for hours through the woods, from which it seemed we would never escape, until we finally came to the Mackinac Straits. We parked the Ford on a ferry loaded with other cars and trucks. The wind and the waves made for a very rough passage—which reminded me of the transport ship that had brought me from Africa to the United States—and we never got out of the car. This trip was only five miles, and soon we drove onto the pier in Mackinaw City.

"There were signs on the ferry," I said. "How do you pronounce these? Mackinac, the straits. Mackinaw, the city."

"The same, just spelled differently."

I nodded. "We have this in Italy, too. The straits, are there more than one?"

She laughed. "No. It's just the way it's spelled." But when I glanced at her she looked perturbed, which gave a depth to her stare. "Your accent," she said. "We're going to have to do something about that."

I nodded.

"We're on the Lower Peninsula. I've never been here and have always thought of it as another continent. We should reach Detroit tomorrow." I knew what she was going to say. I was thinking it, too. "We'll have to stop somewhere for the night."

"I never believed I would get this far from Camp Au Train." I wanted to say *alive*, but instead I said, "With you."

She put her hand on my forearm as I held the steering wheel.

■　　■　　■

As we moved south, the snow turned to sleet and then to rain. Outside of a town called Gaylord, we stopped at a gas station and café, Henry's Roadside Oasis. Along with the money, Chiara had gas-rationing coupons in her handbag. Before rolling down the window, she said, "Don't say a word, and when we go into that diner use that limp." When I looked at her, she said, "Didn't you know you've been limping?"

"It must be from running through the woods from camp."

We were startled when someone tapped on my door. I rolled down the window, and a man leaned down and peered inside. He hadn't shaved in a few days, and water poured off his wide-brimmed hat.

"Fill it up," Chiara said. "And check the oil."

The man looked at me and I nodded.

She pointed toward the café. "Can we get something to eat in there?"

"Sure," he said. "The meatloaf's on special."

"I'll go in and get a table," Chiara said, opening her door. "My husband is a mute."

After she got out, I turned back to the man, who stared at me a moment before going to the gas pump and lifting the nozzle. I sat in the car while he filled the tank and checked the oil. He looked like he'd been soaking wet for days. He came back to my door, and the way he held the dipstick against an oily rag, I felt like I was being shown a fine bottle of wine. "You're down a quart," he said.

I nodded.

He went to the rack of quarts of oil, placed a can on the ground, and jammed a metal spout into the lid with the solemnity of a priest sacrificing a lamb. "Me, I'd rather be deaf," he said as he leaned over the front fender of the car. "Wouldn't have to listen to the wife go on all the day long." He looked back at me through the windshield; I thought he was making a joke and began to smile, but he was dead serious.

When he was finished servicing the car, he came back to my window. "You pull over there, go on inside, and rescue your pretty little wife. I'll be right in. You can pay the whole thing together in the café."

I did as he said, and when I entered the café I favored my left leg. Chiara was sitting in a booth, and from her look of surprise I must have been convincing. A heavy woman in a powder blue uniform was taking her order. The name tag pinned to the lapel read *Phyllis*, and she wore so much makeup I could smell it. We were the only customers in the place.

"*Honey. What. Would. You. Like?*" she shouted.

"Frank's not deaf," Chiara said. "Just can't speak."

Frank.

"Oh, I thought they went hand in hand," Phyllis said. "You always hear people say 'deaf-mute.' Unless of course you are deaf." She laughed. "Oh, I'm sorry—I guess I shouldn't have said *that!*"

"No, it's fine," Chiara said. As I settled in the booth across from her, I nodded and smiled stupidly. "He hears just fine."

"That leg," Phyllis said. "The war?"

I nodded again, but no smile.

"He was repairing a Jeep," Chiara said, "when it came down on his leg."

"Oh, *hon*ey," Phyllis said. "I am *so* sorry."

I shrugged.

"Something to eat?" She said this as though it would cure everything. "Meatloaf?"

I hadn't eaten hot food since leaving the camp and I nodded vigorously.

Phyllis's husband came in out of the rain and sat on the stool next to the cash register. "Henry," she said to him. "Get these folks some coffee while I serve up their dinners." She went around the counter and into the kitchen.

Henry came over with a pot of coffee and filled our mugs. Then he went back to his stool and stared at us as he unbuttoned his slicker. I kept waiting for him to say, *You ain't deaf, that leg, it ain't so bad, and you don't look like no Frank to me.* But he just kept staring at us.

Phyllis brought out two plates: huge slabs of meatloaf and gravy, mashed potatoes, and green beans. In camp I swore I'd never eat potatoes again, particularly mashed, but I was so hungry I went through them without stopping.

Phyllis sat on the nearest counter stool. "He's got some appetite, don't he?"

"Yes, he does." Chiara watched me with genuine wonder in her eyes.

I kept eating. Down at the end of the counter, Henry hadn't taken his eyes off of us.

"Where y'all headed?" Phyllis asked.

"Detroit," Chiara said.

"Oh, you'll *never* make it by nightfall, not in this weather," Phyllis said. "We got some cabins out back. We'll let you have one for three dollars."

Out the rain-streaked window, I watched a police cruiser pull into the station. Chiara and I glanced at each other. "Let us think about it," she said, and then she picked up her fork.

The policeman got out of the cruiser and started toward the café, but he stopped behind our car. He leaned over a moment to look at something—the license perhaps. It was hard to see what he was doing back there, but then he straightened up and came inside. He sat on the stool next to Henry, and Phyllis went around the counter and poured him a mug of coffee. "Any word when it's going to clear, Pete?"

The policeman gazed at us a moment while sipping his coffee. Turning away from us, he said something to Henry and Phyllis.

I cleaned my plate. Chiara picked up her plate and placed it on top of mine. "Go ahead. I'll never get through it all."

I started in on the meatloaf. I ate without stopping, wanting to get as much in me as I could before Pete the policeman came over and arrested us. I was convinced he saw right through the license on our car. Though there had been no houses in sight of that field, I suspected someone might have seen me remove the plate from that old car and they called the police. Chiara stared out the window and I could tell she was thinking the same thing.

Pete and Henry kept talking quietly, and I continued to eat. When the policeman got up off his stool and came toward us, I ate faster. Everything about him was slow and deliberate, and I cleaned the plate just as he reached our booth.

"That your car out there?" he asked Chiara. His hat was encased in a clear plastic rain cap beaded with water, and I thought his eyes were deceptively simple.

"It is, Officer," she said.

"Mind if I ask your names?"

"Of course not." Chiara touched her cheek with her left hand, to make sure he saw her wedding ring. "Frank and Claire Green."

I stared at her, and then up at the policeman, who was nodding.

"You won't make Detroit tonight, Mr. and Mrs. Green."

"Why's that, Officer?" she said.

"You can't drive that vehicle." He looked out the window toward the car. "You have a busted taillight. Gotta get that fixed before you get back on the road."

I leaned back in the booth.

The policeman bent over and put both hands on the table. "Now, Henry tells me that he can call the parts store in Grayling, but a new taillight won't get here till sometime tomorrow." He suddenly took his hands off the table and straightened up, looking regretful. "You drive out on that road, I'm going to have to write you up a ticket."

"I understand, Officer," she said. "And I appreciate your telling us about it."

When I had changed the license plate, I hadn't noticed any broken taillight. I looked over at Henry, who wasn't staring at me now.

■   ■   ■

Our first night together was spent in a musty cabin behind Henry's Roadside Oasis. I was able to take a long, hot bath. Then I drained the tub, and as I was refilling it for Chiara, she came in and we took a bath together. Immediately, there was no shyness between us. The bed nearly filled the room, and its mattress was soft and uneven, the box spring noisy. It didn't matter; it didn't matter at all. Rain pounded the roof on and off throughout the night. It was first light by the time we'd had enough of each other, and then we slept soundly until late morning.

It was a sunny day, with enormous ice-glazed puddles everywhere. When we left the cabin, I carried our one small suitcase, which contained Chiara's clothing and a few things of her father's she thought might fit me. We went into the café, where the small lunch crowd seemed to be mostly truck drivers. The special was cube steak. I didn't know what that was, and there was no way to ask Chiara, so when Phyllis came to our booth I pointed to the breakfast menu.

"Ordinarily we don't serve breakfast after eleven, honey, but for Mr. and Mrs. Green we have the Love Bird's Special: three eggs, bacon, toast, coffee."

I nodded and made a flipping gesture with my hand.

"Over easy? Sure. How you like your bacon, *limp?*" She laughed; she wore so much red lipstick that it had smeared on her teeth. "Claire, how 'bout you, dear?"

"Just coffee, black, please." She looked away, embarrassed.

"You got it, Mr. and Mrs. Green."

After Phyllis went back to the kitchen, Chiara looked at me, and I shook my head.

"She's not talking about your leg, or your bacon, Frank."

During the night we had said a lot of things to each other. One of them was that from now on our names were Frank and Claire Green, and even when we were alone we were to use them. Francesco Giuseppe Verdi, who was named after the genius of the opera, and Chiara Maria Frangiapani, who was named after Santa Chiara, who was married in spirit but not the flesh to Saint Francis of Assisi, no longer existed. It was Frank and Claire Green. There was no grace, no music to these blunt names, just short bursts of sound, like so many American names. If we knew anything that morning, it was that we had to make ourselves into the people who could possess such names.

"Before we leave here," Claire said, "I want to call Momma." She got out of the booth, walked down past the cash register, and entered the phone booth by the front door. Several of the truck drivers along the counter turned on their stools and took notice. Americans seemed so strange to me then. But this—these men watching a young woman walk to a phone booth—was entirely familiar.

Phyllis returned from the kitchen with our order. "She divorce you already?"

I pointed toward the phone booth, then I picked up my fork, but Phyllis was still standing over me.

"You two far from home?" she asked.

I smiled at her and shrugged. Then I broke open one of the egg yolks on my plate. But the woman stayed put, her hands on her broad hips.

"You can never get far enough away, you know."

I didn't understand what she meant, so I continued to eat and nodded. If we had to do this again, I decided that the next time I would be a deaf-mute.

"'Course once they find you, the deed is done. And there ain't nothing they can do about it. There's no going back now, honey."

I stopped eating and looked up at her.

Phyllis leaned down closer and whispered, "I spotted you the moment you walked in here yesterday. Yes, I did. I have this sense about people. You're hiding something. And honey, it's written all over the two of you."

I didn't know what to do, so I picked up the salt and shook some over my eggs.

She came even closer, practically whispering in my ear. "I can see the future, too, and I don't need no cards, tea leaves, or crystal ball. It just comes to me. And I'll tell you right this minute, there will be times when you come to regret having done it, but you'll get through that. You may think you didn't have a proper beginning, but people don't elope unless they can't help themselves. Better to throw yourselves away on each other like this, even if it eventually comes to heartbreak and ruin. At least you had passion, true passion. That's a rare thing, and you seldom see it in some church ceremony where everybody's gussied up and nobody's sure they're doing the right thing."

I didn't understand what she was talking about, so I nodded and continued to shake salt on my breakfast.

"She ain't already knocked up, is she?"

I wanted to speak. I wanted to speak and shock her, but I shook the salt shaker vehemently as I shook my head.

Claire came out of the phone booth and walked back to us, again causing the men seated along the counter to take notice.

As she sat down, Phyllis said, "You want to get him to go easy on the salt, honey. He'll get hardening of the arteries by the time he's forty." She slapped me on the shoulder and then went back into the kitchen.

I put the salt shaker down on the table and looked out the window. A truck pulled out of the gas station and I could see Henry, kneeling at the back of our car, screwing the new taillight in place. He got to his feet and came into the café. After sitting in his usual place by the cash register, he began to scribble in a notepad, and after a moment Phyllis joined him.

"Momma's fine," Claire said. "She says she's going to move back to Sault Ste. Marie. She hasn't been happy in Munising anyway. She has more friends in the Soo. I asked about the Imlachs and she said she wasn't sure, but she thought that fire inspector realized she and George have him over a barrel."

I shrugged.

"Over a barrel? It means he seemed to understand that they both really meant it about his job. You'd be surprised what people will do when their job's at stake. It sounds like something's going to get worked out with the insurance company so the Imlachs can rebuild."

I nodded, and then continued to eat my breakfast. Claire drank her coffee. We were silent, and it was like we were married. We didn't need to talk. It was enough knowing the other was there. I might never have been as content, truly content, as that moment in Henry's Roadside Oasis.

When I finished my breakfast, Phyllis came over from the cash register and placed a slip of paper in front of me. "I see where she carries the purse, but I always hand the bill to the gentleman. Out of respect, you understand." Phyllis laughed as she turned and walked away.

On the slip, Henry had listed everything: gas, oil, taillight replacement, dinner, breakfast, the cabin, with the total underlined at the bottom: *$18.37.*

Claire turned the slip toward her, and her lips moved slightly as she added up the figures, and then she got out her purse and gave me a twenty-dollar bill. We went up to the cash register. I handed the bill to Phyllis, who pressed several keys, which caused a bell to ring and the drawer to slide open. When she started to count out change, I raised a hand and waved it off.

"Why thank you, honey," she said. "You two have a safe drive, and you be careful. I ain't never been there, but I hear Detroit can be one nasty place."

Henry was hunched over his coffee mug and he wouldn't even look at us.

Claire said, "Thank you for your hospitality."

And then we were out the door and climbing into the car. I pulled into the road, heading south, and said, "What's 'elope' mean?" I nearly shouted because I had such a need to speak.

"That's what they thought? We had eloped?"

"What's it mean?"

"Run off to get married."

I laughed. "And I thought they were really on to us."

"Oh, they were on to us," Claire said. There was no humor in her voice, and I stopped laughing. "You know what it means to be taken?"

"Taken?"

"For a ride."

"What?"

"They saw us coming and took us for a ride."

I looked at Claire. She was furious. "They charged too much?" I asked.

"I wonder what the cop's cut was."

"Cut? What is cut?"

"Straits. Cut. Eloped." The joy in Claire's laughter was tinged with dread. "God help us, Frank Green."

12.

We were rounding a bend in the road, doing about forty miles per hour, when I put my foot on the brake and the pedal went straight to the floor. The tires squealed as we drifted into the other lane, where a pickup truck was coming toward us, its horn blaring. I couldn't get the car back on our side of the road, so I swerved left and rolled the car off the pavement, bumping along rutted dirt, as the truck sped close by us on the right. The car descended down the shoulder of the road, plowed through a large puddle of water, and stopped at the edge of a pasture. Water hissed on the exhaust pipes, while beyond a barbed-wire fence, cows grazed as though nothing had happened.

I depressed the brake pedal twice again. "*Non funzione.*"

As we got out of the car, someone behind us called down from the road, "Everybody all right?"

It was the man in the pickup, with a dog. He was wearing bib overalls, and though he was at least in his forties, he had thick, strong hands gripping the steering wheel.

"No brakes," Claire said.

He stared at us through the open passenger-side window for a moment, his jaw working slowly. Turning his head, he spit out his window, and then looked back down at us. "My place is just up the road."

Claire had already begun to get her handbag from the front seat of the car. I whispered, "I don't want to be the mute anymore."

"Okay," she said, clearly disappointed with my decision, and as she started walking up toward the truck, "It's a free country."

I had heard Americans say this before, but while I was in prison it had never had any meaning for me. I looked back at the pasture, where one cow had wandered over to the fence, her head hanging over the barbed wire, not ten feet from me. "I'm free," I said, and she stared back at me as only a cow can.

I got our suitcase from the back seat, locked the car, and walked up to the truck. Claire was already seated in the cab with the door closed. She held the small dog out the window and said, "There's not enough room. Ride in the back with Barney." I put the suitcase in the truck bed, then took the dog and climbed up over the rail, where I sat on the wheel well, holding the dog on my thighs. In the cab, Claire and the farmer were talking, though I couldn't hear what they were saying. The farmer drove slowly, periodically leaning over his window and spitting out a stream of dark juice, while long strands of hair drifted out of Claire's window.

Soon we could see the farm we had just passed: a white clapboard house, barn, and several outbuildings. The truck pulled into the yard, causing chickens to scatter, and stopped in the shade of the one large tree that loomed over the house. The farmer got out and came around to the back of the truck. He let down the tailgate and the dog jumped to the ground. The farmer's teeth were stained with tobacco juice, and he considered me with less interest than the cow in the field, then followed the dog up to the porch door.

Claire climbed down out of the cab, and I said, "Is this all right?"

She stared at the house a moment. "Sure."

"What'd you talk about?"

"Chickens."

"Chickens. What about the car?"

"He says there's a repair shop in the next town south."

I got out of the truck bed with our suitcase, and we walked toward the house. "How come I feel like you're not telling me everything?"

"All I know is his name is Shelby and he lives with Vera. At first I thought she was his wife, but I think she's his sister. I'm not sure. She calls the shots, it seems."

"The shots?"

"The decisions."

"Ah. So maybe that means wife?"

"I don't know."

"Now that you're my wife, Mrs. Green, you call the shots."

A woman came out onto the porch. She seemed younger than Shelby, perhaps thirty-five, and she wore an apron over a print dress. She raised an arm to pull strawlike blond hair back off her broad face, and her forearm was powdered with what appeared to be flour. Unlike Shelby, she had a gaze that was hard but weary, and it seemed to know everything all at once. "Broke down, huh? Shelby'll have to tow you in to Moose's."

"Moose's?" Claire asked.

"Moose Van Voorst. Runs the garage in town. He's also the mayor and dog catcher." She smiled, revealing the fact that she was missing several teeth, as she turned to go back into the house. "Well, come on in then."

Under my breath, I mimicked her. "Well, come on in then."

We followed her into a kitchen, where she was making bread, the loaves in two rows of tin pans lined up on a large table that had a white enameled top. She opened the oven door, releasing heat into the room. Claire and I immediately began to assist her: I picked up each tin, handed it to Claire, who handed it to Vera, who put it in the oven. Twelve loaves, six on each wire rack. Once while leaning over, Vera's dress fell open, revealing her breasts, which swayed freely, smooth and pale as the loaves she was placing in the oven. When our task was finished, she closed the door and straightened up, her hands on her hips. "People come from miles around for our bread, milk, chickens, and meat." I was tempted to tell her the same was true of my family, that we sold primarily cheese and sausage, but would never think of baking bread—that was what other families did. She watched me expectantly, and when I didn't speak she swept her hair off her forehead again, leaving a streak of flour above her eyebrow. "Didn't catch your names."

We both hesitated, and then I cleared my throat. "Frank and Claire Green."

"We were headed for Detroit," Claire said.

Vera smiled as if that were the most absurd notion she'd ever heard. "Well, don't plan on getting there tonight." Then Shelby came into the kitchen, ducking to get through the door, and she said to him, "Best that you get that car into town before this weather comes. South wind," she said, looking at me. "Gunna rain. Or maybe sleet. Or snow. It'll do something."

Shelby got a coil of chain from the barn, and he and I drove back to the car. He didn't talk much, only to give me instructions on how to help as he hooked the car to the truck. Before he got back in the cab, he said, "The one thing you don't want to do is run into the back of me."

I got in the car and steered as he pulled me down the road. We rarely exceeded fifteen miles an hour, and it took almost an hour to reach a small town that seemed to rise right up off the flat pastureland, stands of trees, two church steeples, and a row of silos. We rolled down the main street, past old brick buildings, until we pulled into Moose's Texaco station. Shelby came to such a slow, easy stop that the car ceased to roll yards from the rear fender of the truck.

Moose Van Voorst was bigger than Shelby, and they appeared to be about the same age. His mechanic's jumpsuit was heavily stained with oil and grease. "Can't look at her today," he nearly shouted. "Thirty-six Ford, you're lucky she got you this far. Call tomorrow and I'll tell you what's what." He sat at a desk that was cluttered with boxes of auto parts. The office smelled of rubber; tires were stacked in the corners, and dozens of fan belts hung on the wall behind him, along with a calendar with Rita Hayworth kneeling on a bed in her slip. He began to fill out a form and said, "Name?"

"Frank Green," I said.

"Address?" When I didn't answer immediately, he looked up at me. His large nose was crooked and he hadn't shaved in several days. I was trying to understand how this man could be the mayor of any town. "Got an address, Mr. Green?"

"We are going to Detroit," I said. "We are . . . we have eloped."

"Hear that, Shelby?" he shouted. "Young love! Hot damn!"

For the first time, Shelby showed some emotion, grinning broadly.

"I guess that means you ain't got no phone neither." Out in the garage, someone began pounding on metal, the sound reverberating through the building. As he got up out of his swivel chair, Moose shouted, "You just give us a call in the morning then."

Shelby and I drove back to the farm. He didn't speak until he said, "She'll put you out in the bunkhouse. Hard to find hands now, with the war and all." I turned and stared at him, not knowing what he meant by *hands*. "You can earn your keep by helping out with chores."

"I'll be happy to." But as I said this, I saw that he was grinning because I didn't get the joke. "What would you like me to do?"

"Young love! Hot damn!" He laughed until he gasped for breath, then he leaned out his window and spit into the wind. When he stared back out the windshield he had a long, dark strand of saliva running down his chin, which he didn't seem to notice or to mind.

■   ■   ■

The bunkhouse was a one-room shed next to the barn, with two cots, a table and chairs, and a pot-belly stove. The window in the back wall looked out on a stack of firewood next to an outhouse and the pastures running to the north. Vera was right about the weather; a storm came through during the night, and there were gusts that caused the wood structure to creak and shudder, reminding me of the barracks at Camp Au Train. But Claire and I had taken the two mattresses and put them together on the floor. We opened the vents in the front of the stove, and the soft glow of the fire flickered through the room, its amber light touching her skin. Her dark hair seemed to have lights of its own, tumbling down her back, swinging across her face. There were moments that I would try to lock in my mind, because I knew that this could not last, that our odyssey was destined to end, sooner rather than later, and that whatever followed, whatever sorrows awaited us, the result would be that we would be separated, and that I would only have this, these few images of her, illuminated by the glow of the fire. This realization filled me with fear, which I did not want to show her. I knew she felt the same, and that this shared knowledge, tacit, too vile to mention, fueled our need for each other.

Our lovemaking exhausted us eventually, so we were startled awake when Shelby pounded on the door before dawn. Morning chores involved milking the cows, driving the milk to another farm, where it was bottled, and returning to feed the hogs. Shelby gave me a pair of high rubber boots, which caused my feet to sweat. Claire worked in the house with Vera, and I didn't see her until after eight o'clock when we went in for breakfast that included ham, eggs, and biscuits. Vera tilted her head and chewed on the side of her mouth with the most teeth. Once Shelby leaned sideways in his chair and passed gas loudly. I was so tired and full I just wanted to go to sleep; in fact, I dozed off while sitting in the outhouse. The boots were causing a blister to develop on my right heel, and the rest of the morning I limped, really limped. Vera noticed this at lunch and made me take off the boots. The top layer of skin had peeled off, leaving the heel raw and bloody. She rinsed it and dried it with a towel, and then got out a tin that contained gauze pads and ointments. After she loosely taped a pad over the blister, she smeared ointment on another pad and taped that over the first one. She built up four layers in this fashion, and then gave me a heavy pair of wool socks to wear over my own. When I pulled the boots on again, the gauze pads slid against each other, reducing the friction on my heel, and I could walk almost normally.

After lunch—large bowls of pea soup with homemade bread—Vera called Moose's garage. As Moose shouted into his end of the line, she listened and said, "Uh-huh," repeatedly, and after she hung up she said, "Your slave cylinders are shot." She watched me carefully.

"Shot," I said, not knowing how to react, and I looked at Claire.

"That bad?" she said.

"Moose says they're going to have to be replaced. Parts probably won't get in from Grayling for at least three days, and it's going to cost you about eighty dollars." Vera's blond hair was tied back today, and her face seemed extraordinarily wide, her jaw broad and her cheek bones smooth ridges beneath enormous blue eyes. After studying both of us a moment, she said, "Don't have it, do ya?"

Claire, who also had her hair tied back (they had been cleaning all morning and the kitchen smelled of pine trees), shook her head. "We don't have much money at all."

Vera looked like she'd just won a hand of poker. "I guess you'll be working for us for a while. We can't pay much, but we won't charge you for food and board. We'll give you," she said, nodding at me, "four dollars a day. And you, honey, you get two, though you're so skinny you ain't worth more 'n two bits." She laughed, and after a moment Claire did, too. "Now, girl, you ever kill a chicken?" Vera started for the kitchen door. Before Claire could answer, she said, "Nothing to it. Their necks are kind of like you know what in your hand." She laughed again as she led Claire out across the yard to the barn. Claire was wearing a man's wool shirt that hung almost down to her knees. Viewed from the back, she might have been twelve years old, but I knew otherwise.

Shelby and I drove about a half mile out into the pasture, where we worked on a tractor that had a flat tire. Occasionally, a car or truck would turn in off the road and stop in the yard, setting Barney to fits of barking. Though he hardly looked toward the house, Shelby would tell me who it was: neighbors, shopkeepers from surrounding towns, the Lutheran minister, all coming out to buy eggs, milk, bread, or meat. When we had the tire fixed, Shelby stared toward the house as a black sedan pulled into the yard.

"Who's that?" I asked.

"Forty-two Dodge," he said. "Dunno."

We watched a man wearing a fedora and a gray topcoat get out of the car. There was something on the door, an emblem or insignia. Vera came out from the barn alone and spoke to the man for a couple of minutes. She kept her arms folded because of the cold, but it also seemed intended to fend off the man's inquiries as he leaned toward her in what seemed a familiar yet threatening manner. When he left, he drove south, toward Grayling. Shelby watched until the car was out of sight, and then he climbed up in the cab of the tractor. "Didn't come to buy food," was all he said before he started up the tractor.

I got in the pickup and followed him across the rutted fields to the house.

■   ■   ■

Vera and Claire were at the kitchen table, peeling potatoes. The windows were steamed up, and I could smell chicken roasting in the oven. Claire truly looked like a child now, one who had been chastised and was now determined to be on her best behavior, and Vera stared at me as if she were seeing me for the first time. "Where exactly you say you two eloped from, Frank?" When I glanced at Claire, she said, "The way you look to her for the answers, you'll make one fine husband."

Claire wouldn't raise her head up from her work, and her cheeks were flushed.

I turned to Vera. "I didn't say."

"I noticed," Vera said. "And I thought, 'They're just two kids running away from home.' Well, this agent tells me something very interesting."

"What agent?" I asked.

Before Vera could answer, Shelby said, "I knew it was a gov'ment man."

She cut him a look that might shut him up for a week. "The *fed*eral government," she said. "He says they're looking for an escaped prisoner—a war prisoner. A *Nazi*. And they believe he's traveling with a girl. A dark-haired American girl."

I looked at Claire again, but she still wouldn't raise her eyes. "All right," I said, turning back to Vera. "I'm not a Nazi. I was in the Italian army and was captured in Africa. I ran from the camp because the Nazis were running the prison and they were going to kill me."

Vera lowered her head and continued peeling the potato in her hand. Shelby remained where he was, leaning against the sink with an empty glass in his hand.

Vera took her time with the potato, and then she dropped it in the porcelain bowl that was full of potatoes in murky water.

Finally, Shelby said quietly, "Remember what they done to us."

"I'm thinking about all that," Vera said without looking up. There was a potato peel clinging to the back of her wet hand; its pale side was facing up, and it almost looked like her own skin. She peeled it off her hand, much like the layer of skin that had come off the blister on my heel, and dropped it in the pile on the table. I realized that tears were streaming down her cheeks, and she didn't bother wiping them away.

Shelby turned at the sink, held the glass beneath the spout of the water pump, and began working the handle up and down. After a few strokes there came a gurgling sound deep in the pipe, and soon after, water splashed out and into the glass. When it was full he stopped pumping. He drank the entire glass down without stopping, and then stared out the window above the sink. Though it was late afternoon and the sky was overcast, the light made his blue eyes seem to radiate from within. At the table Vera had lowered her head further, and she was releasing soft sighs as she cried.

"Would you two leave us be for a spell?" Shelby asked.

"Certainly," I said. I was so confused at that moment I'd almost said *certamente*.

Claire got up from the table, wiping her hands on a towel. I opened the kitchen door and we went outside. We didn't speak as we crossed the yard to the bunkhouse. It was beginning to snow, and then I realized that it wasn't just snow, but sleet. In the bunkhouse I put kindling in the stove. Claire sat at the small table by the window, her arms folded against the cold.

"We should leave," she said.

I rolled old newspapers up and stuffed them beneath the kindling. "Where are we going to go?" I opened the box of matches, lit one, and held it beneath the newspapers, which caught fire quickly. "And how are we going to get there? Walk? How far can we get before someone stops us?" I added a log to the fire, closed the stove door, and went over to Claire. I removed my jacket—it had been her father's—and put it around her shoulders. "It'll warm up soon." I got one of the blankets off the mattresses on the floor and draped it over her legs. "You should go back to Munising. They catch me, I'll go back to that camp, I guess. But these people don't know who you are, where you're from. You could hitchhike home—isn't that what you call it?"

"I am not going anywhere," she said. "Not without you."

"Anyone asks you, just say I forced you to go with me. They'll believe that."

She got up from the table, holding the jacket around her shoulders with one hand, carrying the blanket with the other. She lay down on the mattresses, her feet toward the stove. I knelt down and spread the other blankets over her. Her eyes were already closed, and I'd never seen her look so weary before; her face held a suggestion of the woman she would become, and in some ways the lines that formed around her full mouth and the dark skin beneath her eyes made her even more beautiful. I put my hand on her forehead, and she smiled faintly, her eyes still closed. "I have not been cutting trees like you. I scrubbed floors and killed three chickens today. It's exhausting work." Then she turned on her side and curled up.

The stove's heat was already starting to fill the room. I sat at the table and stared out the window. The land was so different from the Upper Peninsula, so flat that I could see a stand of barren trees that was on the far side of an enormous field. The sleet was heavier now, and the gusting wind hurled small beads of ice against the windowpanes.

13.

I must have dozed off, because I was awakened by the sound of footsteps crunching on the ice-covered ground, followed by a soft knock at the door. Claire was fast asleep and didn't stir. I got up from the table, went to the door, and opened it; Shelby stood in the sleet, his shoulders hunched, his collar turned up.

I stepped outside into the cold. "She's asleep."

"Come." He turned and led me to the side door of the barn. Inside there was a workbench covered with tools and half-finished projects—some reglazed windows, a disassembled fence gate. He pointed to several overcoats hanging from a series of pegs on the wall. "You two will need them."

I took one coat, brown corduroy with a sheepskin collar, and pulled it on; it was heavy and smelled faintly of straw and manure. There was a hat in one pocket, a wool hat called a Stormy Kromer, which was a baseball cap with ear flaps. I'd seen Americans wear these in the Upper Peninsula; I put this one on and was thankful for its warmth.

Shelby reached up to a shelf above the workbench, pushed aside some paint cans, and took down a bottle; the label said *Old Mr. Boston*. There were two coffee cups on the shelf also, and he put these on the bench and poured some whiskey in each. Handing me one of the cups, he sat on the only stool at the bench. There was a scarred church pew along the wall, and I sat down and sipped the whiskey. The last time I had tasted anything like it was in Commander Dalrymple's office. It went down hard, but I could feel my face flush with its heat.

Shelby took a pack of cigarettes from inside his coat—Lucky Strikes. He tapped one out, lit it with the matches tucked beneath the cellophane, and then tossed me the pack. We both smoked and sipped from our cups; it was dark in the barn, and though there was a light bulb hanging above the bench, he didn't bother to turn it on. We could hear the cows, chewing, rubbing themselves against their stalls, urinating; occasionally one would give out a long, baleful moan.

"Use to be six or seven of us working this farm," he said. "More during harvest. War changed all that. I can see you ain't no German Nazi. Vera, well, something happened that . . ." He poured a little more Old Mr. Boston into our cups, and then said, "You ain't the enemy. You two can stay here until you can get your car back, and then you go on. I know about them work camps—they have 'em down here too and I've heard stories. Sending you back there to get killed ain't going to win us the war." He threw back the rest of his whiskey and got up off the stool. He went to the door and, as he opened it, he said, "Now you go and wake up that little girl of yours. Dinner'll be on in no time."

I finished what was in my cup. Much of what Americans said seemed curious to me. I thought about *no time* and then went to the bunkhouse, where Claire was just getting up from the mattress. I said, "Dinner'll be on in no time."

.   ■   ■

The routine at the farm started every morning before dawn, and every night Claire and I would crawl under the blankets in front of the stove by eight o'clock. Usually we would fall asleep, exhausted, and wake up several hours later, the room cold as the fire had died down. I'd add wood to the stove, and we'd make love so that we'd have to throw off the blankets.

It was a Friday when Moose Van Voorst stopped by in his tow truck. He nearly shouted, even though he and Shelby and I were standing in the yard with nothing but chickens pecking the hard ground around us. "Them parts," he hollered. "They ain't got the right ones in Grayling. They have to be sent up from Detroit." He pronounced it De*trow*it. "Won't get here till middle of next week anyways."

"I see," I said.

He turned to Shelby and said, "You coming into town tonight for the bas-ketball game? They're playing West Branch. Got this center, boy's six-eight and they say he can jump over a cow without no running start."

"Maybe," Shelby said. "Depends on whether Vera wants to visit with Mar-jorie."

Moose climbed back up into the cab of his tow truck. "Okay, but remember it's your turn to bring the paper bag."

We watched him pull out into the road and head toward town. We could hear him shift gears for half a mile, then we walked back toward the barn.

"Shelby, you mind my asking how he got to be mayor?"

"Nobody else wanted the job." He spit juice on the ground. "Ever been to a basketball game?"

"No. And I've only seen one man who was that tall. He was in Africa and he was dead, burned head to toe. We stopped and looked at him, lying on the side of the road. He had to be seven feet."

"Well, you and the missus can come along if you want."

The word "missus" seemed strange. "Thank you, but I think we should just keep out of sight."

"Up to you. It's a free country." Then he chuckled. "For some of us, anyway. Just as well. Your English ain't too bad, but your accent. I suspect most people would think you were from someplace like Quebec where they got a lot of them Frenchie Canadians."

"I assure you I have never been mistaken for a Frenchman."

"See, it's pretty much all the same round here. There's us and there's *for-ners*."

■   ■   ■

We ate early that night, and then Shelby and Vera went into town. Claire and I stayed on in the kitchen and cleaned the dishes. We had the radio on, and when "Moonlight Serenade" came on we turned the light out and danced, our feet shuffling on the linoleum floor.

When the song ended, Claire took me by the hand and said, "I want you to see something." We went through the living room to a small den at the front corner of the house, where Claire turned on a lamp on a desk. I'd never been anywhere in the house other than the kitchen, but she had spent a lot of time helping Vera clean every room. There was a cabinet with some old china, and on the top shelf there was a photograph of an American sailor. He was wearing a white uniform, his hat tucked under his arm. There was a harbor in the background, with palm trees.

"You see the resemblance?" Claire said.

"It could be Shelby twenty years ago."

"Vera saw me looking at it, but she didn't say anything, so I didn't ask."

"Maybe it's her brother, or it could be her father," I said.

"I think it has to do with what made Vera cry today."

I shrugged.

"I've seen no other photographs that might be family in the house."

Just then a set of headlights swung into the yard and Barney began barking in his pen. We looked out the window and watched the sedan stop in the yard. The official-looking emblem on the door was difficult to see. We left the den and went into the dark living room, but the shades weren't drawn, so Claire led me up the stairs and into a small room where Vera did her sewing. When we heard the car door shut, we looked down through the lace curtains as the agent climbed the porch steps, but he didn't knock at the front door. Though the dog continued to bark, we could hear the agent's footsteps on the floorboards as he moved along the front of the house. He would pause occasionally, probably to look in windows.

Then he came down off the porch and we watched him cross the yard to the dog pen. As he squatted before the gate, he took something from his coat pocket and put his hand up to the chicken wire, causing Barney to stop barking. The agent stood up and walked on to the bunkhouse. He opened the door and went inside. After a couple of minutes he came out and returned to the porch. Claire took my hand and led me into a closet, which smelled of camphor. We heard the kitchen door open, and the agent's shoes made a tapping sound on the linoleum. He came into the living room, where the floor creaked beneath him, and entered the den, which was directly beneath us. There was silence, followed by a sound I couldn't identify at first. Claire stared up at me, and then I made a motion with my hand as though I were sliding open a desk drawer. He opened each one, and closed it with a clap. He was unhurried, and once I could hear the rustle of paper.

He left the den and stopped at the foot of the stairs. "Dogs can always be bribed," he said. His voice was deep, rich, but absurdly playful. "Come out, come out, wherever you are." As he climbed the stairs, he began to whistle.

At the top of the stairs he paused, and we could hear him breathing, the low wheeze of someone who takes little exercise. There were four rooms upstairs, and he went into the one across the hall from ours, his shoes knocking on the hardwood floors. Again, drawers were slid open and shut, and something—I suspected an article of clothing—was dropped on the floor. "Oh, Vera." His voice was almost gleeful now. "I loved to slide these panties down your thighs." Louder, as if to someone else, he said, "It was in the summertime, you know. We were two years out of high school. Lorraine and I had to get married, of course, and she reeked of breast milk all the time. Vera and I liked to use the barn out there. It was a long summer, no rain."

Abruptly he came into the hall and stood for a moment just outside the room we were in, and then he descended the stairs slowly. "But I'll be back, and we'll meet at a more opportune moment."

He went through the living room to the kitchen, where he stopped, and we listened to the silence for a good half minute. I began to worry that he was somehow coming back through the house and up the stairs without being heard. I wondered if he could do that if he removed his shoes. But then there was a trickling sound, which grew more forceful as he urinated on the linoleum floor. When he was finished, he said, "It's too cold out there tonight. Don't want the little fella to catch a chill, do we?"

The door opened again, and he went out onto the porch and crossed the yard to his car. This time Barney didn't bark, but he whined a couple of times, as if he expected more of what the agent fed him. The agent's footsteps crunched on the glaze of ice in the yard. I left the closet, and Claire followed me to the window, where we peeked out through the curtain. He opened the door and got in the car, but he sat there for at least a minute before starting the engine. The car moved in a slow, lazy circle in the yard, turned out into the road, and headed south. We watched until its taillights disappeared.

Claire went out into the hall to the room where he had been; I followed and found her picking up various women's undergarments and putting them back in the dresser. I went downstairs to the kitchen. The floor tilted toward the center of the house, and the puddle had run to the corner by the icebox. I found several towels in a drawer and began to wipe up the floor.

■　　■　　■

Neither of us slept well until early morning. When I heard Shelby swing open the barn door, I got up and dressed quietly. Through the window I could see him walking across the yard to the house. I went over to the kitchen, where Vera had brewed a strong pot of coffee. She must have seen me coming because there were three cups and saucers on the table.

She sat across from Shelby and gestured toward the empty chair. "What is it?"

"That government agent was back last night," I said as I sat down.

Vera's eyes were like I'd never seen them before: startled, frightened, and yet also seemingly vindicated. "I knew he wouldn't stay away," she said.

"Who is he?" I asked.

"Roy Ferris," she said.

"You went to high school together."

She leaned back in her chair. "What happened?"

I looked over toward the icebox. "He urinated on your floor. I cleaned it up with a couple of towels. They're out in the barn. I was going to wash them and not tell you, but I've slept on it and I think you should know." Neither of them moved. "He was in your room, too," I said to Vera. "Went through your dresser."

For a moment I could see anger in her eyes, the set of her mouth, but then it passed into something else, some recognition, perhaps even acceptance.

"Did he see you?" Shelby asked.

"We hid in a closet. There's something about him—don't you say a person is 'odd'?"

Vera fingers worried the edge of her apron.

"I must leave, now," I said. "Can you help Claire go home and keep her out of this?"

"Leave?" Shelby asked. "What, you going to walk?"

"I will what you call hitchhike. South, to Detroit."

We drank our coffee, and when Shelby got out his pack of Lucky Strikes and offered me one, I took it. I'd never seen him smoke in the house before and was sure this was forbidden, but Vera was so preoccupied that she didn't seem to notice the blue smoke gathering about us, until she removed the saucer from beneath her cup and placed it in the center of the table to serve as an ashtray.

"I have to ask," I said, but I couldn't go on. I felt it would be getting too near something that these good people did not want to face any longer, something that their daily routines were designed to avoid.

Vera appeared to come up out of a reverie. "You want to know why?"

"Yes. Most Americans would turn me in."

"Some would shoot you on sight," Shelby said.

"I won't go back to the camp," I said. "My friend, Adino, he was sent back to Italy. I doubt he'll ever walk again."

"The Germans?" Vera said.

"Cut his Achilles tendons. They held a trial and I was sentenced to death." I pushed my chair back from the table. "I must go before she wakes up." They looked at me in a way that caused me to wonder if I'd spoken Italian by mistake. "Please, if you could help Claire in some way." I went to the door, but paused and said, "You are very even people."

As I crossed the yard, Barney poked his head through the kennel gate. He didn't bark, just wagged his tail. I hurried down to the paved two-lane road, the south wind coming straight at me, so I tucked my chin inside the upturned coat collar. It took me at least twenty minutes to get out of sight of the farmhouse. In that time not one vehicle passed, and that was just as well because I wanted to get away from the farm so no one would think Vera and Shelby had anything to do with me. Eventually, sleet began to come in on the wind. When I heard the sound of tires on the road behind me, I turned around and stuck my thumb out.

It was Shelby's truck. He stopped and rolled down the passenger-side window, and Barney stuck his head out, pleased to see me. "Vera has watched from the kitchen window since you left," Shelby said. "It could be hours before somebody drives by here. Come on back now."

"How far is it to Detroit?"

"A ways."

"What's 'a ways'?"

"You'll never get there on foot."

I climbed up into the cab and Barney nestled in my lap. As Shelby turned the truck around, he offered me his pack of Lucky Strikes, and my hands shook as I tapped out a cigarette. "Claire, did she wake up?"

"Not before I left. Vera will just say you and I are doing errands."

After I lit my cigarette, the truck smelled pleasantly of tobacco and wet dog. "Can I ask you about something? You and Vera . . ." I hesitated.

"We're cousins. We were raised together on the farm after her parents died in a fire. That's why Vera sent me after you—she's always willing to take someone in, man or beast." He glanced at Barney. "We found him abandoned in the fields, with a broken leg. Probably thrown from a car. But she's made it clear you have to leave once your car's fixed."

"What about Roy Ferris? He said he would be back."

Shelby just kept his eyes on the road.

.   .   .

Monday morning, Van Voorst's garage called to say that our car would be ready at the end of the day. Shelby and I drove into town that evening. Claire stayed at the farm, packing. We had told Shelby and Vera that we would leave Tuesday morning. Vera only said that she would make us a nice chicken dinner.

When we reached the garage, Shelby said, "Before leaving town, I need to stop by the Elks Club to talk to a fellow."

"We passed it on the way into town."

"It would be better if you drove straight back to the farm."

"Moose? Elk? Is everything here named after a four-legged animal?"

He considered this longer than I expected. "No, some places are named after fish."

I got out of the truck and went into the garage. The brake job cost eighty-seven fifty, and as I drove back out to the farm I calculated that Claire and I had twenty-three dollars left.

When the farm came into view across the fields, I could see a car—Roy Ferris's sedan—parked in front of the house. I pulled off the road, stopping next to a stand of trees alongside the south pasture, and walked toward the house, keeping close to the barbed-wire fence. Cows wandered over to see what I was up to, poking their big heads out between the wires. It was dark when I reached the barnyard. I went up to the kitchen windows. The kitchen was empty, but there was a pot on the stove, steam rising from beneath its iron lid. I walked around to the front door. There weren't any lights on in the rest of the house.

It was not only dark, but quiet—only the sound of chickens, pecking at corn kernels on the ground. I walked out into the yard and saw Barney in the kennel, lying motionless on his side. As I approached I could see blood pooled in the dirt. He'd been shot in the head, the left side of his skull gone.

I walked toward the bunkhouse, but stopped when I heard a sound from inside the barn—something knocking on wood. I went quietly to the barn door, which was open just enough for me to slip inside. At the far end of the barn there was a dim, flickering light—a lantern, casting tall shadows on the wall. I could hear breathing, the sound of a struggle, and moaning.

Tools were kept inside the door and I picked up an axe. I moved toward the back of the barn, keeping close to the stalls on my right. One horse snorted, causing me to stop. The sound from the back of the barn paused, but then, after a moment, it resumed, seemingly more urgent than before—it was a persistent rhythm that I recognized now. I continued on, stepping carefully. The last stall had no gate and was used to store harness, rope, and other gear. When I was close enough to see over the half-wall, I stopped. Roy Ferris knelt behind Vera, who was down on all fours. With each thrust she let out a moan. There was no pleasure to the sound. It was agonized, painful. The front of her dress was torn and her breasts swung freely, jouncing as Ferris entered her harder, faster from behind.

I stepped into the stall and looked into the corners. There was no sign of Claire. Ferris gazed up at me with enormous, bulging eyes, and the word that came to mind was *pazzo*—crazy. He thrust frantically, hurrying now, unable to stop. Vera's hair hung down over her face, which was covered with dirt and straw. For a woman she had a husky voice, but now she let out a long wail. I raised the axe and swung, hitting Ferris's shoulder with the blunt side of the blade. He grunted as he was thrown off Vera, his head slamming into the barn wall. He lay still, crumpled in his overcoat, his trousers bunched around his bare legs.

"Where is she?" I said to Vera.

She was struggling to get to her feet. I reached out to help her, but she held out an arm as if to fend me off. When she was standing, she gathered up the front of her dress to cover herself as she staggered backwards.

"Claire," I said. "What happened to her?"

Her eyes were streaming with tears and her mouth quivered as she tried to speak, but she could only stare at me, until she turned her head toward Ferris as he drew a revolver from the pocket of his overcoat. I swung the axe quickly, and the blade came down on his shoe and sank into the packed earth. Ferris's gun went off and he released a scream that was high-pitched for such a big man. Throughout the barn horses stirred, some kicking at their stall gates. The toe of Ferris's shoe was separated from his foot. He rolled over on his side and began to crawl away on all fours, until he fell on his side and stared up at me. He still held the gun and began to raise his arm. I tried to worry the axe out of the ground, but the blade had sunk very deep and wouldn't release. He extended his arm, his hand shaking, and as he took aim there was a loud gunshot that seemed to go off in my right ear. The blast struck Ferris in the chest, thrusting him down into the dirt. His overcoat and shirt were shredded and soaked with blood.

I looked at Shelby, who still held his rifle over the half-wall, prepared for Ferris to sit up at any moment. But Ferris didn't move, except for his right leg, which twitched rhythmically. Blood issued from the open toe of his shoe.

.　　.　　.

We left the barn and entered the kitchen, which smelled of charred meat—the water in the pot had boiled away. Using a towel, Shelby removed it from the stove and then shut off the burner. Vera was wearing his jacket now, and she sat at the kitchen table, clutching it about her. She was shaking and she wouldn't look up from the floor.

I sat across from her at the table. "Vera," I said, this time speaking calmly. "You have to tell me. Where is Claire?"

She wouldn't look at me.

Shelby went into the pantry, climbed up on a step stool, and reached behind some boxes and tins on the top shelf. He got down a pint bottle, and then came to the table with three glasses. He filled them with whiskey and held one up to Vera. "Come on, now," he said. "Take this, and tell him what happened."

Vera only stared at the floor, her eyes flooded with tears. If anything, her shivering had gotten worse.

Shelby sat down. "Ferris got to her years ago," he said, and then he drank down the whiskey. "She lost it—the child. And he went off to work for the government, but then he came back a few years ago and he's been sniffing around like they had unfinished business."

"She's got to tell me," I said.

He nodded and leaned toward her. "What he do with her, Vera?"

Slowly she raised her head. Her eyes studied the tabletop, and then she glanced at me. "When he arrived she was over in the bunkhouse, packing. I was in here getting dinner ready. I heard the car, and then Barney. I thought it was your car. Then there was the first gunshot and he stopped barking." She picked up the glass on the table and took a sip. Her hand wasn't shaking too badly now, and she was breathing deeply. "When I got to the front door, I saw him in the open door of the bunkhouse. I could see Claire, running out into the pasture. She must have climbed out a back window. He went around the side of the bunkhouse, and he took his time. Pulled out his gun and took aim and fired two, three times." She took another sip and then placed the glass on the table. "She went down in the field once, but she gets up. The next shot, she goes down and doesn't move. Then he turns and sees me."

I got up from the table and went to the door.

Shelby followed me. "We'll need this." He took a lantern from the peg on the wall.

He lit the lantern, and we went outside, crossing the yard to the pasture. It was pitch dark, and occasionally we could hear the cows lowing. We walked about a hundred yards, keeping well apart, and then Shelby said, "Over here." I ran toward him across the wet, icy field and saw him kneel down next to Claire, who was lying on her side in a furrow. When I reached them, he said, "She's alive."

She didn't move.

"It's a long way to carry her," Shelby said, getting to his feet. "I'll fetch the truck."

He gave me the lantern and started across the field. I could see that her jacket and blue jeans were soaked in blood, but I couldn't tell where she'd been wounded. I took off my coat, and when I put it over her she opened her eyes. I touched her hair, which was caked with cold mud.

■   ■   ■

By the time we got Claire in the house, Vera had changed—she was now wearing pants and a flannel shirt—and she had washed her face and tied her hair back. We put Claire on the couch in the den, and then Shelby insisted I come out into the kitchen. "Vera's a nurse," he said. "Let them be for now. We've got to get you ready to leave, and then I'll take care of Ferris."

Vera spent about a half hour with Claire before coming into the kitchen to explain to me what had happened. "The bullet passed through her right thigh," she said. "Fortunately, it was a small-caliber bullet and it didn't hit bone. A lot of blood, but only a flesh wound." Vera went to the sink, worked the pump, and began to wash her hands. "She must have been running away and had turned back when she heard shots, and the bullet just caught her. An inch one way, it would have missed. The other way, it would have been much worse." Vera seemed alert, if tired now.

"Thank you," I said. "How are you?"

She wiped her hands on a dishtowel and didn't look at me. "It's too dangerous to send her to a doctor. The wound is clean, but you will have to change the dressing often." She went to the kitchen table and picked up the glass of whiskey that Shelby had poured for her. "You must go immediately, while it's dark."

I felt extremely weary all of a sudden, unable to think. "Where will we go now?"

"Can't help you much there." Shelby tugged on his earlobe a moment. "Weren't you headed south, toward Detroit?"

I nodded.

"It's your best bet now," Shelby said. "The bigger the city the better."

Vera picked up the pint of whiskey and handed it to him. "I have told you this is not to be in this house."

He took the bottle and tucked it in the pocket of his coat. He opened the door, and I followed him across the barnyard.

"I'm sorry for this," I said. "Vera is angry that we ever stopped here."

"Nope. She's more upset about me hiding whiskey in the house," he said. "As far as Ferris goes—I should have put that dog down years ago."

"What will you do with him?"

"I'll take care of that after you leave." He took the pint bottle from his coat pocket, opened it, and tipped it up to his mouth. When he handed the bottle to me, he said, "Hogs, they eat anything. His car, I'll put it in the barn and deal with it piece by piece."

14.

When I was a boy, my family visited Rome one Palm Sunday. We stood in Vatican Square for over three hours while the pope performed Mass. There were tens of thousands of people there, and my mother insisted that my sister and I hold hands and stand between her and Papa. "Otherwise someone might steal you," Papa said, and I couldn't tell whether or not he was joking. "Right during the Offertory, when everyone has their heads bowed and their eyes closed, a gypsy will grab a child, and take him away and sell him. So while we're in the city, you two hold hands and stay between Momma and Papa."

I remember the look of fear in my sister's eyes, and how damp her small hand became in mine, and that's how I felt when we approached Detroit. Claire was exhausted, and we had pulled off the road and slept in the car several times, so we didn't arrive in the city until late the next afternoon.

"How is it?" I asked.

"Sore," she said from the back seat, where she'd been lying down.

"Should we stop again to change the bandage?"

"You keep driving. I can do it. Vera gave me what I need. You might turn the heat up, though. We want to continue south until we reach downtown."

I had never seen such traffic. It was stop and go, a traffic light at almost every intersection. Finally, we found a parking space on a busy street. We got out of the car, and I said, "I won't play a mute here."

"All right, and now it's my turn to limp."

As we walked away from the car I held her arm. Though it was painful to walk, she smiled, glad to be out of the car. We passed by stores, and at the end of the block, she asked, "So, what do you think?"

"*Non é Roma o Milano.*" When she looked at me, she seemed angry, and I added, "Rome and Milan are the only other cities I've been to, and this looks nothing like them."

"Frank, listen: no more Italian. Your English is accented enough as it is. Otherwise, I'll make you a mute again."

"Okay," I said. The sidewalk was crowded and everyone seemed in a hurry. "Do you know anyone here?" Claire shook her head. "I do," I said, which caused her to stop walking. "We've never met, of course, but—" I pointed toward a bar and restaurant called Jake's Pub. "Would they have a telephone in there?"

The place was dimly lit and we went up to a polished wooden bar. I ordered a draft beer called Stroh's, and Claire asked for a Coca-Cola. We went to a phone booth in back, and it took several calls, but finally I reached Professor June Stillman, at Wayne University. At first she didn't understand me at all, and then, after a pause, she said, startled, "You're the Italian soldier—the one taking the correspondence course?" In our correspondence I imagined that she was an elderly woman, but her voice was young, perhaps in her early thirties. "Where are you calling from?"

"Detroit. Near downtown, I think."

"I don't understand. You're a prisoner of war."

"Yes." I hesitated. "But, you see, I'm free now." I thought she would hang up.

"Where are you?" she asked.

■   ■   ■

When I gave Professor June Stillman the address of Jake's Pub, she said she would meet us at six o'clock. Claire was tiring, so we went back to the car, and she slept in the back seat while I sat behind the steering wheel. It was early evening and people were getting out of work, hurrying along the sidewalks. At the corner they stood in line to board trolley cars, and I envied them—I wanted to ride such a trolley car; I wanted to take one to a place I thought of as home.

I was having second thoughts. I told Claire we had to be careful about June Stillman. It was possible that she had been contacted by the authorities and she would lead them to us. Professor Stillman must have understood my hesitancy, because on the phone she'd said, "I'm short—four-foot-ten. Everybody looks at me twice, and then they try not to stare."

The bar in Jake's Pub was crowded when we returned, but some of the booths were empty. There was a jukebox—I'd never seen one of these new contraptions and I was fascinated by it. Patrons frequently played big band tunes, particularly numbers by Glenn Miller's orchestra. Claire suggested that she would make contact with the woman first. There were two booths near the back; Claire sat in the first one, facing the front door, while I sat with my back to her in the next booth. She ordered a Coca-Cola and I got another Stroh's.

Ten minutes after six, I said over my shoulder, "I don't think she's coming."

"That clock is on bar time. It's fast. Give her a bit longer." Then she paused, and said, "Wait. This must be her."

I was afraid to turn around, so I sipped my beer. I could hear her footsteps— short and quick—as she came down the bar. Claire said, "Professor Stillman?"

"Yes?"

"You're here to meet Mr. Verdi?"

"Yes, I am." She sounded confused.

"Won't you please sit down?" Claire said. "He'll join us in a moment."

I could hear the woman slide into the other side of the booth. "I thought he was alone," she said.

I got out of my booth and turned around. "I'm afraid I wasn't very clear over the phone."

She wore a gray suit and everything about her was tiny. Her straight black hair was chopped off at the shoulders, and she wore thick glasses. She looked like she could have been fourteen just last week, and now she was at least thirty. She seemed startled and confused as she glanced back and forth between us. "What's going on here?"

If I had been there alone, I would have simply walked out of the pub. But Claire seemed unable to move from her side of the booth.

Professor Stillman had a double chin, and her teeth were large and rather crooked. Her eyes were curious, intelligent, and she seemed delighted. "You escaped," she said to me.

I sat down next to Claire. "That's right."

"Wonderful. Did you tunnel out?"

"No, I ran off into the woods."

"He had no choice," Claire added.

"Of course you didn't. In war, the only choice is to survive." She looked at Claire. "And you helped him?"

We both stared at this small woman in a gray suit who sat across from us. Behind those glasses, her eyes turned solemn and sincere. I felt desperate to make our situation clear. "We have not eloped."

At first I didn't think she understood what the word meant, but then she said, "The thought never crossed my mind." She paused, and then with great patience explained, "It's not *elo-ped*, it's *elopt*. The *ed* sounds like a *t*. It's called syncopation, and—" A waitress came to the booth, and the professor ordered a drink called a Manhattan and asked if she could buy us another round, a term I'd never heard before. After the waitress went to the bar, Professor Stillman leaned toward Claire. "Honey, are you all right?"

"She should be in ta doctor," I said.

From the professor's expression, I could tell that I had not spoken correctly again. "See the doctor," she said.

"Ta doctor."

Shaking her head, she said, "You must work on the *th*. It's hard, just as it's hard for English speakers to learn to roll their *r*'s when they try to speak Italian or Spanish—it takes a lot of practice." She studied Claire a moment. "What, you're pregnant?"

"No. I've been shot," Claire said softly.

"What?" She glanced over her shoulder and then leaned toward us. "Shot, with a gun?"

We had no choice then but to explain everything to her, which we did over several rounds. She wanted to know why I had contacted her. When I said that she was the only American I knew, she laughed. "You don't know what I am? You have no idea? I'm a pacifist," she whispered. "And a member of the American Communist Party."

"This is curious," I said. "Why are you not in prison?"

She finished her Manhattan, an awful-looking drink with a red cherry in it. "Honey, they would love to land me in prison."

■   ■   ■

She offered to let us stay at her apartment for a few days. She also said she would take Claire to a doctor she knew at the university. And she talked about people who might be able to help us find work and a place to live. When we left the pub we walked several blocks, slowly, but stopped when we turned a corner: a policeman stood on the sidewalk next to our car, writing a ticket.

"The license plates," I said to the professor. "They're stolen."

"Then we need to leave it," she said.

"But our suitcase," Claire said. "It has everything in it—"

"It won't be safe to go near that car now," the professor said. "We'll take the DSR."

"The DSR?" I said.

She pointed at the trolley car coming around the street corner, its steel wheels squealing on the curved track. "It's short for Department of Street Railways," she shouted above the noise. "The thing you have to learn about Americans is that anything that can be abbreviated will be. It's how we view time, really."

"Time?"

"Time, Francesco. Minutes, hours, days, weeks, years. Life, if you will."

She led us down the sidewalk to where the trolley had stopped, and as we boarded the crowded car, I was curious more than frightened. I'd never seen so many women wearing nylons. Next to me, a man in an overcoat was reading a newspaper. At the top of the page, in small print, it read: *I am paper. SAVE me. I am ammunition for war. Don't waste or throw me away.* Farther down the page was an advertisement for the new Disney movie, *Snow White*, but what caught my attention was the headline: "No Sign of Miller's Plane in English Channel."

As the trolley started to move, the interior lights flickered occasionally, but no one seemed to notice. Claire held me by the arm and a couple of times she glanced at me, her eyes asking if we were again being taken for a ride. I could only grip the smooth metal bar overhead and set my legs apart for balance as the trolley, picking up speed, seemed to not just hurtle through the city night but through time itself.

III. 1956

15.

closed the shop as usual at five-thirty. It was one of the first days of the year when a warm afternoon breeze came off the Detroit River. On the sidewalk, men carried their suit coats slung over their shoulders, and women seemed to push through the heat, their skirts shifting languidly as they walked to the DSR stop at the corner. As I locked the front door, I saw his reflection in the glass: he was leaning against a signpost across the street. His dark suit coat was buttoned up, despite the heat, and a folded newspaper was tucked beneath one arm. He had been there at least an hour ago, when I had glanced out my showroom's plate-glass window.

This was nothing new. A day hardly passed when I didn't see someone I suspected might be watching me. They often employed the usual props, a newspaper or a book, and they never seemed to be looking directly toward me. They were always men. In the warm months they often wore sunglasses. I could never be certain if their surveillance was real or a figment of my imagination. Still, I had no choice but to play it safe. I had developed different means of escape, all requiring that I do nothing to indicate I knew I was being watched.

Instead of crossing the street to the DSR stop, I walked south until I reached the pawn shop near the end of the block, where the RCA Victor Victrola console radio and phonograph player was still on display. I studied the mahogany cabinet, and then the window's reflection of the street behind me. The man in the dark suit deposited the newspaper in the trashcan on the curb, but he didn't move on. I did. Halfway down the next block I went into Tony's Grill, where I often went for lunch or a beer after work. Tony's was the first place I had worked after we arrived in Detroit. The bar was crowded with its usual rush-hour patrons. On a shelf behind the bar, Tony had the Tigers game on the radio. During the war he had been stationed in the South Pacific, which he commemorated by wearing Hawaiian shirts every day of the year. Today's was red, with large green palm fronds. He spotted me and went to the tap and began to draw a glass of Stroh's. I sat at the far end of the bar, where I had a good view of the front door.

Tony came down and placed a coaster and my beer in front of me, and said, "One-one, eighth inning, Frank." He moved back up the bar to wait on other customers.

I sipped the foam off the top of my beer. The front door opened and a woman, followed by a stout man, entered the bar. If it had been the man in the dark suit, I would have left a quarter on the bar, turned around, walked down the corridor past the restrooms, and through the kitchen, where Paolo the cook would not have taken much notice as I opened the door and stepped out into the back alley. But the couple came in, and as they approached the bar they were silhouetted against the bright light coming through the plate-glass window—everybody seemed to be getting plate glass installed these days, and Tony and I had recently joked that we ought to go into business together, starting our own firm, Detroit Plate Glass. We were often dreaming up business ideas, and though this one wasn't very exciting, I suspected that we could probably make a killing.

I drank my beer and listened to the ballgame. Tigers manager Bucky Harris came out to the mound and took the ball from Jim Bunning. They were changing pitchers—Virgil Trucks was warming up in the bullpen. I liked him because he was a veteran and this was clearly his last season, and because fans called him "Fire" Trucks. In America, Tony liked to say, everything changes, and while the Tigers changed pitchers, WJBK's play-by-play announcer Mel Ott said that they would pause for a commercial. Ott was the new play-by-play announcer that year, replacing Dizzy Trout, who also had a name I liked, and from whom I had learned a great many American colloquialisms. Everything in America changes, even during commercials. I took my time with my beer, thinking about the potential of plate glass.

When my glass was empty, I decided to go to the men's room before walking back to the DSR stop. I went down the corridor, pushed open the men's room door, and stepped up to the urinal. It was filled with ice, another sign that summer was coming. I don't know what the pleasure is in pissing on ice, watching it melt rapidly, but it's real, and I was concentrating on boring a hole right down to the porcelain when the door behind me swung open on a creaky hinge. I finished up and, turning, found the man in the dark suit standing in front of the door.

I went to the sink, washed my hands, and pulled down on the towel dispenser. For once it worked (another of Tony's business schemes was to find a company that made a good, reliable towel dispenser and sell it throughout the Midwest—he claimed, with a smile, we would "clean up"), and I dried my hands slowly, hoping the man would step over to the urinal.

But he said, "Hello, Frank."

I looked at him in the little mirror in the towel dispenser. "I know you?"

He shook his head.

"Didn't think so." My hands dry, I faced him. This was something I had learned since arriving in Detroit: if you faced Americans straight on—they would say "confront them"—usually they would back off. If they didn't, you had a problem.

"Frank, I'd just like to have a few minutes of your time." He didn't appear to be backing off. In fact, he seemed pleased with the situation.

"You want to talk?" I said. "In here?"

"Frank Green, your accent's very good. Sounds almost like you were born here. You've always been good at picking up languages, I understand. Let me buy you a beer and we'll have a little chat." He held out his hands as if to show that he wasn't concealing anything. "Just a talk and then you walk."

"I walk?"

"Yeah, Frank. It's a free country. Everyone can walk, they play their cards right."

I shrugged. "Sure. Okay."

I followed him back to the bar. He was not a big man, about five-eight, but he was compactly built. His thinning dark hair smelled of Brylcreem, combed straight back. There was nothing threatening, nothing imposing about him, but still the way he walked it looked like he knew exactly where he was going.

We took the empty booth in the back corner. I sat facing the front door, as was my custom. Tony's wife, Ginger, came over and took our order: beer, and coffee, black.

On the radio it was the top of the ninth, the Red Sox were ahead, 3-2, and Ike Delock was still on the mound at Fenway Park. I was irritated that I couldn't just listen to the game. "You know my name; I ought to know yours," I said.

"Fair enough. James Giannopoulos. I'm with the INS."

"Not the IRS?"

He shook his head. His stare was direct, slightly amused; it said he was willing to play games if necessary, but it was just a waste of time. "INS, Frank. Immigration and Naturalization Services."

Ginger came to the booth, her bracelets jingling, and as she placed the coaster and beer in front of me, she said, "There you go, dear." She put the cup of coffee on the table without ever looking at Giannopoulos. "Delock," she said. "Michigan native. Highland Park. Wish the Tigers had him. You don't get him out off the mound by the seventh, you're cooked."

"'Fraid so," I said.

Giannopoulos watched her walk back to the bar, but it was not like the way most men watched Ginger. He was waiting for her to get safely out of range. He was about my age, in his mid- to late thirties. Greek complexion, heavy beard, which he probably had to shave at least twice a day. He looked like a man who took little interest in his appearance. His suit, his hair, the thin gray tie, it all seemed designed not to be memorable.

"You've been following me," I said.

"I've been anxious to meet you, Frank." He didn't look anxious about anything.

"Why's that?"

"Well, to express my admiration, among other things."

"Admiration for what?"

"For being a model American citizen."

"The government sends someone out to congratulate its citizens for good behavior?"

"No. But you're an unusual case." He picked up his cup. The coffee was lousy at Tony's. I'd been telling Tony and Ginger for years they should do something about it. After James Giannopoulos sipped his coffee, I expected to see some sign of dissatisfaction, perhaps even revulsion, but there was nothing as he put the cup back in its saucer. "You are an extremely unusual case, Frank. Very impressive."

"That so?"

"Your file is that thick." He held his thumb and forefinger about an inch apart. "Please don't say, 'What file?'"

"Then perhaps we could just sit here and listen to the ballgame."

There was the faintest smile. "That would be nice." He seemed sincere, but with regret he added, "Though it wouldn't be in your best interests."

I drank some beer, deciding that it might be wise to remain silent, at least until I had a clearer notion of what he was up to, what he was after.

"You written to Adino Agostino lately?" When I didn't answer, he said, "He sends you postcards from Naples. And sometimes envelopes stuffed with newspaper clippings about Italian soccer. He doesn't write much, of course. I suppose it's his daughter's hand. She must be old enough to learn how to write, so he dictates something to her, just a note about the weather, the family. That was a terrible thing they did to him up there at Camp Au Train. I understand he was really a gifted player. Of course, soccer here in the United States—nobody understands this sport. It's all baseball and football. Games where you can use your hands." He took another sip of his coffee. "It's all in the file, Frank. And what makes it truly extraordinary is it's still open—you're still out there, walking around."

"I thought you said it was a free country, everybody walks."

"Most files have been closed, Frank. They've been captured, they've turned themselves in, or they're dead. A few managed to get home, back to wherever they came from. You're one of the few still living here, a free man. You are to be congratulated." He looked over his shoulder a moment, though there was no chance that someone was within hearing range. "But it won't last much longer, Frank. It's for your own good, really."

I finished my beer. "What is?"

He looked disappointed but not surprised. "All right. If I were in your position I'd react the same way. You don't know who I am, where I'm really coming from. You only got this far because you're careful. Have another beer, and I'll set the record straight." He turned and raised his hand to get Ginger's attention.

■   ■   ■

After a fresh beer and a second cup of coffee were delivered to the table, Giannopoulos said, "When you and Claire—Chiara, a very pretty name—first arrived here, you got in touch with June Stillman, who taught at what was then called Wayne University. Not much remains the same in America, Frank. This year they changed the name to Wayne State. We've never been sure if Professor Stillman knew you were coming, if you had communicated your intentions before getting out of the camp in Au Train, or if it was just part of your good fortune. No matter. She took you in and introduced you to her friends, people at the university, people who were pacifists or members of the party. They helped you because otherwise they could only sit around and theorize. They could actually *do* something about you. You became like their pets. If they could save you, they could feel a lot better about themselves. They found you jobs, and soon you were able to get your own apartment. And then they got you in touch with people who could provide you with a new identity, because you understood that things don't remain the same here, and that your survival depends on it. So you became Frank and Claire Green. You bought documents that look as genuine as mine. Believe me, you're lucky you found a girl like Claire. As the songs say, it must be love. By the time the war was over, you were model citizens. You went from working in the kitchen here to that shop down the street, which you now own. Claire worked in several offices as a secretary. She got pregnant—the first time in '49, but she lost it. The second time, in '51, but again there were complications. She was in the hospital for a week. Now it's five years down the road and still no kids. During all this you drifted away from those commies who helped you at first. It's just getting too hot for them in this country, thanks to people like Joe McCarthy. But you remained loyal to Stillman. When she took ill, you visited her regularly. I had a cousin who had to go into one of those iron lungs, and I know it's a blessing when they finally die."

Giannopoulos paused and sipped his coffee. For a moment I thought he was through, but then he said, "Two years ago you returned to Italy. You and Claire took a train to New York and a steamship across the Atlantic. Your mother had died. You didn't go home when your father died in '46, but this time it was your mother. And your sister was getting married. So you stayed nearly four months, and we thought that you had decided not to come back. You liked being Francesco Verdi again, and Chiara Frangiapani came to like it in postwar Italy. My guess is you considered going into the family business, which would have been fine by us: good luck and we close your file. But you come back. And you bring some money—I suppose you let your sister and brother-in-law buy you out of your share of the store, the house, and the olive grove over there—and you have enough, twenty-five thousand dollars, to buy that shop down the street. Business is getting better all the time. You wear a nice suit, and those Italian shoes are very sharp. They're easier to afford over here, anyway. You even have an assistant. And Claire, she doesn't work as a secretary anymore, though a couple of times a week she comes downtown and does the bookkeeping for you. You run your shop, you pay your taxes. The crying shame of it is we don't have more citizens like Frank and Claire Green."

The bar had emptied out and Sinatra was playing on the radio. I realized I had no idea who had won the ballgame, though I suspected it was the Red Sox.

"So, Mr. Giannopoulos," I asked, "what do you want?"

"I want to help you."

"From what you say, it sounds like I don't need any."

"I wish that were so." Giannopoulos sipped his coffee. "We've learned something about Vogel. We've learned that he's after you, Frank."

"Vogel." I had picked up my glass, but put it down.

Giannopoulos smiled, but only just. "He's still in America, Frank. They have men planted here who have been given orders to find the rest of you. I have to tell you that we even have suspicions about some of the men working in our own agency. Between the communists and the remains of the Nazi Party, you don't know who's who in this country anymore."

"Maybe you're one of them?"

"You better hope not. If I were you—well, you're just going to have to decide who to trust. I realize that up to now you have acknowledged none of what I've been saying. You've just listened, because you're smart. But you have to ask yourself this: if I wasn't here to help you, why would I bother to convince you that I know so much about you?" Giannopoulos waited, and when I said nothing, he showed the slightest disappointment. "All these years, Frank, you've been looking over your shoulder. Every day. It's got to wear you down—both you and Claire. But you know that this will never go away because they never forget. At Camp Au Train, Vogel had you tried, first on charges of treason; but then, again, after you ran, he also tried you for murder of a member of the Nazi Party. Now I'm not here to suggest that you're the one who actually killed Otto Werner. It's very possible that it was that Russian, Dimitri Sabaneyev. In fact, I'm inclined to think that that's the case. But it really doesn't matter. The point is you're on their books, you're still out here, and Vogel has an obligation. Even after all these years, with their little Führer dead and gone, men like Vogel are more devoted and loyal than ever. If they weren't Nazis, what would they be? They don't know how to be anything else."

"You said this Vogel's in America?"

"A lot of them are in South America, and they have good lines of communication between there and here." Giannopoulos considered his coffee but then thought better of it. "We have learned that Vogel is in Detroit."

"How would you know that?"

"Remember a guard named Shepherd? I believe the prisoners at Au Train called him *the* Shepherd. He lives down here now. Has for years. Out of the blue he comes to us and says that he's seen one of the officers who had been imprisoned at Au Train, one of the hard cases that was supposed to be sent back to Germany to be tried: Vogel. But Vogel never got to Germany. Somehow they lost him. These people run through your fingers like water. Nobody had seen or heard of Vogel for years, and then the Shepherd says he saw him not two weeks ago. Frank, I know you know what I'm saying here. Vogel's been given his orders and he'll come after you. Like I said, you're going to need help."

I looked down at my empty beer glass.

"We think he's been given orders regarding you and another one here in Detroit."

"What 'other one'?"

"Escaped POW. An Austrian named Klaus Stemple. He now goes by the name of Carl Simmons. Lives up off Gratiot."

"Have you told him all about this, too?"

Giannopoulos shook his head.

"Why not?"

He seemed undecided, but then said, "My new boss, they sent him out from D.C. Named Taggart. It was his position that we tell both of you. But I said, 'Let's just go with Frank Green first. See what happens.'"

"Why?"

"All I can say is Simmons is different—he's Austrian, and I don't think he'd be as receptive as you." Giannopoulos leaned forward and said, "If we're going to find Vogel, we're going to need your help."

"You're looking for bait."

"I'm afraid so."

"And you have two kinds out in the water now, me and this Simmons: one knows, the other doesn't."

"You could look at it that way. Would you rather I had told Simmons and not you?" Giannopoulos pushed the coffee aside, making the slightest face. "I know this is not what you want to hear, but there it is, Frank. You help us out and we get Vogel, then we'll let you stay. Legit. For good." Giannopoulos took a billfold out of the pocket of his suit coat and put two dollars on the table. "You sleep on it, Frank. Think it over." He began to slide out of the booth.

"If I am who you say I am, Claire and I could just disappear tonight."

Giannopoulos paused at the edge of the seat. "You could. But I think you'll realize it would not be in your best interests. It was one thing back during the war to run off and become Frank and Claire Green. But now it's not so easy. You're older. You got something to lose. You walk away from the shop, you go empty-handed. Besides, I think you like who you are—am I right?"

"What makes you say that?"

"The shoes. The good Italian shoes. You can afford them here." Giannopoulos slid out of the booth and stood up. "I'll be in touch." He walked toward the front door, a silhouette against the failing light coming though the plate-glass window.

16.

It was twilight when I took the trolley home. I usually read the paper or sometimes dozed during the trip, but that night I simply stared at my reflection in the window, thinking about a man named Phillip Brick. Since the end of the war there had been numerous articles in newspapers and magazines about escaped POWs in the United States. Over twenty-two hundred prisoners had escaped, and by the early fifties all but a handful had been captured. They were usually caught by the police, but there were also instances where they had been turned in by private citizens, Forest Rangers, and even Boy Scouts. One man's mother-in-law dropped the dime on him. Some men, when things got too close, surrendered voluntarily.

Three years earlier, in May 1953, Reinhold Pabel had become a national sensation. During the war, Pabel, a former German infantry sergeant, had escaped from a camp in Washington, Illinois. He had only fifteen dollars, a road map, and an article by J. Edgar Hoover on the government's procedures for tracking down escaped POWs. Pabel hitchhiked to Peoria, where he took a train to Chicago. Using the name Phillip Brick, he found work—the usual thing, dishwashing, shipping clerk—but soon he managed to find work in the circulation department of the *Chicago Tribune,* and eventually he opened his own book store. He married an American.

One day FBI agents walked into his shop and arrested him, a story that made the news across the nation. An interview with him appeared in *Time* magazine, and he wrote an account of his escape for *Collier's* magazine, which was entitled "It's Easy to Bluff Americans." Claire and I followed all of this closely, and for months I expected that I too would soon be caught. But nothing happened. For months, the press covered Pabel's bureaucratic odyssey, which, if possible, was more bizarre than his actual escape: legally, he was not a criminal, because he had been brought to the United States involuntarily, and as a soldier it was his duty to escape. There was no law designed to deal with a prisoner of war who escapes and remains in the country after the war has ended. The court finally issued a verdict of "voluntary departure," which would require Pabel to return to Germany, while at the same time his name was placed on a priority reentry list, so that six months later he was allowed to return to the United States and rejoin his American wife. The *Collier's* article ran photographs of several other German POWs. Somehow, fortunately, an escaped Italian POW didn't warrant the same attention. During these months, Claire and I often discussed what we should do. I considered turning myself in, but we were in the process of establishing the business, which had taken all of our money. That would be lost. And we didn't want to give up who we had become, so we continued to be Mr. and Mrs. Frank Green.

It was later than usual when I got back to our third-floor apartment. Claire had set the table with our good wine glasses, and the kitchen smelled of pesto. I knew what this meant. She was past thirty now, and putting her arms around my neck, she hugged me tightly. Her face was perhaps fuller, but her features were more delicate, even fragile, than when she was nineteen. Her hair was shorter, cut at the shoulders, soft as black silk.

"Sorry I'm late."

She kissed me. "This is one meal I'd rather not start by myself."

"Do we still have time for dinner?"

"Not sure. I think I'm still ovulating, so we may have to skip dessert."

"Do I have time to open the wine?"

"Yes, but we shouldn't let it breathe too long."

We ate fettuccine with pesto and took the second half of the bottle of Chianti to bed. That winter Claire had said she wanted to try once more to have a child. After her second miscarriage, the doctor had cautioned us about another pregnancy and the possible complications that might result. But once Claire had made up her mind, she refused to discuss the dangers involved. Since then we had made love according to her cycle, and each month when her period began there followed days of silent disappointment.

"We could pretend we're in the cabin at Henry's Roadside Oasis," she said as she lay down beside me.

As I had done many times over the years, I first kissed the scar on her right thigh. After the bullet wound had healed, there was a small, puckered scar, which I had tended to avoid. I was afraid of it. I was afraid that to touch it would hurt her, but I was also afraid to touch it because of what it meant to her—it was because of me, because she ran away with me that she had become disfigured. But then one night she pressed the scar against my mouth, and my tongue came to know its every fissure and crevice.

After a while, I got up off the bed.

"What is it?" she asked.

"I don't know." I opened the window. The air was cool against my skin.

"Come back here and talk to me." I sat on the edge of the bed. "You're having second thoughts about this, because of what the doctor said?" There was the faintest light coming from the window, and I could see the side of her face and one large, inquisitive eye. "Maybe you don't want to have a child?" she said.

"That's not it," I said. "The risk—it is a concern, yes." I took hold of her hand. "Listen, I don't think it's safe for you to stay in Detroit." She sat up, her back against the headboard. "I'm afraid my past has finally caught up with us." I wanted to leave it at that, but I knew I couldn't. We had been in this together for years. I told her about how I had been followed from the shop to Tony's. She knew I often suspected that I was being followed, but as I told her about my conversation with Giannopoulos she never spoke, but only watched me in the near dark. When I explained about Vogel being in Detroit she became still, stone still. Our fear—rarely mentioned all these years, but always present—had been that the government would find me one day, that some agent would tell me they had a file on everything that had happened since I ran away from the work detail in the woods in Au Train, and I would be taken away from Claire, suddenly, without warning. But this was worse than that fear. This was not just a tidy man in a dark suit who represented the United States government; this was Vogel and what he had represented at Camp Au Train, and what he continued to represent now, more than a decade after the war had ended. It was no surprise to me that when I was finished, we sat together on our bed in silence, until she whispered, "It never ends."

"I want you to leave the city for a while. Couldn't you go back up north?"

"Me? Just me?"

"Just you."

"I haven't been up there since Momma died."

"But she had good friends in Sault Ste. Marie."

"The Zampas, yes. They're like family."

"Go there. Until I sort this out."

"Will you?"

"I don't have any choice, do I?"

I leaned over and kissed her mouth, and her arms came up around my neck.

.   .   .

The next morning I called the shop right at nine, when we opened, and my assistant Leon Cune answered. I told him I'd be in late. Then Claire called Carmen and Louisa Zampa in Sault Ste. Marie; they had been her mother's neighbors and closest friends for years. As she suspected, they were more than willing to have her come and stay with them. Then I helped her pack and we took the trolley down to the Greyhound terminal. We said little until she was about to board the bus.

"I don't like this," she said.

"I don't either, but you look nice in that outfit." It was her green dress with wide shoulders and broad lapels.

"Why don't you come with me? No one would find us up there."

I reached inside my suit coat and took out my billfold. I counted out two hundred dollars and gave it to her. "I'll send more soon."

She looked away. "I'm not going to cry."

"No, you're not."

I held her in my arms and her shoulders trembled slightly, but when she pushed me away she was all right. She climbed the steps into the bus, and I handed up her suitcase. When the bus began to move slowly, I walked alongside. Staring down at me, Claire's eyes were somber and frightened. And angry.

■   ■   ■

I got to my shop a little before noon. It had been an appliance repair shop, owned and operated by George Sturges for over thirty years. I'd been working for him since early in '49. He frequently talked about retiring to Arizona, and I told him that somehow I would buy the business from him. When I returned from Italy after my mother's death and my sister's wedding, I had the cash to buy Sturges out. He took his asthma to the desert and I changed the name of George's Electrical Repairs to Made in the Shade.

Leon Cune had worked for Sturges for years; he could fix anything and I kept him on to handle repair jobs. I sold lampshades. The showroom behind the new plate-glass window was stocked with every conceivable style, color, and size lampshade, and within weeks my walk-in business was brisk. What really took off, though, was the commercial work. The Big Three plants were turning out millions of cars a year, and Detroit was a boomtown. I took orders from restaurants, hotels, businesses that needed dozens of identical lampshades, which I sold wholesale.

Leon was in his high swivel chair at the workbench. The shelves behind him were filled with radios, toasters, blenders, sewing machines, and televisions, each tagged and awaiting his attention. "Another year or so and I'm going to stop with the small appliances," he said. "Do nothing but TVs. It's like an invasion." Leon was in his fifties, and his voice seemed to burble up out of his throat as a result of decades of smoking Pall Malls. He wore a Tigers ball cap and thick, heavy-framed glasses. His tiny hands, the backs darker than the palms, were perfectly suited to working in and around wires and coils. "Ja'ever read this book by George Orwell, *1984*?" he asked as he wiggled a tube free from the back of a Zenith TV. "Thirty years from now these things are going to be everywhere."

I picked up his pack of cigarettes, tapped one out, and lit it with his Zippo. I had been trying to quit for several years. Claire wouldn't allow smoking in the apartment, and I could go for several days now without giving in—but not today. "I keep smoking these, I won't ever see 1984."

"We're talking twenty-eight years from now. I'm not betting on making it myself," Leon said. "You were really smart, Frank, you'd go into TVs instead of shades."

"Maybe. But pretty soon everybody'll be selling TVs. The competition'll kill you."

"Never be as much in lampshades."

"But there are millions of lamps in Detroit, and every one of them needs a shade."

Leon slid down off his stool, walked over to the parts bin, sorted through some cartons, and brought one back; he removed the new tube from the carton, put it on the workbench, and then climbed back up in his seat. Once, when a customer's boy had come into the shop he screamed when he saw this black man who was four feet tall. Leon was unfazed, and he began talking to the kid like Donald Duck. "*Mommy, Mommy,*" Donald said, "*Look at the cute little man. Can't we take him home with us?*" The boy began to laugh, though his mother, when she stepped into the workshop, was flustered to find her son standing eye to eye with a dwarf, a Negro dwarf. Then Leon's voice changed to something you would hear on a radio (or now a television) commercial, a deep, suave voice that said, "That's right, kids! You've got to do what Mommy tells you and drink your milk at *every* meal if you want to grow up *big* and *strong*." And then in yet another voice, something that sounded desperate and squeezed, he said, "*Milk! Yuk! I always hated milk! And look what happened to me! But it's not too late for you, kiddo—go home, do what your mother tells you, and drink your milk!*" The boy went into hysterics, and his mother, now apologizing desperately, tugged him back out into the showroom.

Leon fit the new tube in place and gently pushed down until it was snug. "The thing about all these TVs is that by 1984 you not only see people in them, they can see you. All the time. It's a government thing, of course. It's called Big Brother."

"Maybe you read too much, Leon."

"Yeah. I ought to take in a movie more often?"

"Wouldn't hurt."

"There's some good ones out there now. *The Invasion of the Body Snatchers*, *Godzilla*, and *It Conquered the World*."

"This country is so full of choices."

"I'm kinda interested in the one called *The Black Sheep*," Leon said. "About a mad scientist who kidnaps people so he can open up their brains in search of a cure for his wife's brain tumor."

"Sounds like a winner." I took one more drag on the cigarette and crushed it out in the tin ashtray. "Any calls?"

"One."

I waited. Leon loved to do this. "And?"

"Eventually, they hung up."

"They leave a message before hanging up?"

He picked up the notepad next to the phone and made a production of flipping through the pages. "Nope, guess not."

"I'm not in the mood today, Leon. What was the message?"

"I told you, they hung up."

"Didn't say anything?"

He shook his head. "I was expecting some heavy breathing, but zilch."

I went across the hall to my office and sat at Sturges's old roll-top desk, which was littered with paperwork. I dug out the phonebook and looked up a number for C. Simmons on Sarnia Avenue. When I called, there was no answer.

I left the office and paused in the hall, where I could see out into the showroom. The light from the plate-glass window gave the shades a soft glow—pastels and burgundies and at least a dozen variations on white. "Leon, I'm going to be away from the shop for a stretch."

"I should start taking long lunches, too." For years, he brought a lunch box to work.

"I'm talking a few days, Leon. I'll check in now and then."

He finished setting a screw in the chassis of the television and then turned his thick glasses on me. "If Mrs. Buzzbee comes in looking for that perfect shade to match her peek-a-boo negligee, can I run my hand up her skirt?" With Leon, every customer was named Buzzbee, and every woman's secret desire was to be seduced by a dark-skinned dwarf.

"Long as you don't blow the sale, Leon."

I walked out into the showroom, pausing once to straighten a shade, and then went out the front door. When I heard a tapping on the glass behind me, I stopped on the sidewalk and turned around: Leo stood behind the plate-glass window. There was a sign in the shape of a television screen, which read "Expert TV Repairs." Leon pressed his face up against the glass inside the screen, flattening his nose and lips, and then Donald Duck quacked, *"Little Brother is watching you! Little Brother is watching you!"*

■　　■　　■

I walked down to Tony's Grill and ordered a beer and a pastrami sandwich. The place was quiet and Ginger came over to my booth, sat down, and lit a cigarette.

Today her blond hair was worked up into a beehive, and her nails and lipstick were a matching hot pink.

"How's the sandwich, hon?"

I nodded, taking another bite. "Best pastrami in Detroit."

"We pay for it, believe me."

The one customer at the bar left, and Tony came over to the booth and slid in beside his wife. "How's the sandwich?" Tony asked.

I shrugged. Tony laughed. Ginger picked a shred of tobacco off her tongue.

"This shade," I said, looking at the wall lamp above the table. "It's developing a chronic case of bulb burn. I'll bring over another one. You know, if you went with a different color, you could completely change the atmosphere in this place."

"You mean make it brighter?" Tony asked.

Ginger exhaled and said, "No, dummy. Something mellow, sexy. Sure, Frank. Bring over something in . . . blue. Yeah, blue—it'll enhance my cleavage. You know, the deeper the cleavage the better the tips. Some guys'll stay for an extra drink just for another peek."

"Okay, I'm broad-minded," Tony said, laughing. "Let's try the blue."

Ginger rolled her eyes.

"She doesn't appreciate my jokes," Tony said.

"There are three types of men," Ginger said. "Comedians, wannabe comedians, and straight men. Tony's a wannabe. You never see Jack Benny or Milton Berle laugh at their own punchlines."

"She just doesn't appreciate my material," Tony said. "What about Frank? Straight man."

"Hundred percent," Ginger said. "Never even tries to tell a joke, 'cause he's not stupid."

A couple came in the door and sat at the bar. As Tony got out of the booth, he took a small envelope from the pocket of his Hawaiian shirt and dropped it on the table. "That guy you were talking to last night? Stopped in earlier and left this." He went around the bar to wait on the couple.

I picked up the envelope, tucked it inside my suit coat pocket, and went to work on the second half of my sandwich.

"Funny he doesn't just stop by your shop down the street," Ginger said. "Maybe he's got a thing for you?" She took a drag on her cigarette. "Or he's a spook." She watched me eat, trying to maintain disinterest, but then she said, "What's going on with you, Frank?"

"What do you mean?"

"Something's different." As I finished the last of the sandwich, Ginger stared at me, one elbow on the table, propping up her cigarette. "Everything all right with Claire?"

"You're a very perceptive woman, Ginger."

"I like to exercise my woman's intuition. That's how I ended up in this joint with the Tone."

"You'll find out eventually—Claire's left town for a while. We're not splitting up."

She tapped her cigarette into the ashtray. "Where'd she go?"

"I'd rather just leave it for the time being. We're just taking a break."

The front door opened and a half dozen people came in and sat in the first booth.

"Bluehairs," Ginger said, getting up. "Real big tippers, no doubt. Cleavage don't do squat for them." She reached across my table, giving me a peek, and turned the lampshade until the brown spot was facing the wall. "Yeah, let's go with the blue."

Her bracelets sang as she walked down to the first booth, one hand tucking a wisp of hair up in back.

I took out the envelope and opened it. The slip of paper inside was folded once. *Tony's tonight, 10 p.m.*

17.

took the trolley on Gratiot and found Simmons's apartment building, an old brick house behind a wrought-iron fence. At the next corner there was a pharmacy with a phone booth. I dialed Simmons's number and he picked up on the second ring, his voice devoid of any European accent. I waited, and when he said hello a second time, I said, "Vogel's here, looking for you." I hung up and left the store.

It was mid-afternoon with a cool breeze coming off the Detroit River and the sidewalk wasn't very crowded, mostly old women pulling grocery carts and a group of school girls singing "Que Sera Sera." Halfway down the block I saw a man come out through the wrought-iron gate. He headed west, with the stride of someone who intended to waste no time. Tall and lean in a brown double-breasted suit and a tan fedora, he had the bearing of a military officer. When he reached Gratiot, he hailed a cab, and I did the same. After about fifteen minutes of jogging north and west, his cab stopped in front of a Catholic church. I got out of my cab farther up the street, and as I paid the driver I saw Simmons enter the rectory.

There was a park across the street from St. Stanislaus's Church. I spent a half hour on a bench, watching pigeons and children. Many of the kids spoke Polish.

Finally, Simmons and a gray-haired priest came outside and opened the garage behind the rectory. I walked out to the sidewalk as they pulled into the street in a black DeSoto Firedome and headed west. It was late afternoon and traffic was getting heavy. I found a taxi at the next corner and told the cabbie to drive west. I couldn't see the DeSoto up ahead. We went for several miles, and I began to think that Simmons and the priest must have taken a turn somewhere behind me, until I saw their car parked in front of a restaurant called the Black Forest.

Inside, I sat at the bar and ordered a beer, which came in a stein. The bartender wore lederhosen, and the waitresses all wore traditional German dresses. There was plenty of cleavage, and the clientele—mostly businessmen—looked like heavy tippers who could afford to stay for an extra peek. In the back corner, Simmons and the priest sat at a table with one of the waiters, an overweight man in a black vest and white shirt. By the way he spoke to the waitresses coming and going from the kitchen, I assumed he managed the place. I could keep my back to their table and watch the three of them in the long mirror behind the bar as they drank coffee and schnapps. They spoke quietly, hunched over the table. The waiter had a large head with heavy jowls and dark hair—too dark for a man his age, and oiled, so that it was slicked down on his scalp. His stubby fingers nervously touched his face and smoothed his hair back. The priest said very little. Finally, Simmons got up and came to the end of the bar. His right cheekbone was more pronounced than the left, seemingly from a permanent bruise, and a scar ran down his forehead, terminating in his right eyebrow. Using the phone on the bar, he made a call, and after a few minutes he became impatient. I heard him say in German, "We told you this would happen someday." He hung up abruptly then and returned to the table. They talked for another few minutes, and then the waiter went back into the kitchen. When Simmons and the priest got up to leave, I paid for my beer.

I left the restaurant and walked down to the intersection. Waiting to cross the street, I could see the two men come outside. They spoke for a minute on the sidewalk before the priest got in his DeSoto. Simmons watched him pull out into the traffic, and went back inside the Black Forest.

■   ■   ■

I returned to our apartment and called the number in Sault Ste. Marie that Claire had left by the phone. Carmen Zampa, an elderly man who always sounded like he was about to clear his throat, answered; I had met him once, when we had returned to the Upper Peninsula for Momma's funeral. I could hear his wife Louisa in the background, speaking Italian. When Claire came to the phone, she said, "I called the shop and Leon said you went off and he didn't know when you were coming back."

"It's been a busy day. How was your trip?"

"Exhausting. There was a long wait at the straits because the ferry had some engine trouble. I fainted on the bus from St. Ignace to the Soo."

"You did the other times, didn't you?"

"Yes, every time, the day after I've fainted I've turned out pregnant." Neither of us spoke for a moment. "Can't you just come up here?" Then, lighter, as though trying to not sound desperate, she added, "You know there's still snow on the ground here?"

I looked out the kitchen window: the maples lining the street were budding. It had been another warm day in Detroit and it was starting to rain. "This won't go away by itself."

"So what will you do?"

"I don't know, Chiara." I hadn't used that name in a long time. "You're all right?"

"The Zampas are taking good care of me, though I'll get fat the way they feed me."

"Get some rest, get nice and fat, and see a doctor."

"They have an apartment over their garage. I'll be fine there, though lonely."

"I'll call again soon."

"This is the only time I'm going to say it this way: *Ti amo.*"

"*Ti amo.*" I hung up.

I went to the icebox and found that there was some fettuccine left over from last night's dinner. I sat down at the kitchen table and ate it cold.

■   ■   ■

I got to Tony's one beer before 10 o'clock. Tony and Ginger had gone home and the night shift had taken over. The place was quiet. I sat in the last booth with a Stroh's, facing the door. The Tigers game had been rained out that afternoon and no one had bothered to turn on the radio. A few minutes after ten, Giannopoulos came in with another man; he was younger, with a military brush cut, and he remained by the front door—he looked like he'd been trained to stand watch in doorways—while Giannopoulos peeled off his raincoat and sat across from me in the booth.

"Your friend with INS, too?" I said.

"Jack? My assistant."

"Your protégé. You go to the same tailor."

The waitress, one of Tony's cousins, this one named Annette, came and took our order; I had another beer, and Giannopoulos had coffee again. After she went back to the bar, I asked, "How long have you been in the INS, since the end of the war?" Giannopoulos looked displeased, though not surprised. "You think you know a lot about me," I said. "It's only fair I know who I'm dealing with."

Giannopoulos had a large gold ring on his right hand; he twisted it for a moment. No wedding ring. "Fair enough. I began working for the Allies, first as a translator and then in interrogation. I was all over Europe, but I was primarily based in Trieste."

"I had an aunt in Trieste," I said.

"Strange town," Giannopoulos said. "It was Austrian, and then after the first war it went to Italy. It's now what we call here a melting pot. In warm weather I used to like to eat outdoors at the restaurants on the canal, across from the Orthodox Church."

"I remember that church," I said. "My aunt took me inside once, just to see it. I remember lots of gold, and candles. There were women weeping, and when I asked my aunt why, she said it was because the church was so beautiful."

Giannopoulos nodded. "Grand buildings over here, but they don't bring you to tears."

We waited as Annette came to the booth and put the coffee and beer on the table.

Giannopoulos sipped his coffee, his eyes, dark brown with heavy lids, showing complete disinterest now. "I want to make something perfectly clear," he said. "You're an escaped prisoner of war. There are only a few of you still out there walking around in the United States. I can pull you in any time."

"You can then always go to Stemple." He didn't bother to answer. I took out a fresh pack of Lucky Strikes, broke the cellophane, and offered him a cigarette. He took one. I lit our cigarettes and said, "Stemple knows Vogel's in Detroit."

"How?" And then he said, "You told him?"

"I called him."

"Just to piss me off."

"Sure," I said. "Plus I wanted to see what he would do."

"That wasn't part of the plan."

"It's me Vogel's after, so don't talk to me about *your* plan."

"So. You called him. Then what?"

"I said Vogel was in town and hung up. He left his apartment immediately and I followed him. Ever hear of a German restaurant called the Black Forest?"

"Sure. Stemple owns it—we know that." Giannopoulos shook his head in disgust.

"He met a priest."

"What priest?"

I smiled, and after a moment he did too, almost. "I don't know his name," I said. "He's at St. Stanislaus Church. And there are others. At the restaurant they sat and talked with the manager, who was nervous. And Stemple called someone from the restaurant and spoke German. They're all worried."

"All right." Giannopoulos began to slide out of the booth. "I'll check out the priest."

"I'll go back to the restaurant. My wife is out of town and I have little interest in cooking for myself."

Giannopoulos stood up. "You know I didn't have to tell you about Vogel at all."

"Don't try to tell me you were doing me a favor. I'm bait, remember?"

"Where'd you send your wife?" When I didn't answer, he said, "It's the first smart thing you've done."

As Giannopoulos walked to the front of the bar, Jack opened the door for him.

■　　■　　■

The following day I spent in my office, and mid-afternoon I walked down to Tony's, watching the cars pass on the street. Detroit built cars; Detroiters were obsessed with cars. In 1956, who you were was defined by what you drove. I didn't own a car, so for several years Tony and I had an arrangement where I could use theirs, a '54 Pontiac Chieftain V8 4-Speed Hydra-Matic, lime green with a white roof. My part of the bargain was to keep the tank full and the oil changed regularly. I took it to the car wash every week and stored my sample books in the trunk.

I drove the Pontiac to the Black Forest. It catered to a very different crowd from Tony's Grill. The men all wore suits, and there were some pricey-looking women: jewels, necklaces, mink stoles. Again, I sat at the bar and ordered a stein of beer.

After a few minutes Stemple came out from the kitchen. He made the rounds, talking to customers at various tables. As he came along the bar, he paused by my stool. "You look familiar," he said pleasantly. "Weren't you in here . . . yesterday?"

I nodded.

"Back for something to eat?" His eyes began to scan the tables. "There might be something open in, oh, ten minutes." He took one of the menus from under his arm and handed it to me.

There were small lamps on the bar; I looked at the nearest one. "You have too much ambient light in here."

"Ambient light?"

"Right. These shades, they let too much through this fabric. If you went to something denser, say, a forest green with pleats, or maybe a nice Venetian linen, the light would be contained, creating a distinct pool on the tablecloth or bar. More shadows, which would make the place more romantic and, well, forgiving, if you know what I mean."

"Yes," he said vaguely.

"Plus, these shades are looking a little worse for wear. See these little runs in the fabric? It's sort of like a nylon stocking—once a run starts, there's no stopping it." He was looking at me now with genuine curiosity. "Sorry," I said. "Can't help it. It's the salesman in me."

"Lampshades."

"That's right. My name's Frank Green." I keep business cards in my coat pocket for just such moments. I took one out and placed it on the table, and he glanced at it as we shook hands.

"Carl Simmons," he said.

I put the menu on the bar. "How about the pork chops, Mr. Simmons?"

"Excellent choice," he said, looking across the dining room again. "Yes, I think we can get you seated in a minute."

Simmons found me a table for two, back by the kitchen door, where I wouldn't feel too conspicuous as the only person eating alone. The pork chops were done perfectly, accompanied by applesauce, Brussels sprouts, and späetzle. Simmons waited on me personally, and I could see as he moved around the room, he was looking over his lampshades with a critical eye.

When I finished my meal, he brought my coffee and two snifters of schnapps, and sat down across from me. "You do this every time you walk into a place, knock their shades?"

"Only if they've seen better days."

His smile was stiff, formal, something acquired to survive in America. "I've been thinking of having the place painted, but I wonder if I could get by for another few years if I reduced this—what was it, ambient light?"

"Exactly," I said. "The right shades will provide a most forgiving light, and it would prove less expensive than a paint job." We sipped our schnapps and coffee, and I offered him a cigarette. When I had both lit, I said, "You're a member of St. Stanislaus's parish? I saw one of the priests in here yesterday."

"Yes, Father Brosnic. Louis is a dear man."

"Ah, that's right."

"If you know him, why didn't you come over to the table? I don't believe he recognized you." His eyes were wary now.

"I don't really." I waved a hand through the cigarette smoke drifting between us. I leaned toward him, and said, "You both seemed . . . worried. It's very understandable, under the circumstances."

"What circumstances?"

"I mean Herr Vogel."

Stemple was trying to look as though he didn't recognize the name, but he must have realized it wasn't working. "You know this Vogel?"

"The Bird," I said. "Yes, he's here, in Detroit—yesterday you told Father Brosnic, and you called someone else. At least three of you are concerned, and rightly so."

His face was now slack with dread. "You work for Vogel?"

"Of course not, Herr Stemple." He leaned back in his chair. I got my wallet out and put a twenty on the table.

"Please, it's Simmons. Or maybe I could call you by your real name?"

"Folks just call me Frank."

"Yes, America is so informal—and new: new identities, new possibilities."

"And no one has a past," I said, "until a man like Vogel shows up."

"How do you know about Vogel?" he asked.

"Word gets around," I said. "What is it that you and Brosnic have in common? Faith? I think it's more than that. And this other person you called—you were all members of the Nazi Party?"

"I did my duty, Mr. Green. We all did."

"Vogel believes he's still doing his."

"How did you know him?" he asked. "Were you in the Wehrmacht?"

"No, I was in the Italian army. I knew him in prison. But you and Brosnic, you knew him during the war?" He merely stared at me. "And perhaps even before?" Still nothing. "And you did something—something that he has never forgiven."

"The Bird does not forget, or forgive."

"Like the Party. Long ago you and the others were tried and sentenced."

Reluctantly, Simmons nodded.

"Vogel is here to carry out your execution."

He was staring at me, helpless. "And the same is true for you?"

"The same for me, Herr Stemple."

"So. We are condemned men. New identities mean nothing. We cannot conceal our flaws, our runs in ambient light." He took a drag on his cigarette. "The war isn't over for men like Vogel. They're all waiting for the opportunity to rise up again."

"Your eye and cheek," I said. "You were wounded."

"Like so many, I sustained many wounds, some that are visible, some that are not. Scars and physical disabilities may not be the worst things we took away from this war. We are all blind men here, groping in the dark."

"What will you do? Run?"

Now Stemple got up from the table. He seemed weary, even exhausted. "I would like to think I am through with running. This is a great country, is it not? We live here now, but we are from a different time and place." He picked my business card up off the table. "We sell pork chops and lampshades. But we all still carry the past with us, concealed like a secret, hoping that it doesn't come back to haunt us. Maybe we can help each other?" He tried to smile, though with little conviction. "Perhaps, Mr. Green, you are the one who should run?"

"I ran once before. Not this time."

"Very well then." He gave me a curt, polite nod, a formal Old World gesture that here seemed savagely out of place, and then he walked back through the swinging kitchen door.

18.

The following morning I was getting dressed for work when the doorbell rang. I finished knotting my tie as I opened the door. Giannopoulos stepped into the apartment and handed me a copy of the *Free Press*. "See this yet?" On the front page was a photograph of Father Brosnic, wearing his vestments as he stood in front of St. Stanislaus, welcoming parishioners to Sunday Mass. "He's dead," Giannopoulos said. "Heard confession from six to eight last night, and about a half hour later he was in the sacristy. The church janitor found him. The police believe that two men entered the church and repeatedly stabbed him in the hands, feet, and chest. That symbolic enough for you?"

I got my sport coat and we went down to the street to Giannopoulos's Ford Customline. Jack sat behind the steering wheel, and once Giannopoulos and I were in the back seat he pulled out into the street and headed west.

"I talked to a friend with Detroit police," Giannopoulos said. "There was a lot of blood in that sacristy, and the police found two sets of footprints. One set—the smaller of the two men—seemed accompanied by a series of red dots."

"Red dots, in the blood?" I said. "Dots—a cane?"

"I've never seen anything about a cane in Vogel's files," Giannopoulos said. "Another thing: Brosnic wasn't any priest. We've been checking him out and he never attended a seminary, was never ordained. His real name was Mile Ionescu and he donned the collar to get himself out of Europe after the war. A lot of Nazis traded one uniform for another. In their fear and abhorrence of communism, the Church provided their only refuge. Nice irony there, I suppose." Giannopoulos took out a pack of Lucky Strikes and offered one to me. After lighting them, he said, "You know what this means."

"Vogel's only begun," I said, "and he won't stop until he's taken care of all of us—and it doesn't matter who dies as long as it leads you to Vogel. Nobody'll be sorry when it's my turn. America will be a safer place without us, right?"

"I don't believe that, Frank."

"Where're we going?" I asked. "The Black Forest?"

"Thought we'd drive by."

"I doubt it's the kind of restaurant that serves breakfast."

When we reached the Black Forest, it wasn't open, but Giannopoulos told Jack to park in front of a coffee shop down the block. We left Jack with the car and went into the coffee shop. We sat in a booth by the windows, where we could watch the street. After he ordered coffee, Giannopoulos said, "Tell me about Vogel, when he was in that prison camp up north."

"Don't you know? You think you know everything about me—why not Vogel?"

"Oh, I know what he did before he was a prisoner of war. I know why he's still on a list of war criminals that are wanted to be brought to trial in Europe. Israel wants him, too. And I know that he has a lot of support over here—financial support that has kept us from finding him. A lot of these Nazis that get into the United States find a small, inconspicuous life and become model citizens. Smart, like you. But not Vogel. He leaves no trace. We have nothing in terms of employment or an address. No driver's license or checking account. What was he like up at Camp Au Train?"

"Kommandant Vogel ran the place," I said. "You told me you know about my friend Adino, back in Italy. What happened to him in camp says it all. When Vogel finally got fed up with him, he had Adino's Achilles tendons slashed. It's the same thing with Brosnic—the stab wounds through the hands and feet. Vogel doesn't just carry out a sentence, he makes a statement. Mere execution isn't good enough. Tell me, what do they want to try Vogel for?"

"The Romanians want him bad, but so do the Germans. When Hitler's army first went into Romania, Vogel was an officer who worked with the Croat Iron

Guards. It was their job to round up Jews, Gypsies, and Serbs. This is before the concentration camps had been set up. Executions were mostly carried out with a bullet in the brain. To save ammunition, they sometimes lined people up in two rows, one standing and the other kneeling right in front of him, so the bullet would pass through the brain of one and into the chest of the other. But the Iron Guard wanted blood and they used knives. They held competitions. One of them cut the throats of over thirteen hundred people in one night—in one night. There's evidence that Vogel helped organize and promote such events."

The waitress came to our booth and asked if we wanted a refill. Giannopoulos said yes as he tapped out two cigarettes. I was lighting up when I saw a delivery truck stop down the street. The driver, wearing a tan uniform, got out and went to the front door of the Black Forest. He knocked, and after a moment the door was opened and he was let inside the restaurant.

Giannopoulos turned and looked out the window. "What?"

"Someone's over there. I saw Stemple there yesterday. He tells me that he refuses to run. So your money's on Stemple. Stick with him and Vogel will show up eventually." I put the unlit cigarette on the table and began to slide out of the booth. "Thanks for the coffee."

For the first time I saw genuine surprise on Giannopoulos's face. "Where are you going?"

"I'm through with this. You and Jack are on your own now."

"You're going to run, too?"

"I've told you everything I know."

"You don't understand, Frank." Giannopoulos took some coins out of his pocket, put them on the table as he got out of the booth. "We're not sure what Vogel looks like."

"If you know his war record, you must have photographs."

"Well, it's like this," he said. "There *were* photos, but they're gone. This is not the first time that our files have been tampered with. There are people in our agency—throughout the government—who help these Nazis out. You might think that we've been infiltrated, or you might think that since the war, some of these Nazis have been put to work by us—the CIA, the FBI, whatever—to fight against the communists. I think it's probably both. The fact is, we have no photo and no idea what Vogel looks like these days."

"I haven't seen Vogel in twelve years. He must be fifty, at least."

"He's going on fifty-two."

"I probably wouldn't recognize him if he sat down next to me. Sorry."

I went out to the curb and began looking up the street for a taxi. Giannopoulos stayed right with me. Jack stood by the car, alert. When a cab pulled up, I opened the rear door and was about to get in the back seat, but Giannopoulos took hold of my arm.

"Just go over there with me now," he said. "I want to see this Stemple. Do that, and then if you want, you run and hide, I won't bother you anymore."

"Is that a promise?"

He nodded as he shut the taxi door. We walked across the street, leaving Jack with the car. There were Venetian blinds in the windows of the restaurant, all closed. The delivery truck was still idling at the curb.

"They must have a door around back," Giannopoulos said.

We walked around to the alley behind the building and found the back door wide open. The kitchen was clean—stainless steel tables washed down, pots and pans hanging above stoves. Giannopoulos pushed through the swinging door and led me into the dining room, which was dimly lit and empty. I walked past him, quickly weaving in and around the tables, toward the front of the room. When I reached the window I grabbed the cord, yanked up the Venetian blind, and watched the delivery truck pull away from the curb. At the intersection, it barely slowed down, causing other cars to stop suddenly, horns blaring, as it burst through a knot of traffic.

Giannopoulos had already opened the front door, and he was jogging across the street to his car, shouting instructions to Jack. I ran outside, and we got into the car and followed the delivery truck through the intersection. We went for about a half mile without seeing the truck ahead of us. Giannopoulos hunched forward next to me in the back seat, and we looked down each side street we passed, but didn't see any sign of the truck.

After another dozen blocks Giannopoulos told Jack to turn around. "Did you see who got in the truck?" he asked him.

"Not well," Jack said. "Two men, but someone else could already have been in the cab of the truck. The driver wore a uniform, like a delivery man. Couldn't see the other one because he got in the passenger side."

"He didn't have a cane?" Giannopoulos asked.

"I didn't see any cane, but then I didn't really see him at all. Just the driver."

Giannopoulos sat back in the seat and took his pack of cigarettes from his coat pocket. "At St. Stanislaus, two men went into the sacristy. One with a cane.

If he's blind, he's going to have a hard time stabbing someone through the center of the palm. Maybe being blind, he leaves it up to the other man. He's only there as a witness."

"More like a judge," I said, taking the offered cigarette pack. "To them, this is an official act. Vogel's there to pronounce sentence before the execution is carried out."

. . .

We went back to the Black Forest, leaving Jack in the car at the curb. Inside, before my eyes had time to adjust to the dark, a woman said, "We're *closed.*" Her voice was young and peevish.

Like a couple of blind men, Giannopoulos and I felt our way around the tables and moved toward where her voice had come from—and I began to make out the woman standing at the far end of the bar.

"You cops?" she asked.

"Immigration and Naturalization Service," Giannopoulos said. He flipped open his wallet, but she barely looked at it, turning her head away in disgust. I could see her now and realized she had waited tables the night before—in her mid-twenties, with her blond hair pulled back in a bun. "I'm looking for Carl Simmons," Giannopoulos said.

"Well, he's not here," she said. "Just me, it seems."

"Why's that, this early in the morning?"

"Hans calls me and says get down here right away, and he's not here."

"Hans?" I asked.

"The manager."

"Simmons is the owner," I said. "Hans, he's the manager. Waits tables as well. Large man. Oiled hair."

"He's always here early, always punctual." She gestured toward the kitchen with a graceful hand. "I get here and the back door's wide open."

"How long ago did he call you?" Giannopoulos asked.

"Maybe forty minutes."

"When's the last time you saw him?" he asked.

"Last night, when we closed. What do you want with him anyway?"

I eased myself onto a bar stool. "He say why he wanted you here early?"

She lit a cigarette, and I could see her face clearly as she leaned into the flame. She had green eyes and dark red lipstick, painted on to make her mouth look fuller than it really was—and when she took the cigarette from her lips her front teeth were slightly pink. "Yeah," she said sarcastically. "One of the cooks is sick, and he needed me to come in and help with the prep. I hate prep. You chop onions and you can't get the smell off your hands all night, plus your eyes run, messing up your mascara. I told him forget it, I closed last night, but he was insistent. Then I show up and he's not even here."

Giannopoulos walked back toward the kitchen. "Mind if we have a look around?"

"Why should I mind?" She watched him push through the swinging door. "While you're back there, grab an apron and take care of those onions for me."

"A couple of nights ago," I said, "I was in here. You waited on that table back there. Three men: Simmons, Hans, and a priest."

"So?"

"You know the priest's name?"

"Everybody calls him Father Lou."

"You haven't heard," I said.

"Heard what?"

Giannopoulos came out from the kitchen. "Simmons didn't mention it when he called?"

She was still staring at me, and I believed she really didn't know. "Mention what?"

"Father Lou's dead," I told her.

At first it didn't seem to register. She just looked at me with those green eyes, and then her entire body went slack. I was off my stool and caught her as she fell and eased her down to the floor.

Giannopoulos stepped around her, went behind the bar, and began sorting through the bottles of liquor. She opened her eyes and tried to sit up, but then she started to cry, burying her face in my shoulder. Giannopoulos came to the end of the bar and poured out a shot of Scotch. "What's your name?" he asked.

After a moment, she lifted her head off my shoulder. "Braun."

"Right," he said. "And it's followed by?"

She put a hand on my shoulder to steady herself as she sat up. "Collins."

"Father Lou was your uncle?" Giannopoulos asked. "So you knew his name was really Mile Ionescu."

She looked at me, and I took a handkerchief from inside my coat pocket and handed it to her. She daubed the mascara coursing down her cheeks. "No," she said. "I knew his name was Mile Ionescu, a name I was never to repeat. Never, because he was my father." She started to gather her feet under her, and I helped her stand up. "Simmons, he's my uncle."

"Klaus Stemple," I said.

"Yes, yes," she said wearily. "We must tell *Onkel* Klaus."

"And Hans?" Giannopoulos asked. "Tell me he's related, too."

"No, just a good friend. He grew up with my father and uncle, so he's like family."

"What's Hans's real name?" I asked.

"I think I'm saying too much."

"New names don't always work, Braun, even here," I said. "Whatever his name was, Hans was taken away just now. By Vogel, or someone working with him."

"Vogel," she whispered. For a moment I thought she was going to begin crying again. But she straightened her shoulders, picked up the shot glass, and drank it down. "They're all so afraid of him. It has to do with the war. Where would they take Hans?"

"We don't know," Giannopoulos said. "It would help to know his real name."

She touched her fingertips to her forehead a moment, and then said, "Krantz."

"Hans Krantz?" Giannopoulos looked pleased. "Used to be one of Hitler's chefs," he said to me. "Until he was suspected of plotting to poison his vegetarian dinners. Somehow he managed to slip away and get to the States, where he could serve Wiener schnitzel."

"What will Vogel do to him?" she asked. When Giannopoulos didn't answer, she said, "Vogel. He killed my father, and now he'll kill Hans?"

"The other night," I said, "Stemple came to the bar here and made a phone call. Spoke German. Who would he call?"

Her eyes began to well up again, and this time when I offered her the handkerchief she waved it away. "My mother," she whispered. "She has refused to speak to my father for years, so it's always Klaus who communicates between them."

Giannopoulos leaned toward her and spoke softly. "Braun, we should find your mother before Vogel does. She goes by Collins now? Where is she?"

"She lives in Grosse Pointe Farms," she said. "She's married to an American. Her name is Elena Collins."

"And before?" I asked. "What was her name before she married Mile Ionescu, who became Father Lou Brosnic?"

"And before?" Braun said. "So many names, but nobody really changes, do they. My mother's maiden name was Saller." She wiped the tears away with one hand, smearing red lipstick across her cheek, which was already streaked with black mascara. "But before the war, before Mile, she married when she was very young, younger than I am now."

She stared at me, waiting, and when I said it, it wasn't a question but an answer, the answer none of us wanted to hear. "Her name was Vogel."

19.

Jack drove north and east, Braun sitting between Giannopoulos and me in the back seat. In daylight, with her makeup fixed, Braun was even younger than I had originally thought—early twenties at the most.

"Your mother," I said, "she was in her teens when she married Vogel."

"She wasn't sixteen."

We didn't speak after that until we took Moross into Grosse Pointe, when Giannopoulos said, "Elena married well this time around."

"My mother likes to say, 'It's not Bavaria.'"

"Mr. Collins, what's he do?" I asked.

"Cars," she said. "Larry designs them. Wait till you see next year's Chrysler. Says they're going to come out with these big tail fins."

"Fins?" Giannopoulos shook his head. "What is happening to this country?"

Braun directed us through a neighborhood full of mansions set back on well-maintained lawns, until we turned into a long pea-stone drive that took us to a large house in mock-Tudor style that overlooked Lake St. Claire. She had called ahead from the restaurant and spoken to her mother briefly in German. I understood enough to realize that things between them weren't exactly warm.

An English butler greeted us at the front door. He led us through a series of large rooms, where several maids polished and dusted antique furniture, and finally we were shown through a humid atrium full of enormous plants and squawking exotic birds to a glassed-in studio overlooking the beach. Wearing a paint-splattered smock, Elena Collins stood before a large canvas with a brush in one hand, a palette in the other. She looked as though she received regular facials, maintaining high cheekbones and flawless skin beneath the slightest protective sheen. Her silky blond hair draped both sides of her face, reminding me of a Saluki. She stood before a painting that could only be described as abstract: swirls and eddies of thick black and gray oil, layered on like cake frosting, broken by an occasional streak or splotch of crimson.

As Braun introduced us, her mother continued to stab the canvas with her brush. "What do you think, gentlemen?" Her German accent was still very much in evidence. "Wouldn't this cheer up your living room? I'm trying to think of a title. Something like *Smoke Gets in Your Eyes*, perhaps?"

Braun wandered back into the atrium, keeping out of her mother's range. She coaxed a parrot to drop down out of the giant fronds and perch on her forearm.

"You've heard about Father Lou?" Giannopoulos asked.

"I saw the papers this morning."

"Hans Krantz was abducted from the Black Forest an hour ago," Giannopoulos said.

Elena Collins didn't look away from her painting. "Vogel will kill him. Slowly. Symbolically. Nothing abstract, I'm afraid."

"Vogel is carrying out sentences on both men," I said. "What were their crimes?"

"Disloyalty," she said. "Disloyalty to the Reich is absolutely unforgivable. You would have to know Vogel to understand how much this means to them."

Giannopoulos said, nodding toward me, "He did."

Elena Collins put her palette and brush down on a small table cluttered with paint tubes, and then she turned to me. "How?"

"We were in a POW camp together in the U.P."

"Vogel ran the place, no doubt," she said. "But you survived them, Mr. Green."

"I escaped."

"I thought I had, too—long ago, before the war even began, when things were still being set in motion. The Reich was growing stronger all the time, and it consumed my first husband. I was lucky, I thought, to escape. He let me go—he had his women anyway. But when I got pregnant by Mile—you know we all grew up together—it was too much for Vogel. Particularly after what Mile did later."

She went to a door and led us outside. Giannopoulos and I followed her down a set of wooden steps to the beach. She walked between us, her arms folded. "Mile did his job. He didn't find it particularly tasteful—that would be his word—but he did as he was told, at first. His father was Romanian, and when the German army went into Romania, Mile was sent in to oversee interrogations because he understood the dialects so well. It was Klaus Stemple who got him the position, him and Hans Krantz—we were all in Romania at first."

"With the Iron Guard," Giannopoulos said.

"It would all be swift and clean—we truly believed that at first. It was like an operation: a brief period of pain, followed by extended recovery, but the end result would be strength. The New Order would save Germany, and we would create a new Europe—a new world. The Jews were treacherous. They controlled so much capital. We were convinced we had to do something extreme—it was a matter of our own survival."

"Stemple, Krantz, and Mile Ionescu," Giannopoulos said, "their jobs were to find Jews and—"

"Relocate them," she said vehemently. "Now everyone sees these films and they think that the concentration camps were there from the beginning. They believe that we all knew about it—that we were all present every time they turned on the gas. No one wants to believe that some of us were appalled, too. There is no doubt that through their work they sent many people to their deaths. But when they realized what was happening, the extent of it, they changed. By the end of the war, Mile had saved hundreds, maybe thousands of Jews. Stemple and Krantz, too. They helped find them hiding places. They arranged for them to be transported. In some instances they drove trucks out of Romania—they had the authority. Several times they personally took people to Trieste. There was a great business in passports and other documents. They would board a ship and sail down the Adriatic. Many went to Istanbul. Odd, isn't it, Jews seeking shelter in a Muslim country?"

"They delivered people to Trieste?" I asked.

"Jews. Serbs. Gypsies. I tell you people are alive today because of these men." Elena Collins paused, and we all stared out at the flat plane of blue water. On the horizon there was one long, rust-streaked ship, an ore boat, heading north. "After Vogel was sent to Africa, we learned that he had been captured. When the war ended, there was this massive search by the Allies. We were interrogated, much as we had done ourselves. Everyone was a war criminal. We got out of Europe any way we could. By then Mile and I had separated—the war, the pressure, it was too great. He disappeared, and I thought he had been killed or imprisoned by the Allies. I managed to get to the States with my daughter. A year or so later, I hear from this priest: Mile has become Father Louis Brosnic. I tell him it's too late to reconcile. He understood—I had met a GI who was going to be an engineer in the auto industry, and for our daughter it would be better that way. But there was always the bitterness. I could live with it, but I don't like what it has done to Braun. She is so . . . I raise her up here, and as soon as she can, she moves into the city and goes to work in that restaurant where she will be near Mile and the others. I guess I can understand her wanting to be close to her father, but it is so much safer up here. The suburbs, they are a great American invention, no? No history, no past, nothing that can hurt you. Comfort that can strangle the life out of you."

"And you," I said. "You remember."

"Yes, Mr. Green, I can't forget. There's a difference, isn't there, between remembering and not being able to forget."

I nodded. "Then Vogel found out that you were all here in the States."

"Mile called me," she said. "It was perhaps seven, eight years ago—one of the few times we have spoken directly to each other since we split up. Somehow he had heard about Vogel—that he was in South America. The Reich was still alive, waiting to reemerge. They still maintained their judicial system, if you can call it that. There were crimes against the Party, and it is Vogel's job to see to it that punishment will be carried out. It is imperative that he pursue his former friends, even his ex-wife. To do so is to maintain the purity of it all. Of the dream. It's what motivated so many of them, this dream, and when the war was over, they could only survive defeat by clinging to the dream. They *still* believe, and none of us can be exempt. I knew it would only be a matter of time." Looking back toward her house, she said, "So in truth, even in this suburban fortress there is no real safety. But my daughter—I wish for her to be safe."

"I might be able to help," I said. "I know a place that's safer."

"You have done this before. People you can trust."

"Yes," I said. "People I can trust."

"Trust. That is more valuable than money. You must be a most fortunate man." Elena Collins turned to me. "This is a great country, is it not, Mr. Green?"

"It is," I said.

"We come here, we change our habits, our dress, our accents—some of us, anyway. We change our names, do we not, Mr. Green? And for this, perhaps we even prosper."

"Some more than others," I said.

"But still, the money does not conceal you, and it becomes necessary to hide."

"I'm afraid so," I said. "You could both leave."

"No, Mr. Green," she said. "But thank you for your kind offer. I will keep Braun with me for now, while we make arrangements for her father's funeral."

"And I'll make some arrangements for her," I said, "and let you know."

"This I appreciate. Very much." Elena Collins put her hand on my sleeve—a courtly gesture, it seemed—and arm in arm we led Giannopoulos back toward the house overlooking Lake St. Claire.

. ∎ ∎

"One minute I feel like throwing up," Claire said through the static on the phone. "And then suddenly I'll get the chills, and five minutes later I'm breaking out in a sweat."

"But you're all right?" I said loudly. I was standing in the bedroom, looking down through the white sheer curtains at the sidewalk. Occasionally someone would pass beneath the streetlamp, but there was no sign that the apartment was being watched. "I mean the other times you ended up feeling really bad—you could sense that things weren't right. Remember?"

"I know, but so far it's fine." She added something that I couldn't understand.

"What?" I nearly shouted.

"At night I have these dreams of you and me—pretty hot stuff." She laughed, which made me realize how far away she really was, up there in Sault Ste. Marie. "We're usually in that little cabin, or sometimes the bunkhouse, and the rain is always pounding on the roof. Can't you come up here?" Claire was not one to plead, but now she was coming pretty close. "Or I could return to Detroit."

"Stay there. Please. We'll be together soon."

"You know it snowed here last night? There's often no real spring in the U.P. It's winter, and then—all of a sudden—one day the bugs are driving you mad." Her voice had become falsely pleasant.

I sat on the bed. "You're not alone now."

"That's right!"

"The Zampas are treating you all right?"

"Oh, just fine." Then she laughed. "But if I don't see you soon, I'm going to run off with this guy who works down at the locks. All day he catches the lines thrown from the ore boats and ties them around these big cleats."

"Well, maybe you can have hot dreams about him tonight."

"I'll try." There was a long pause and I began to think we had been cut off. "I only pray for your return to me soon," she said.

I listened to the static in the phone line from Sault Ste. Marie. "It won't be long."

"What?"

Louder, I said, "I'll call again soon."

.   .   .

I must have fallen asleep, because I was suddenly awakened by the phone ringing. It was after one in the morning. I picked up the receiver, and before I could say anything, a voice said, "Mr. Green?"

It was Stemple, his voice deliberate and careful. "Yes?"

"I have spent the day helping with the arrangements for Father Lou's funeral tomorrow morning." He sounded fairly drunk, and I could hear ice clicking as he took another sip of his drink. "And then tonight I received a phone call from Vogel. He says he intends to 'bring all of us to justice'—that is what he called it. You, me, Elena—her daughter, even."

"Braun? What offense has she committed against the Nazis?"

"Eliminating entire families has always been part of their solution."

"Why would Vogel contact you? Why not just kill you?"

"Good question. This is also part of their 'justice.' We must understand that it is not simply murder—that it is in fact a sentence to be carried out. It creates this powerful psychological effect."

"It's called fear."

"Precisely. And there's more," Stemple said. "Krantz—he is still alive. Hans is being skinned alive. *Very* slowly. It is imperative—that was Vogel's word—that Hans have time to contemplate his atonement." I could hear Stemple pick up his glass; he took a drink and put it back on the table. "Vogel mentioned St. Florian. You know who this is?"

"He was a Roman military officer who became a Christian. He carried out the violent persecution of many Christians for the Emperor Diocletian. But eventually Florian adopted Christian beliefs—secretly—and this meant he could no longer carry out his orders. So the Romans—his own soldiers—tortured him and tried to get him to recant, but he refused. So they skinned him alive, burned him, and then a millstone was tied around his neck and he was thrown in the River Enns."

"You Italians, with all your saints."

"Each one has a story, Herr Stemple. There is another saint, St. Bartholomew. I saw his statue in the cathedral in Milan when I was a boy. The statue, he stands erect, boldly so, with his skin draped over one shoulder, like a cloak. I remember there was a small crowd standing before it. Some people prayed, of course, but there were two priests standing behind me. They were whispering, talking about how the statue was a remarkable study of the human anatomy. For weeks after, I had nightmares."

"For Catholics, you're supposed to offer your pain and suffering to Jesus—correct?"

"Yes," I said.

"But this does not make it all right for Krantz. He will never be canonized a saint."

"No."

I could hear his labored breathing. Finally, he asked, "What did you do during the war?"

"I was an Italian officer. After being captured I was in a POW camp here in Michigan."

"You never imagined this life for yourself."

"This is true, Herr Stemple."

"For all of us. At first, during the war, I thought I was fighting, too. We all did. But then we began to realize that we were only doing terrible things to people. War was no excuse. And when we understood this and tried to help these people, it made us fugitives. All these years I have been waiting for someone like Vogel. Of *course* he is *blind*—he has always *been* blind. At least we became able to see. Sometimes I wish that weren't so. It would have been easier, really. Vogel—he still believes, he still has that, and in a strange way I am envious of his blindness. Brosnic, Krantz, and I, we talked about this often, the fact that it is now so hard to believe in anything. Democracy, capitalism, communism,

God—it doesn't matter what it is, Mr. Green, just so you believe in something. It gives you strength and conviction. It makes you righteous. For Vogel, believing in the Führer is the same as believing in Jesus."

20.

Rain pounded the slate roof of St. Stanislaus's Church, which smelled of damp wool and incense, a very Catholic combination. The church was filled beyond capacity, so I stood in the back of the balcony. Through the distortions of a stained-glass window directly behind me, I could see hundreds of people huddled beneath umbrellas on the sidewalks and in the park across the street. Had they known the truth about Father Lou Brosnic, that he was not an ordained priest, that his daughter and ex-wife sat next to his coffin, and that he had at one point in his life, when he was Mile Ionescu, labored for the Nazi regime, they probably would have stood in the rain nevertheless. Why? Because before the offertory of the Mass, several parishioners climbed the pulpit and told of Father Lou's devotion to St. Stanislaus's Parish. They recalled numerous acts of generosity and kindness. For his parishioners, these acts would be sufficient penance for whatever sins he might have committed.

Stemple was right: the Führer was Jesus to the Nazis, but the difference is that Christians, true Christians, believe in forgiveness. Nazis don't. They believe in strength through retribution. They cannot tolerate weakness, let alone failure, and are incapable of forgiveness. This, they believe, is their greatest virtue. It's what makes them so horrifying. Somewhere in the city of Detroit a man was being skinned alive, slowly. I remembered the statue of St. Bartholomew in the cathedral in Milan, how it frightened me as a boy. But it's different, thinking of St. Florian and St. Bartholomew. They were flayed alive centuries ago. Their pain has become legendary and has lost its real human element. They were martyrs, and then they became saints. It's not the same for a man named Hans Krantz, who was being skinned alive in Detroit in 1956. They must have taken him to a remote place, a warehouse or an abandoned building, his mouth gagged so that as the blade of the knife peeled away his skin, his screams could not be heard. I thought of the moment when I'd sliced my finger, which happened often when I'd worked in the kitchen at Tony's Grill. Just a little slip of the knife opening the skin is a terrible sensation, the sharp steel separating the flesh so cleanly, so easily. What was happening to Krantz was unimaginable. Maybe his body would go into shock. Maybe, if he was lucky, he would die of a heart attack.

At the end of Mass, I managed to inch forward until I found a place at the balcony railing. I could see Braun and her mother, standing in the front pew, both wearing black veils. The people who filled the central aisle parted as the pall bearers carried the coffin out of the church. There was only the sound of the rain, shuffling feet, and the occasional cough. In the years since the end of the war, Claire and I had attended Mass regularly. One Sunday, as we walked home, she told me, *You don't pray anymore.* There was no reprimand in her voice, only curiosity. I said, *Since becoming Frank Green, it seems I have forgotten how.* She held my arm, as she often did when we walked together, and her fingers tightened around the sleeve of my coat as she said, *You will remember, one day.* And we didn't speak of it again.

When the church was empty, I knelt, with my arms resting on the balcony railing, and closed my eyes. I knew how to say the Hail Mary, the Our Father, the Act of Contrition, but recitation wasn't what I needed. I thought of Claire. I thought about her voice coming through the static on the phone the night before when she said, *I only pray you will return to me soon.* I could pray for that.

When I opened my eyes, I stood up, blessed myself, and moved toward the narrow balcony stairs. Pausing at a stained-glass window above the landing, I looked down toward the street. There were many shades of brown in this window, the pieces of glass constituting the robe of St. Francis of Assisi. There was a car at the curb, and I kept moving my head, trying to look through a piece of glass that would offer a less distorted view. I found one pane of pale amber glass near the bottom of the window, and through it I could see a blind man being helped into the car. He wore a fedora, so I couldn't see his face. But there was something in his shoulders, something rigid that reminded me of the man who stood in the woods of northern Michigan, and I was sure it was Vogel. Just as the door was about to be closed, he raised his head. It was his face, which always reminded me of a fist, but older, the lines deeper. He wore sunglasses, as so many blind did, and his hands expertly folded up the sections of his white cane, which he held in his lap. And then the door was closed. The man who assisted him also wore a fedora and a dark raincoat. He walked around the front of the car and got in behind the steering wheel. I could not see his face, but by the way he moved, it was clear that he was much younger. And something in his bearing, too, was familiar. I went down the balcony stairs quickly, but when I pushed open the front doors the car was gone.

Before the funeral Mass started, Elena's butler had approached me as I entered the church. He whispered that the Mass would be followed by a private burial, and Mrs. Collins would appreciate it if I would come out to the cemetery and take Braun away after the graveside service was concluded. The cemetery was twenty minutes north of the church, and I waited by Tony's car. There was a small crowd gathered beneath the canvas top that had been erected over the grave. Elena stood arm in arm with her husband, Larry Collins, one of these beefy Americans who insist on wearing dress shirts with a collar a half-inch too small. Braun stood next to her mother, splendidly erect in black high heels. And Klaus Stemple stood beside Braun, wearing sunglasses despite the overcast sky.

When the ceremony was finished, everyone walked slowly to the black limousines that were parked along the curb. Braun spoke briefly with her mother and then hugged her, a formality; Stemple took her by the arm and they came over to my car. The butler fell in beside them, carrying a small suitcase, which he handed to me as I opened the back door of Tony's car. Braun and Stemple climbed in the back seat and I drove out of the cemetery.

"We have tried to convince Braun to reconsider," Stemple said as he removed his sunglasses. I looked up at him in the rearview mirror, at his prominent cheekbones, at the scar that ran down into his eyebrow.

"I am *not* leaving Detroit," Braun said as she continued to daub her eyes with a handkerchief. "I told you, I told Mother, I'm staying here."

"Such youth, such bravery," Stemple said to me, attempting a smile. "Where are you going to take her, Mr. Green?"

I turned left at a traffic light.

"You won't tell me because you don't trust me?" he asked. "Or perhaps it's too dangerous for me to know, in case I encounter Herr Vogel."

"Take your pick," I said.

Stemple gazed out the side window. "I suppose, should I meet our friend the Bird, he might have the means to persuade me to talk. Certainly, I am no longer young, no longer brave—if, indeed, I ever really was."

"Where would you like me to drop you?"

"As things are, I can't go to my apartment, and I can't go to the Black Forest. I too must go into hiding."

Braun lowered her handkerchief. "You're leaving Detroit?"

"I don't know, my dear. No, not immediately. At least not until my nerve runs out. At this point we must all—as Americans like to say—make ourselves scarce." Stemple leaned forward and laid a hand on the back of the front seat. "There's a cab stand at this next corner. I'll get off there." When I pulled over to the curb, he asked, "Will I be able to contact her by phone?"

I shook my head.

"What about you, Mr. Green? Where might I reach you?"

I glanced up at him in the mirror. "You could always leave a message at my shop."

"Yes, of course, you gave me your card," he said vaguely. "Made in the Shade, was it? Something about ambient light, I believe. Mr. Green, this is not the new life we envisioned for ourselves, is it?" When I didn't answer, he said, "Right, it's the one we've got."

He turned and embraced Braun, kissing her on the forehead. It seemed a formality to be endured; she only glanced at him with a perfunctory smile. After he got out of the car and walked to the nearest cab, I pulled out into traffic.

"It feels odd sitting back here alone, like you're my chauffeur," she said. Leaning forward, she draped one arm over the back of my seat, her silver wrist bracelet chiming. "Well, you might at least give me a cigarette."

We smoked as I drove, and the rain came on again, sweeping in gusts along the streets. Smoke filled the car, and she said, "Sometimes a cigarette is the only thing, though pretty soon I could use a drink."

"There'll be something where you're staying."

"With you?"

"You'll be staying with two friends of mine, Tony and Ginger."

"In Detroit."

"Yes." I stopped for a red light and turned to look at her. "You have to stay put. You can't contact anyone, can't call anyone. *Anyone.* Understand?"

"Okay, Dad."

I faced the windshield and gazed out at the street. The rain was now backing up the drains, causing water to rise above the curbs. When the light turned green, I said, "What about your mother?" I spoke loudly because of the sound of the rain drumming on the roof, the slap of the wipers.

"For now, she'll go downtown. Larry has this swanky apartment there, but I guess they won't even stay there. If I know them, they'll be sunbathing on some remote island in the Caribbean. We're all going to just run and hide." She rolled down her window and tossed her cigarette out into the rain. "What about you? Where will you hide, Frank?" When I didn't answer, she said, "You won't say, or you don't know?"

■ ■ ■

After I dropped her at the apartment—Ginger was there and she treated Braun like a long-lost sister, while eyeing me with suspicion—I spent the rest of the afternoon at the shop. Leon and I took delivery of new stock and I called Giannopoulos, but he wasn't in, so I left a message. After closing up for the day, I walked down to Tony's and sat in a back booth. The scampi, one of Paolo's better dishes, was on special.

I was sipping grappa and coffee when Giannopoulos walked in with Jack, who took up his usual station by the front door.

"You called, Frank?" Giannopoulos said, sitting down across from me.

"I did."

He looked up at the waitress, Tony's cousin Annette, and said, "Just water, lots of ice." After she went back to the bar, he said, "You've got the girl tucked away?"

"Yes."

"Fine. Because I have more good news."

"Let me guess: Hans Krantz."

Giannopoulos nodded, and waited as Annette placed the glass of water on the table. He watched her walk back to the bar, and then said, "He was pulled out of the Detroit River a couple of hours ago."

"Flayed?" I asked.

"How'd you know that?"

"Stemple called me last night," I said. "Called me because Vogel called him. Vogel's not going to stop until he's got all of us."

"That's two down. Yesterday you wanted to leave Detroit. Might be wise, Frank."

"I'm not helpful as bait anymore? You don't want any more martyrs?"

Giannopoulos just looked at me as he sipped his water.

"Tell me something," I said. "How did Krantz die?"

"How?"

"Was it something like a heart attack?"

"No, he drowned," Giannopoulos said. "There was water in his lungs."

"So he lived through it."

"He did. Flayed alive."

"I won't run. There's no point."

"What about Stemple?"

"I can't speak for him."

"Yesterday you were ready to hit the road, Frank."

"That was yesterday."

"We can't guarantee protection. I'm sorry."

"Hide?" I said. "If Vogel can't find us, he'll wait. The war ended years ago. He's a patient man."

"We could at least put a man on you again." When I shook my head, he lifted his hands off the table, palms up, suggesting that he was giving up on me. "You have a gun?"

"Think I need one?" He considered the glass of water between his hands as though he didn't know how it got there.

"I take that as a yes."

Giannopoulos leaned forward and whispered, "We've warned you. We can't help you beyond that, until Vogel has been dealt with. What are you going to do, wait around till he nails you? You going to stay in your apartment, where it's easy to find you? Do you have any idea what Vogel might do to you? I mean, in the eyes of the Third Reich, what is your crime?"

"That's a very good question." I took my cigarettes out and lit one. I thought about what Braun had said about a cigarette being the only thing. "I'm an Italian who saves American babies—making me a treasonous commie pinko. What kind of punishment would that warrant?"

"I were you, Frank, I'd at least check into a hotel."

"I'm considering it."

"The bit about saving the baby . . ."

"Maybe they'll work it into my obituary?"

"Listen, Frank, there are things I'm not allowed to do."

He glanced over at the bar, and then stared at me again.

"Murder," I said.

"You think of another solution?"

I picked up my coffee cup and then put it down. "No."

"Well, then I can't help you, any of you." Carefully, he placed his elbows on the table and pressed his hands together, just at the fingertips. It was an effort at calm, something to avoid exasperation. "Frank, I want you to understand this. I admire you. I admire what you've done. You've survived all these years, where so many others have . . ." He pulled his fingertips apart as though to suggest loss, oblivion. And then he laid them on the table, again wrapping his hands around his glass of water. "You've done so because you have this trait—it's real independence, of thought and action. To tell you the truth, I'm a bit envious. I don't have such independence. Everything I do is determined by someone else. I'm given my orders and I do them."

"You're a good soldier."

"If I could, I would take out Vogel in a minute. But I can't. There are re-straints—there are always restraints." He paused and inhaled slowly. "But you have no restraints."

I shook my head.

"You can. And then you can continue to live as you have. Free, independent."

"First bait. Now the hook."

"I can make sure that no one will ever look for you again. I can pull a few files."

"What files?"

"First time we met, I mentioned the thick folder we had on you? It contains all sorts of documents." Giannopoulos took his hands off his glass of water. The condensation had moistened his fingertips and he rubbed them together for a moment. "One doc in particular is labeled 'Grayling.' Toward the end of the war, there was an agent up there who disappeared. Guy named Ferris, Roy Ferris. He wrote a report that mentions a POW who might be staying at a farm. This Ferris, he worked out of Grayling and he just vanished, not a trace."

"You think I did that?"

"It doesn't matter if you did. It's what can be done with that file. It can be made to look like you did something, whether you did it or not. Or it can disappear. Forever."

"You've got a great democracy here. Be careful it doesn't slip away, because if it does you'll have a hell of a time getting it back."

"You'll be doing your country a great service." Giannopoulos pushed his glass toward the middle of the table as though it was the culminating move in a game of chess, and then he got out of the booth.

"My country," I said. "I don't know what my country is any more than I know who I really am. That's as free and independent as you can get."

He walked to the front door, which Jack held open for him.

21.

iannopoulos was right about a number of things. One of them was that, like Braun and Stemple, I had to make myself scarce. I returned to my apartment and packed a small suitcase. My pistol was in the bedroom closet, tucked in the shoulder holster, which I strapped on. In the lobby, I checked the mailbox—a phone bill and a letter from Claire—and then, after watching the street for a few minutes, I went out the back door of the building and down the alley that led to the next block, where I took a cab downtown. Thirty minutes later I was checked into the Huron Hotel, a short walk from my shop and Tony's Grill. When Giannopoulos said he admired me for my freedom and independence, he was really complimenting me on my ability to be nondescript. The Huron offered weekly rates for salesmen and was about as nondescript as they come.

Dear Frank,

There's a gorgeous fog here again tonight. From my apartment above the Zampas' garage I can see the lights along the locks, and the ore boats sound their horns down on the St. Mary's River. Louisa and Carmen have been splendid. Louisa wants to fawn over me but I think after a couple of days Carmen has convinced her that I'm not their daughter and might not want to spend every waking moment in their loving embrace. I'm spending longer periods in the apartment without one of them ringing the bell and calling up the stairs to see if I need something. The garage has three bays, for their car, the truck and snowplow, and Carmen's workshop. Upstairs there's a living room, kitchenette, and two bedrooms—bigger than our apartment in Detroit but it seems empty without you. I wish we knew how long this "arrangement" will last.

I walk a great deal. Sault St. Marie is not a big place. Fortunately, along with the fog the weather's been cool (slept with a sweater on last night). There's a park nearby where I sit and read. Afternoons it's filled with children and their mothers, who sit on benches gossiping. I've been away from the U.P. long enough to be keenly aware of the local accent. It's not the same as over around Munising, but more Canadian. Today in the park I spoke with a woman who said she went for weeks without seeing her husband who worked on the "oor boots." Her name is Gwenn and she has two little girls and she's expecting her third. She broke away from the other mothers and sat with me a while (she as much as told me that she was sent to reconnoiter, and then report back to the loud, chatty one named Alice). Gwenn was quite nice and I think she welcomed sitting with someone new. She had a copy of Peyton Place, *which she said was splendidly trashy, and when she saw that I was reading* East of Eden *(I already have a library card!) we started talking about members of the Trask family.*

Before leaving me on the park bench she said something that kind of floored me. "When are you due?" I mean it's only been how many days? Finally I managed to ask what made her think I was pregnant and she laughed, saying she had considerable experience in this area. So then I told her that I wasn't sure but hoped that in fact I was pregnant, but it was still too early to be certain. And she said she could see it when I walked into the park. "See what?" I asked. She said something vague about my posture, though of course I'm months away from possibly showing.

But then the thing that really got me was when she said, "You've tried before, but it hasn't worked out." When I asked her how she knew that, she simply said, "Your eyes." Anyway, before she left the bench she jotted down the name of her doctor and tucked it in my library book, and I have an appointment next week.

The fact is, this time it feels different. Already. Little signs. It makes me a bit jumpy (I'm trying to lay off the coffee). One minute I want to scream out in a park that I'm pregnant, and the next minute I'm in the bread aisle of the A&P fighting back tears for no apparent reason. But it's ok. There's a joy to it that radiates from within. I just wish you were here to bask in the glow.

I'll sign off now. It seems so strange writing a letter to you, when we were together only days ago, eating pesto fettuccini, never dreaming that we'd suddenly be apart indefinitely. It's what I live for, being with you, Frank. You don't have to write (I know you won't), but I wait for your calls. Please call soon.
Love,

Chiara
(I'm back in the U.P. and I can't help it—up north, I'm still Chiara.)

. . .

First thing in the morning I walked over to the shop, stopping at a newsstand to pick up a newspaper and a postcard of the city lights reflected in the Detroit River. I wrote on the back, "*Ti amo. Ti amo. Ti amo. –Francesco*" and dropped the card in a mailbox. There was no more hiding. If I wanted to say I love you to my wife in Italian, what's to stop me?

. . .

Hans Krantz's murder was on the front page of the *Free Press*. I was reading about it as I walked into the shop (the door was unlocked, though it was just past seven—early, even for Leon). I went back through the showroom and stopped in the workshop doorway. Leon was sprawled on the floor, unconscious. His stool was knocked over, lying across his short legs. I knelt down beside him and lifted the stool off of him. His jaw was swollen, and there was a nasty bruise next to his left eye.

I got a cup of water from the cooler in my office. When I returned to the workshop, he was sitting up, his back against the file cabinet. He drank the water down without stopping, and then said, "What they do with my glasses?"

I looked under the workbench and found his dark-framed glasses lying amid TV and radio parts, one arm broken off. "They need a little repair." I took the roll of electrical tape down off the pegboard, sat on the floor next to Leon, and began taping the arm back on his glasses. "What happened?"

"Last night. I was just finishing up that Zenith. It musta been elevenish. There was a rap on the door, and when I went out, there were two men, one young, one old."

"The old one blind?"

"Guess so." Leon took the glasses from me and bit off the roll of tape. "You never could fix anything, Frank." He slid the glasses on and said, "That looks rather stylish, huh? Sorta Cary Grant. Or Sammy Davis Jr."

"How young?"

"Oh, everybody looks too young to me now. Late twenties—thereabouts."

"What they say?"

"Say? Not much. They were looking for you, surprise-surprise. German accents, or maybe Austrian? I did my best Bogart, and the young one—his name's Anton—bopped me good. This could be a father and son routine? The old man asks all the questions while his boy does the heavy work."

"He had a cane."

"That's your man." Leon's glasses sat at an angle on the bridge of his nose.

"You want a doctor?"

"No." He rubbed the back of his neck. "Lying on this friggin' floor all night. What I could really use is a cup of coffee, laced."

I took him by the arm and helped him to his feet. "Let's go down to Tony's."

"They're not open this early."

"No, but they'll be there prepping for the day." We went out into the showroom. Then I paused and said, "Wait here a sec."

I went back into my office and unlocked the safe. We didn't have a bank account and nearly everything we had was in there. I took out all the cash, bills wrapped in elastic bands. No time to count it, but I did a rough tally and figured there was something over eight thousand dollars. I switched off the light as I left the office. "We're going to be closed for business for a while," I said. "And you're going on a paid vacation."

"I am?"

"Don't you have a sister—Saint Somewhere?"

"St. Louis."

I counted out two thousand dollars and handed it to him. "Have a swell time."

■   ■   ■

We walked over to Tony's Grill and they were all there, preparing for the day, Tony behind the bar, Ginger and a couple of cousins setting up tables. The smell of onions and garlic came from the kitchen. Ginger got out of the booth where she had been refilling all the sugar bowls. "Your girlfriend," she said, squinting against the cigarette hanging from the corner of her mouth, "said she didn't want to sit in our apartment all day, so she's out back helping Paolo." Then taking Leon by the arm, she turned him so she could see better by the light from the front window. "What the hell, Leon?"

"Had a little run-in with this great pair of knockers. I mean cleavage with an echo like the Grand Canyon." He rose up on his toes and leaned toward her white satin blouse. "*Hellooo!*"

Ginger took her cigarette from her mouth and cocked her head, disappointed. "You pay for that sort of thing on the street, Leon, this is what happens. Dope."

"No, no, I was doing pro bono work." He touched his jaw tenderly. "I think this was more of a knee-jerk reaction. Know how it is when you tall girls hit the bull's-eye—they constitute a physical threat."

She looked at me, her eyes both curious and angry. "It's you, isn't it? All this, this *crap*—it's because of *you*."

"Guilty." Looking over at Tony behind the bar, I said, "How 'bout a couple of coffees, and doctor his."

"Sure thing," Tony said.

Ginger helped Leon into the booth and then sat down next to him and resumed filling the sugar bowls. After each one was filled, Leon flipped closed the stainless steel lid, which made a nice solid clink. The cousins got back to their chores.

I went over to the bar, where Tony was filling two mugs of coffee. One he topped up with Irish whiskey. "Splash?" he said.

"Thanks, no."

I took the mugs over to the booth and gave Leon the laced coffee. He was content helping Ginger. I was going to sit down across from them, but Ginger fixed me with an eye and I thought better of it. I went up to the front window and worked on my coffee. This hour of the morning, the sun, rising over the river a dozen or so blocks east, floods the street with angled light, long shadows. Back in the kitchen I could hear the rapid knock of a knife blade on butcher block, and the radio that Paolo kept on while doing prep. After a commercial jingle ended, the news came on, leading with the story about the police finding Hans Krantz's flayed body in the river. The chopping ceased; there was the clatter of something—a knife?—falling to the floor.

Paolo swore in Italian, nothing unusual around Tony's.

I followed Tony back to the kitchen. Paolo and Braun were at the sink, and he held her left hand under running water. There was blood on her apron, on the floor, smeared by shoes. She was white, her eyes streaming tears, but she was quiet, perhaps in shock. We were like a surgical team. First, we wrapped the cut finger in one clean towel, and after several minutes, when it had been used up, we got a second towel. Paolo continued to swear in Italian, and at one point he said to me and Tony, "*È cucina mia*. Is no good."

"It's a little cut," Tony said. "You get cuts and burns all the time."

"No." Paolo walked away and began checking his pots simmering on the stove, a gesture that suggested he was washing his hands of further involvement.

Tony and I continued to work on the cut, putting pressure on the finger. Braun stared at her hand as if it wasn't hers. When the bleeding had pretty much stopped, Tony went into the office for the first aid kit.

"They skinned him." She continued to stare down at the towel wrapped around her hand. "Skinned him alive, and then they threw him in the river. Do you think—"

I knew what she was going to ask, so I said, "It's my fault. I should have thought to come in and tell you, before you found out—" I nodded toward the radio, which was perched on a windowsill.

"This little cut hurts," she said, a note of fascination in her voice, "but *that*. How can they *do* that to someone?" She looked at me for the first time, her eyes pleading.

"Don't ask me to explain it. The war, it did things to people."

Tony came back with the first aid kit and got out gauze pads and a roll of white tape. I assisted as best I could, but Tony had done this before, and we talked about how often I almost lost a finger when I had first started working in the kitchen. When the finger was bandaged, Tony said, "Five years I wrapped wounds in the South Pacific. Trust me, you'll be fine in a few days."

I said to Tony and Paolo, "Give us a minute, will you?"

They both understood and left the kitchen.

"You're getting out of Detroit," I said. Braun continued to stare down at her bandaged finger. "This morning. I'm going to take you back to Tony and Ginger's apartment. We'll pack up your suitcase, and then I'm taking you to the bus station."

Her lips tightened, and for a moment I thought she was going to cry, but then she asked, "Where?"

"Sault Ste. Marie."

"That's, like, way up north."

"Exactly. My wife's up there, and she's alone in this apartment with an extra bedroom. It'll be fine. You'll be there by tonight." I waited a moment, until she looked up at me. "Besides, I want you to take something up to her."

"How long?"

"I don't know that. Until it's over."

She then did something I wasn't prepared for: she stepped into my arms and hugged me tightly. I placed my hands on the small of her back and she laid her head on my shoulder. After a moment, she asked, "These lumps under your coat—what is that, Frank?"

"It's the money I want you to take up to my wife so the two of you will be all right."

Then she stepped back and patted the holster on my left side. "And this is not money. I know what this is. This is the thing you need even more than money. You should get out of Detroit, too."

"I'd like to. But somebody's got to stay."

■   ■   ■

I borrowed Tony and Ginger's Pontiac and, after a brief stop at their apartment, took Leon and Braun to the bus station: Leon to St. Louis and then Braun to Mackinaw City, where she'd take the ferry across the straits and catch another bus from St. Ignace to Sault St. Marie.

"Funny," Leon said before boarding his bus, "how many places in America are named after saints."

"Why funny?" I asked.

"Don't know." He glanced up at me, and I half expected him to wink. "You'd think we were in Spain. Or maybe Italy." Then he climbed on the bus, humming "That's Amore." He paused at the top of the steps. Turning around, he seemed to enjoy the fact that for once I had to look up at him. "Frank," he said. "I'm onto you."

"Onto me what?"

He shook his head. "Listen, brother, you can't go on like this."

"Like what?"

"Like underestimating a dwarf." Dead serious for the longest moment, his brown eyes enlarged by his glasses, which were still taped at one corner and were slightly crooked on his face—and then he smiled.

"You take care, Leon."

"I always do." He started down the aisle, and though he was out of sight, I heard him say in his most pleasant television voice, "Why, ma'am, would you mind if I sit next to you in this vacant seat? I do like to be near the front of the bus, you know, so's I can keep an eye on our driver. It just makes me feel safer, you know?"

I waited for the woman's response, but then the bus doors closed with a hiss and a sigh.

■   ■   ■

As I walked Braun to her bus, she said, "In the movies, I've always liked those scenes at the bus or train station. Broken hearts and imminent danger."

"The best ones are when they manage not to make a scene."

"I feel like the heroine." She leaned forward and kissed me on the cheek.

After we had seen Leon off, she had gone to the ladies' room; I took it as an opportunity to go to the men's, where I stuffed the wads of bills inside her suitcase.

"Don't let that out of your sight," I said as I handed her the suitcase.

"I could take the money and run. Denver. San Fran. Rio."

"You could, but it's not what heroines do."

"Your wife, what's her name?"

"Claire, but she'll appreciate it, now and then, if you call her Chiara."

"Will this be all right with her?"

"It's nice of you to ask. It will be fine with her. She's all alone up there. You'll get along fine. I'll call her, and she'll be at the station when you get in tonight."

"When you call, tell her I'm the girl who looks like she's carrying the loot." Braun gazed down the platform, searching for a last impression to take with her. "This would be better in a train station—all that steam shrouding the platform in mystery."

"You are a romantic."

"I'm nervous, I think." She tried to smile. "I've never been that far north."

"You'll like it. She says it's . . . cooler than down here. You'll need a sweater."

"A sweater?"

"There's still snow on the ground."

"You kidding? It's May."

"I'm not kidding."

"Snow," she said, as though she'd never really considered what the word meant before, and then she shifted her suitcase to her other hand and boarded the bus. I stepped back on the platform and watched as she got settled. She put the suitcase in the rack above her seat, and then sat down next to a window just as the bus began to pull out of the station. As she looked down at me, her eyes seemed disinterested but resigned, and it reminded me of how during the war, before I was captured, things would happen suddenly, we'd be ordered to prepare to march. You just did it. You had no choice. And you never knew whether you were headed toward safety or harm. You just didn't think about that, then.

22.

econd lives, second thoughts. When you live a second life, you think about things later. Which too often means regrets. Things you should have done, things you shouldn't have done. But eventually you arrive at the place where you are—all these things you might have done, or might not have done, they don't matter, because you're here now, and that's the only important thing to keep in mind. Klaus Stemple had said, *Did any of us ever think this would become our new lives?* Of course not. How could we? I was the boy who once played an A-minor chord on the maestro's piano. I never imagined leaving Italy, and certainly not spending years—decades—here in America. I hoped to one day meet someone like Claire, but had no idea it would be under such circumstances. For that alone, for her, I could never have any real regrets.

My only second thought, actually, had to do with my gun. I'd bought it from a guy Tony knew: Louie. He was so insistent about not giving his last name that people called him Just Louie. A few months after I'd started working at the grill, he came into the kitchen one night as I was cleaning up, and said, *Just call me Louie, and my friend Tony out at the bar tells me you might be interested in some personal protection, so I would like to be of assistance, if I may.* He was short and wide, and wore a good tweed overcoat and a black fedora that had snow melting on its stingy brim, which sported a small red-and-white feather in the hatband. He placed his briefcase on the stainless steel table I had just finished wiping down, and when he opened it, there were four handguns displayed on what looked like black velvet. I remember glancing toward the door, fearing that someone might intrude (though Paolo had already left for the night—first thing you learned from Paolo was it was his kitchen, and he didn't stick around to clean up at the end of the night). *Not to worry*, Just Louie said, *we will not be disturbed during our consultation.* And then he proceeded to display his wares. He had the natural delivery of a salesman. Never actually assertive, always seeking the customer's opinion, trying to home in on the option that would close the deal. *You like the fit of this one in your hand? You comfortable with this weight?* And ever suggestive. *Have you considered how you plan to carry it?* With a flip of a latch, he opened the inside of the briefcase lid, which offered a display of several styles of shoulder holsters. Just Louie was a true salesman in every detail, right down to his trimmed mustache and manicured fingernails. I learned more from him about sales than about weapons. The secret was to deal with the customer as though you shared a secret. He could have sold anything: firearms, automobiles, even lampshades.

Ultimately, I decided upon the Beretta 1934, which was the pistol I'd been issued in the army. However, my eye kept wandering to the Colt Python, which Just Louie explained had gone into production the previous year, and in his opinion might be the best double-action revolver ever made. He picked it up and placed it in my hand and said, *Now don't you feel like a cowboy?* I agreed that it had good heft, but I wasn't a cowboy, and it was too expensive. The used 1934 wasn't as powerful, but Just Louie sensed that I was familiar with it, so he talked up the fact that the Berettas had been making firearms since the Middle Ages. *You're not a cowboy but a man with history on his side*, and he gave it to me at what he claimed was an incredible discount (a nice way of saying he was dumping it), which included the convenience of easy financing.

That first year in Detroit, what little money we made went toward food, rent, and obtaining the necessary papers—birth certificates, wedding license—that would legally declare that we were Mr. and Mrs. Frank Green. But every day when I stepped out onto the street, I looked both ways up and down, expecting someone to handcuff me or, worse, shoot me. I had such second thoughts about the Beretta that I considered asking Just Louie if I might trade up. But as the months passed, and we had been Frank and Claire Green of Detroit, Michigan, without any difficulties, I began to leave the pistol in a shoebox on the shelf in the bedroom closet, and from that moment on I really began to think—and act—like any law-abiding citizen. It was my best bet. But now I wished I had that Colt Python, because I kept thinking I shouldn't get too close. With Vogel and his assistant, I needed to somehow see them from a distance before they saw me. I needed something with long-range accuracy. But what I had tucked under my left arm was going to have to do.

I was going to have to get close.

I couldn't afford second thoughts—not now.

■   ■   ■

And I was not accustomed to talking to Claire on the phone. Not long-distance. A quick call from the office to say I'd be home half an hour late and could I pick up something on the way—that was one thing; but Detroit to Sault Ste. Marie, over a crackling phone line, it was impossible to say what you meant. It was harder to understand what she meant. The result was we both said very little. I told her that I had moved out of the apartment. I told her that I appreciated her letter, but wouldn't be collecting the mail from either the apartment or the store for the time being. I told her I would call her whenever I could, which was met with a lengthy silence.

"Where are you now?" she said finally.

"Phone booth in the lobby."

"No phone in your room?"

"This is not exactly the Ritz."

I was looking out the front windows of the lobby, watching three buses pull up in front of the Huron Hotel. I told Claire about Braun, about her arriving on the bus in Sault Ste. Marie that night, about the five thousand dollars she had in her suitcase.

Again, the silence, the static.

"I couldn't ask you first," I said. "There wasn't time."

"I understand."

"Do you?"

"I do."

"It'll be all right, the two of you there together?"

Slight pause. "You did the right thing, Frank."

"I just didn't know where else—"

"It's fine, really, Frank. You're always . . ." Static.

"Always what?"

"You've always made quick decisions under pressure. It's how you've kept us safe. It's how we've gotten from there to here."

The buses pulled away from the curb, leaving dozens of men and women standing on the sidewalk in front of my hotel. They had luggage, they were gesturing excitedly with their hands, and they seemed in complete confusion. Conventioneers. Christ. They'll make a racket all night in the hotel.

"Her bus gets in at eight-thirty," I said. "I'll call tomorrow."

"Yes, all right."

"*Ti amo.*"

"*Ti amo.*"

A click and the line went silent. I had this hollow feeling. I suspected we had not really talked about what we should have talked about. She wasn't telling me what was on her mind, and I hadn't asked.

I left the phone booth as the people who had gotten off the buses began to crowd into the lobby. Some were gathered at the front desk; others stood in small groups. I started for the elevators but stopped and looked around. There was no sound, nothing. It was like a silent movie, the way they gestured with their hands, their arms. Facial expressions seemed overly theatrical. A suitcase fell over, making a loud booming sound that reverberated off the mock-marble columns. No one noticed. Their hands and arms continued to move in the air.

Deaf-mutes. A convention for deaf-mutes.

I got on the elevator with several of them. They nodded and smiled at me, and I nodded and smiled back.

∎   ∎   ∎

The silence kept me awake. I could hear them in the hall, their footsteps, doors opening and closing, but there was no sound, just movement. The hotel seemed haunted.

A little after midnight I gave up trying to sleep and went out, thinking I'd get a drink. But I just walked, thankful for the sound of traffic, music coming out of the open doors of bars and night clubs. Eventually, I found my way to Tony's Grill. Ginger was alone behind the bar, cleaning up. There was one customer, sitting in a booth. She drew my beer and I took the glass to the phone booth.

I wanted to make sure Braun got into Sault Ste. Marie all right, but it was too late to call. I took out my wallet and found Klaus Stemple's number, which I dialed just out of curiosity. At the very least, he wouldn't be anywhere near his apartment, and I wouldn't be surprised if he'd already left Detroit. But the phone rang twice and then someone picked up—no hello, just soft breathing coming through the line.

"Stemple?" I said.

No response. Just the breathing, and it went on like that for an eternity, or so it seemed. Whoever was on the other end of the line heard the sound of running water as Ginger washed glasses. When she finished, she dried her hands and put her bracelet back on, which tinkled lightly. The one customer, an old man, shuffled to the front door and disappeared into the night. Still, there was nothing but soft breathing at the other end of the line. I didn't think it was Stemple. I wasn't sure if it was a man. I just couldn't tell.

I took my hotel key from my coat pocket, looked at the number on the tag, and said, "Cedar five-five-oh-six-two, noon tomorrow," and hung up the receiver.

Ginger had just wiped down the bar when I sat down, careful to place my glass of beer on a coaster. She poured herself a Scotch on the rocks and said, "What's going on with you, Frank?"

"What do you mean?" I sipped my beer.

"Come on," she said. "You have these quiet meetings with this suit while his watchdog guards the door. And Claire's suddenly out of town—"

"Don't let your imagination get carried away."

She lit a cigarette, watching me. "And this blonde kid, there's nothing going on there?"

"That's right." I studied the foam as it slid down the inside of my glass.

"I think you got some problems you don't want to admit to."

"That so?"

"Yeah, Frank. You avoid talking about the war. Which is not unusual. Some men, it's the first thing you learn about them, where they were, what outfit, what they did, the whole thing, until you want to scream *stop with the war stories*. Tony, he doesn't go on and on about it too often, thank God, but sometimes, like the other day, he's unloading meat from a delivery truck out back, and as he picks up a side of beef he says its weight reminds him of Ned Peterson, a kid from Arizona, or what was left of him after a mortar hit his foxhole on Okinawa. Tony will wear a Hawaiian shirt every day for the rest of his life because it's something he promised himself he'd do if he made it back from the South Pacific. Fine, that's how he deals with it. But you're one of these guys who doesn't like to broadcast it, doesn't wear it on your sleeve, so to speak, if you'll excuse me. And I'm guessing you were in Europe; I'm guessing that this guy that sits in the booth and talks with you real quiet, he's got something to do with it. I don't know, Frank, you were something—intelligence, or a spook, something like that. With you it's not what you say, it's what you don't say. Tony wrapped a lot of wounds, saw a lot of blood, but he says sometimes the worst wounds are the ones you don't see. He says your war's none of our business, so I'm not asking here, just making an observation, you understand?" She picked up her drink, rattled the ice a bit. She was done.

"Ginger, you know how many friends Claire and I have in this town? Real friends?" I asked. "Three: you, Tony, and Leon."

"You're a strange guy, Frank. Lots of people wouldn't count Leon as a friend. But that's the thing about you I've noticed: you're like us, but somehow you're not one of us."

"I'm not sure I know what that means."

"Come on, you understand English, Frank. It means what it means."

For a moment I wanted to tell her just how strange I was, how strange it all was—how being an American, being like them, didn't come naturally for me. I wanted to tell her that I was a distant relative of the great Giuseppe Verdi, the streets of Detroit were a long way from the hills of Le Marche, and for years I'd been living a life that wasn't my own life. "We all got problems, Ginger." I finished my beer and stood up, placing a dollar on the bar. "And it's late. See you tomorrow."

■   ■   ■

The deaf-mutes proved to be a blessing. The hotel was quiet and I slept soundly until almost eleven o'clock. When I got up, I showered and then went down to the phone booth in the lobby and called Claire.

"Did she get in all right?"

"Yes," Claire whispered. "We were up late talking and she's still asleep."

"Okay, I'll make this quick. Is it all right?"

"It's fine. It's nice having her here."

"It won't be forever."

"How are things there?"

"Everything's fine."

"So everybody's fine, only everybody's in hiding and we're hundreds of miles apart."

"As I said, it's only temporary." I looked at the clock above the hotel's front desk. "Listen, I've got to get off—I'm expecting a call at noon. I'll call again later."

"All right. It's fine—she's fine, really."

"Good."

"I love you."

"I love you."

It was a few minutes before noon when I hung up. I remained in the booth with the receiver wedged between my ear and shoulder and one hand holding down the hook, waiting for the phone to ring. Through the folding glass door I looked across the lobby toward the coffee shop. People eating, people working. A weekday morning—everything was business as usual, but something about it reminded me of the deaf-mutes. Body language spoke volumes. Nobody quite looked at anybody else. Ginger said I was strange. She was right. But we are all strange. No matter what life—or lives—we lead, we're all strangers.

The phone rang, and on the third ring I released the hook but didn't speak.

"Captain Verdi."

Despite all the years, I knew it was Vogel. I wanted to hang up but didn't. I just held the receiver to my ear and listened to the silence. Finally, I said, "Where's Stemple, Kommandant Vogel?"

"How good of you to call last night." His German accent seemed as strong and angular as I remembered it, but there was something oddly pleasant to it. "I've been trying to reach you."

"I'm sure you have."

"No one can hide forever."

"True. Neither can you."

"Obviously you have been in communication with Herr Stemple. Where is he?"

"I don't know. Guess you've missed him."

"You know where he's gone?"

"No idea. What do you expect? I'm sure he's a long ways away by now."

"No one can avoid justice forever."

"I hope that's true, Vogel."

"Well, you are still in Detroit. I must commend your ability to remain . . . I believe the term is 'at large.'"

"Yes," I said. "It's an amusing phrase."

"And I admit that I have come to admire your courage. This is something you displayed when we were in the camp in Au Train, but unfortunately yours was grossly misguided. You insisted on working at cross-purposes at a time when it was essential that we remain unified in our resolve."

"I remember this speech, Kommandant. You used to give it several times a week."

"You raised too many questions then. And now it appears everyone has disappeared—Stemple, Elena, her daughter. Everyone except you."

"Perhaps you should give up. It's pointless."

"That is not possible," he said. "Justice is not pointless, and it is timeless."

"Then we should meet. Sooner than later."

"You always struck me as a realist. What do you propose we do at this meeting?"

"Talk."

"Perhaps you wish to beg for mercy?" When I didn't answer, he asked, "And where do you propose we meet?"

"Someplace public."

"But of course."

There was a poster on the easel across the hotel lobby, which listed various group events for the deaf-mutes' convention. One included a trip to Belle Isle in the Detroit River before dinner that evening. "Belle Isle," I said. "There's a fountain. Let's say five this afternoon."

"Very well, Captain Verdi. *Va bene*."

■   ■   ■

I spent the rest of the afternoon in my hotel room. Once I went back down to the lobby and called Giannopoulos, but he wasn't in, and when his secretary asked if I would leave a number, I hung up. Back in my room, I considered packing up and walking to the bus station. But eventually one of them—Vogel or Giannopoulos—would catch up with me. Giannopoulos had given me an out: do his dirty work. Alone. It was the only option. You're a soldier until you do, then a soldier no more.

At four o'clock, I went downstairs to get a cab, but there were about two dozen deaf-mutes lined up to board a bus parked at the curb. A woman in her forties, wearing a yellow dress with a lace collar, smiled at me and made a series of signs.

"I am not with the convention," I said slowly.

The man standing in front of her in line turned and she exchanged signs with him, and then they both looked at me and made motions toward the bus.

"I do not want to intrude," I said.

They waved this off vigorously.

"According to the schedule in the lobby, you're going to Belle Isle, right?"

The woman nodded as she took me by the arm and walked me toward the open door of the bus. So I got on board. There was a great deal of signing between the woman and the others who were already seated. They nodded and smiled: I was more than welcome to join them. The woman guided me to an empty bench and we sat down together. I looked about the bus; there was something odd about it that I couldn't put my finger on—not that all the passengers were deaf-mutes, but something else, something about the way they *were* together. She dug into her purse and produced a small notepad and pen; flipping the pad open, she wrote: *Audrey Vickers. Librarian. Bettendorf, Iowa.*

She had a weak chin, enormous teeth, and very pink gums. When I reached for the notepad, she shook her head and gestured toward her mouth.

"Frank Green, Detroit," I said.

Suddenly arms were extended toward me and I shook hands with people seated behind us, in front, across the aisle. And then I realized that there were whites and blacks on the bus—that was not unusual. But in Detroit, in 1956, a bus was a segregated public space; whereas here, these deaf-mutes were sitting on this bus together. Some whites and blacks, in fact, shared the same seat bench, and they signed to each other enthusiastically. It was quite a remarkable thing, really, though to them it seemed the most natural thing in the world. I imagined asking Leon—who had tried to take a seat in the front of the bus to St. Louis—if he thought this was ever possible, and could see him push his glasses up his nose as he let out a laugh. *Frank, you are some kinda fool.* I suspected he believed, or hoped, it was possible, but he'd never let his cynical humor down enough to admit it. When the air brakes sighed, the bus lurched forward, causing applause to break out among the passengers.

There was rush-hour traffic and the bus made slow progress toward the river.

I learned from Audrey that this was her first visit to Detroit. She was one of the organizers of the convention, which attracted people from all over the Midwest. There was no wedding ring on her left hand, and something about the way she sat next to me suggested that she had already established possession—I might have been a stray dog she'd found on the street and decided to take home and feed. Everyone on the bus gestured constantly—talking—often pointing to something on the streets or sidewalks. At one point, the man who had helped me aboard stood up and made a series of gestures, which concluded with his dropping his suspenders off his shoulders, which must have been a punch line to some joke because some laughed aloud (to my surprise), while others nodded their heads, grinning broadly. Audrey wrote on her pad: *Neil loves randy jokes.*

I nodded, but when I looked up from her notebook, she had a genuine look of concern in her eyes. For years I had been living a lie. I'd altered my habits, my speech. I'd even once pretended to be a mute. All was deception. And here, this deaf-mute woman from Iowa was able to see right through it.

■　　■　　■

The bus crossed the General MacArthur Bridge, and when we reached Belle Isle the group was met by a guide, a tall, elderly woman who was also a deaf-mute. She had the bearing of a schoolmarm, and after a few curt signs, the group obediently followed her down the path into the park. When I lingered behind, Audrey took me by the arm, but I withdrew it.

"Thank you, Audrey, but you go on with the others." She looked doubtful, so I pointed at my wristwatch. "I must meet someone here. I hope you enjoy your visit to Detroit."

I began to back away. She appeared distressed, perhaps even heartbroken, but then reluctantly she started up the gravel path after her group. When she glanced over her shoulder, I smiled and waved. Still she didn't seem convinced.

I went in the other direction, toward the Scott Fountain. A warm breeze was coming off the river, and there was the pleasant smell of freshly cut grass. Couples lay on blankets, dozing, reading, some cuddling, while families occupied picnic tables, eating. I climbed a wide set of stairs and entered the open area that surrounded the large fountain, which was brilliant white in the late afternoon sun. Park benches encircled the fountain, and the sound of the water slapping and splashing had an odd effect: it was so loud that people seemed to be performing mime. Old men and women sat on the benches, gesturing, while young children ran about in defiance of their parents' warnings.

I walked around the fountain, but stopped when a man got up off a bench and came toward me. He had to be Vogel's son. Certain features—the set of his mouth and the unflinching stare—were reminiscent of the Kommandant I had known a dozen years earlier, but there were other aspects of this man that were different, utterly unknowable. With the Kommandant you knew where he was coming from, as Americans like to say. He possessed a consistency that made him transparent and therefore quite predictable. Nazis were nothing if not predictable. But I immediately realized there was something incomprehensible, something perplexing and unfathomable about his son. He was not just unpredictable, he was completely opaque. He might have been another species, one that I had never encountered before, and as I thought of the things he'd done to Mile Ionescu and Hans Krantz, I had no doubt that this man was capable of such horrors. Yet he didn't give me the impression that he was some insensitive, unfeeling being. Nor was he some twisted monster who took perverse satisfaction in administering pain and suffering. He was not a man who performed such acts without the slightest concern or doubt. On the contrary, his eyes carried it all. The knife wounds, the flayed skin, the blood—he bore it all and it had taken its toll.

"Captain Verdi?" His voice was uncertain, burdened with complexity. "My father will grant you a brief interview." Past him, I could see Kommandant Vogel sitting on a park bench, an old man in an overcoat and gray fedora, wearing sunglasses, his face turned toward the sound of the fountain. "You will make no attempt to touch him. Keep your hands in sight at all times."

I took in the rest of this young man—he was taller, more muscular than his father had ever been; to me, someone who had spent years trying to blend in, it seemed admirable yet bizarre that he was so effortlessly dressed like an American, a nondescript tan jacket and dark slacks. His haircut, too, was perfect in its innocuous precision. "What's your name?"

This took him by surprise, and briefly he seemed disarmed, so to speak. "Anton."

"I understand, Anton."

Almost reluctantly, he stepped out of the way, allowing me to approach his father. Kommandant Vogel's white cane lay folded up next to him on the park bench. At the sound of my footsteps, he patted the seat beside him. "Please, Captain Verdi."

I sat next to Vogel, keeping to the other end of the bench. Anton had taken up a position some ten yards away, standing by a trimmed hedge. Vogel continued to look straight ahead, seemingly admiring the fountain. He was sitting to my left, and I could easily pull my gun from the holster under my left arm and fire. I glanced at Anton, who was scanning the grounds. "I see a resemblance."

"He is my son, yes."

"He's what, thirty, give or take a year? You have trained him to do your butchering."

"He has learned obedience."

"When will this stop?"

"When we are told—we all have our orders."

"The war is over, Vogel. It was over years ago. For you and me it was really over while we were in Au Train."

His skin was waxy, pale, and when he shook his head slowly the cords in his neck seemed to vibrate with the effort. "Anton read to me from a brochure about this fountain. It's quite a technological marvel—you know I was trained as an engineer, so I can appreciate such things, even if I can't see them. Fountains are interesting, don't you think? They are a very public form of art. People flock to them because they represent something about a country, its culture, the dreams and ideals of its citizens. The Führer had a great belief in the power of architecture, how it would unify the German people. Since his death we must be even more vigilant in pursuing and protecting his dreams and ideals." Vogel turned his head slightly in my direction. His attempt at a smile was more a grimace. "Wars never really end, Captain Verdi. You should understand that, coming from Italy. Now that there are so many communists running your country, do you not think people are putting up resistance? Of course, here it is different. There is something about democracy that makes people weak, forgetful. This is such a hollow place—I'm sure you've observed this. There's very little sense of the past, just shallow children's stories about cherry trees and never telling lies. A people without a history—they always talk about the future, but the future will not be theirs. You must see that this won't last. They have no real strength, no discipline." He raised his face to the sunlight. "Instead they would rather enjoy themselves. They are more interested in sitting by a fountain, mindlessly basking in the sun."

"What you are doing," I said, "what you did to Mile Ionescu and Hans Krantz, this will not lead to some sort of victory. Orders or not, you are merely exacting revenge. This is all you have left."

"People who disobeyed orders must be brought to account."

"Tracking down people like Stemple and me, it will not bring the Reich back. Your Führer is dead, Vogel, and so are his ideas."

"We must carry on. Our work is not finished."

"So you take orders. Where are your commanders? South America?"

"We are gathering strength. This democracy is very useful, very pliable."

"They must be eating and drinking well in Brazil. They ran off with whatever money and valuables they could carry with them and they are in hiding, while you and your son are up here. You're still a prisoner, Vogel. You've never really gotten out of Au Train."

He tilted his head—a gesture of sympathy. "And you actually believed that you could escape? If that were so, you would not be here. Alone. We are both still in that prison camp, Captain Verdi, and the sentence that was passed twelve years ago is still valid today. Time does not diminish justice."

Anton was staring straight at me. His hands were in his jacket pockets, and I had no doubt that he was holding a gun. If I moved quickly, I could pull out my revolver and fire at Anton first. Vogel would be helpless. And this was what gave me pause—even if I managed to take down Anton, I would be left with a frail, unarmed blind man sitting on a park bench. Ideology didn't matter, nor did any responsibility for the pain and suffering of others. I realized that to shoot him would be as wrong—and ultimately as pointless—as what he had done to people like Hans Krantz. Even the knowledge that shooting him might prevent the execution of others didn't work. I couldn't do it.

I looked toward the fountain. In the setting sun, plumes of gold water arched above the wide pool. "I wish you could see this fountain," I said. "The colors right now, with the sun setting behind it. But for you there is only the darkness."

"Captain, do you ever hear from your friend in camp, the little fellow, the communist?"

"Adino Agostino."

"Yes, that's him."

"The one whose Achilles tendons you had cut." Vogel almost appeared amused—I was incapable of comprehending the true significance of such an act. "He has spent all these years with his family, handicapped. He is the one with real courage."

"I recall he was quite talented in the football matches. He had promise."

I could have shot him then. At that moment, I could have reached inside my jacket, pulled the Beretta out of its holster, pressed the muzzle against his ribcage, and pulled the trigger. But still, I didn't. "It's just occurred to me," I said, looking at Vogel. "I'm not here because of what you might do in the future. That I simply can't know. You're right—it is all about the past. That's all we have, the past. In this, you and I are the same." Vogel turned his head toward me slightly. "But your son," I said. "He must be very obedient, and it has been difficult for him." Anton could hear what we were saying, and something in his posture stiffened. Not threatening, but threatened. "His mother, Elena?" I asked Vogel. "You will have him kill his own mother? And his half sister? Will it come to that?"

I can't say with certainty what happened next. I've thought it over, tried to visualize the exact sequence of events, but I can never be sure. All I know is Anton moved, and I suspect he did so because I must have done something, given some indication of my intent at that moment. But I don't exactly recall reaching inside my sport coat.

All I know is the result: Anton drew a gun from the pocket of his jacket. I think I might have stood up, though I'm not sure. He held his arms outstretched toward me, and then I was staring at the sky. I was lying on my back—I remember that the ground was hard and uncomfortable. Pebbles pressed into my shoulder. I was having great difficulty breathing. There was chaotic movement around me, and through it all the jets of water rose high above the fountain and crashed down into the pool, creating a sound as loud and persistent as a waterfall. There were voices; there was screaming, it seemed, but it was difficult to tell with the noise of the fountain.

The sky above me was blue. Cloudless. A rich, early evening blue. I tried to concentrate on that blueness. It was getting harder to breathe, and there was this pressure on my left side. I could not tell exactly where, though it occurred to me that my heart might be damaged—certainly my lung, because there was fluid interfering with my breathing. I was gurgling every time I inhaled, and I could taste blood.

And then she was there. Audrey Vickers. Librarian. Bettendorf, Iowa.

She was leaning over me, her wide face blocking the blue sky. She was wearing glasses, and I couldn't remember if she'd been wearing them before, on the bus. Plain, wire-frame glasses, a type you rarely see women wear anymore. She looked confused, horrified, but also remarkably self-possessed. I was aware that there were others around me—other deaf-mutes—and by comparison, I could tell that they were in a panic. I wondered how they had come here to the fountain if they couldn't hear the gunshot. Or was it gunshots—again, I wasn't sure.

Audrey Vickers must have touched me, because when she raised a hand to push her glasses up her nose, her finger left a smear of blood on the corner of the right lens.

I remember trying to speak, but it was impossible.

My breathing was becoming more difficult.

I closed my eyes, for how long I don't know.

I opened them when Audrey Vickers touched my face with her hand. She had this inquisitive look on her face. There was now a policeman crouching beside her, his expression grim and hard, very hard. I turned my head slightly—it was a real effort—and saw a revolver—my revolver—in his hand. Beyond him I could see the park bench and the hedge. There was no sign of Vogel and his son Anton. When I looked back at Audrey Vickers I tried to speak, but couldn't. She leaned closer. I opened my mouth again. My lips must have been covered with blood. I could taste nothing but blood by then. She was looking at my mouth, and I realized she wanted to read my lips. Finally, I whispered, "*Dov 'è?*" She came even closer. "*Dov'è Chiara?*"

Audrey Vickers straightened up. She looked at the policeman and shook her head.

IV. 1991

23.

I died.

The doctors told me: I was dead on the table for several minutes, until they managed to get my heart beating again. It wasn't sleep with its landscape of dreams. It was nothing. Nonexistence. Nothing.

And then I was alive again. For days afterwards I lay in a hospital bed, in pain, heavily medicated, and I kept trying to understand the fact that I had died. But I couldn't understand it. I only knew that I was alive again. I wanted to thank God for that.

. . .

Now, years later, I still don't know exactly what happened at Scott Fountain on Belle Isle. What I do know is that I had survived, and that Vogel and his son Anton had disappeared. People who were there at the fountain gave different accounts to the police and the newspapers. A few said there seemed to have been an argument, which resulted in the shooting. But most said that they hadn't noticed anything unusual until shots were fired and a man was lying on the ground in a pool of blood. There followed panic and confusion, and no one took notice as a young man led a blind man away from the fountain.

What I do know is this: the bullet missed my heart by inches, and the damage to my lung has adversely affected my health ever since.

Those first weeks after the shooting, while I was in that hospital bed, I insisted that Claire remain in Sault Ste. Marie. Braun returned to Detroit, thinking at first that she would stay there, that it was possible to resume her life there. But none of us, it seemed, would be able to resume the life we'd led before the shooting.

As soon as I was able, I left the hospital. I was weak, my breathing difficult. My left arm was in a sling. My dressings had to be changed regularly. Braun accompanied me on the trip to Sault Ste. Marie, thinking that she would stay with us only until Claire and I were settled. But the weeks turned into months. Braun kept saying that she would soon return to Detroit, but there was always a reason to stay a little longer. I suffered infections and bouts of fever. Claire was having increasing difficulties with her pregnancy and was in no condition to care for me by herself. We were, all three of us, hiding out in the apartment above the Zampas' garage. We received no mail. We had no telephone. If we needed to make a call, we went over to the Zampas' kitchen.

Giannopoulos had no idea where Vogel and Anton were, and he took care of my gun. The unregistered Beretta on Belle Isle didn't exist.

∎   ∎   ∎

Most fall afternoons we'd take a walk through town—an unusual sight in Sault Ste. Marie, then in the mid-fifties. On the sidewalks and in the stores we couldn't miss the furtive glances and the overt stares.

"We're a freak show," Claire said one afternoon. "The pregnant woman, the wounded man, and . . . what are you?" she said to Braun.

"The tart," Braun said. "The Detroit tart."

They laughed, while I avoided doing so because it only caused searing pain in my chest.

We entered the park that bordered the locks. An ore boat, which had come up the St. Mary's River, slowly rose on the flooding waters. This was our daily entertainment, watching these massive ships, some a thousand feet long, rise and fall in the locks, before heading out into Lake Superior or downriver to the lower Great Lakes, transporting taconite to Chicago, Detroit, or Toledo. Beyond the locks, the harbor was a marvel of industry, boats and barges passing beneath a smudged sky. The ominous, perpetual racket of the blast furnaces at Algoma Steel thundered across the water from Sault Ste. Marie, Canada.

"You should go back before winter sets in," Claire said.

"To Detroit?" Braun said. "I don't think I can live there again. Everything's different up here. I'm different up here. In Detroit, I was spoiled and pampered. After my mother married Larry Collins we lived in Grosse Pointe Farms, and when I was fourteen I was packed off to a private school in Boston. It was the kind of place that was supposed to straighten out rich girls and help us find rich boys at nearby colleges and universities. With me, it didn't work. I got kicked out of school."

I wanted a cigarette, but my doctor had forbidden them. The lake was twenty-one feet higher than the river and we watched the ship rise as tons of water gushed up from beneath the lock gates. We never ceased to marvel at the pure force of water. "You're staying because you feel needed," I suggested.

"That's something I've never experienced before, being needed," Braun said. "But it's also that my whole life I've been trying to escape. I always thought things would be better somewhere else. Here, I don't need the clothes, the makeup, any of that. Strange, isn't it? Here, you don't care how things are somewhere else. Here, things just are."

Claire and I knew what she meant, and we didn't speak of it again. Most afternoons we walked to the locks to witness the activity on the harbor. An ore boat is not a beautiful or graceful ship; its design is purely functional, its purpose to convey iron ore, limestone, and coal. Yet watching these vessels pass through the Soo became an essential ritual, equally sacred and visceral, providing momentary respite from our own lives, which lacked definition or direction.

So Braun stayed, nursing us both through the U.P. winter. The wind off Lake Superior often drove the temperature down to twenty, thirty, forty degrees below, and the snow—hundreds of inches of snow, drifting so high that some people came and went from their houses by a door on the second floor. Most mornings Mr. Zampa's truck would rumble beneath us while it was still dark and we were huddled under our blankets. Sometimes, when I was feeling strong, I'd make the rounds with him as he plowed driveways and parking lots through the night, sharing a bottle of grappa. The winter was as beautiful as it was brutal. The cold pared our desires down to the need for food, clothing, and shelter. The days were hard, exhausting, and we became bound to our neighbors by a shared sense of survival.

■ ■ ■

The baby was due the third week of February.

Those last few weeks we were all in a virtual state of hibernation. Claire could barely get out of bed. At that point I was sleeping in the other bedroom and Braun was on the foldout sofa in the living room. Though the central heater rattled away and there was a wood-burning stove in the living room, we still could see our breaths most mornings. Long johns, two pairs of wool socks, baggy corduroy trousers, flannel shirts, sweaters, scarves, hats, gloves with the fingertips cut off—that was how we dressed indoors. And we combated the cold with food: meats, breads, potatoes, and Mrs. Zampa's pasta in a ragù sauce made with ground venison. Throughout the fall, gutted deer carcasses hung from trees about the neighborhood. By December, backyard rinks had been erected and flooded, and after school the cold air was filled with the sizzle of skate blades, the knock of hockey pucks. Frequently I walked to the grocery store, pulling the Flexible Flyer I used to transport food and supplies back to the apartment. I had cash. Cash for food, cash for the rent. I had cash because Leon had bought my business, and he'd arranged to have our belongings sold off from the apartment. I resisted calling Tony and Ginger, believing that it was safer if they didn't know our whereabouts. Our life in Detroit ceased to exist.

By then Claire was in great discomfort, often pain. Dr. Muse was making regular house calls. He provided some pills that made her drowsy, and for hours she'd be fast asleep beneath a heap of blankets. She couldn't keep anything down other than a little toast and broth. It was the middle of the night, during a blizzard, when her water broke. I remember the smell of her soaked bedsheets. She said, "Get me to the hospital before everything freezes." It had all been prearranged: Mr. Zampa drove us in the pickup, the plow pushing fresh snow aside. Mrs. Zampa called Dr. Muse, who arrived at the hospital before us. Braun and I spent hours in the waiting room, drinking coffee spiked with grappa, which Mr. Zampa kept in his truck. He was too nervous to stay, so he went out and did his rounds of plowing and returned at first light with Mrs. Zampa, who had her rosary beads wrapped around her wool mittens.

A little after seven a.m., Dr. Muse came out into the waiting room. Though he was in his hospital greens, he still wore his heavy rubber galoshes, the loose buckles jingling like coins in the pocket. He asked to talk to me alone, and we went out through the swinging doors to the corridor, where he talked about the complications. He was noncommittal about Claire's chances. "It's a girl," he said, almost as an afterthought. "Five pounds, seven ounces. Congratulations."

．　　．　　．

The next couple of days we kept a vigil at the hospital. I stayed in Claire's room day and night. She looked shriveled and her breathing was shallow, constricted with crackling phlegm. She could barely lift her head off the pillow, and I had to hold the glass of water in front of her face and direct the straw toward her mouth. Her eyes, large and glossy, were saying something to me, something I didn't want to acknowledge. But her gaze was so persistent that finally I nodded my head.

"The baby," she whispered. "We name her Mary, after the St. Mary's river. Or would you prefer Marie, after Sault Ste. Marie?"

"I like either."

"Mary, I said it first. And, listen, we have to think of Mary, right?"

I looked away, nodding my head again.

Mary lay on her back in the nursery. Her eyes were blue-gray, and they searched the ceiling above her relentlessly. Her bassinet had a plastic housing; an oxygen tube was fitted to her tiny nostrils, and she was attached to a series of wires and an IV. Mr. Zampa said she looked like they were going to launch her into outer space like one of those Russian dogs. Her lungs were underdeveloped and there was an irregular heartbeat. I worried that she wasn't feeling the touch of human hands, other than the brief visits to Claire's room and when a nurse's aide changed her diapers. She didn't cry—not when I watched her—though she made little grunting noises. Every moment was a struggle to exist.

．　　．　　．

Claire died in the afternoon. She fought for each breath for a minute or so. Though I had pressed the buzzer pinned to her bedsheets, a nurse didn't come to the room. And then Claire was still. Hospital staff arrived and asked me to wait out in the hall. I sat on a bench across from her door until the doctor came out and told me what I already knew.

Braun had gone back to the apartment to get me a change of clothes, and when she came down the hall and saw me, she must have known immediately. She sat down beside me and we didn't move, didn't speak. Finally, we helped each other stand up and walked out of the hospital.

·   ·   ·

In so many ways, Mary was a blessing. The immediate job of organizing Claire's funeral was complicated by the fact that the baby was still in the hospital, which meant that Braun and I continually returned to watch her through the glass. The doctors suggested an operation to deal with some constriction in her lungs, but several days after Claire was buried, Mary made remarkable progress. Nine days after she was born, we brought her back to the apartment.

There was a period of sorrow, confusion, and dismay where I don't think either of us was seeing things too clearly. We were too busy, too exhausted, too buried inside ourselves. The days and nights were devoted to diaper changes and feedings. The apartment became a cocoon that smelled of baby powder and milk formula. We more or less worked in shifts, twenty-four hours a day. There were, however, moments of unexpected solace: dancing with Mary in my arms while on the radio Vic Damone sang "On the Street Where You Live." By late April, winter showed signs of loosening its grip.

It was Mr. Zampa who managed to help me break through all this. Afternoons, when Mary was napping, I'd often go downstairs to his workshop. He believed anything could be fixed—furniture, windows, any appliance—and I liked to give him a hand. He would keep a bottle of grappa on the shelf.

One day we were gluing the joints of a footstool and he said, "You looked in a mirror lately?" Before I could respond he said, "The pants, they're like flags snapping in the breeze, you've lost so much weight. The girl, too. It's not healthy, but I realize some men like it when a woman gets that way." He had thick, calloused fingers, but there was a delicacy to them when he handled wood. After applying a daub of glue to a leg of the footstool, he inserted the end into a slot in the frame, and then I held the clamp in place as he tightened it. "*Dio mio*, she loves that child like she was her own. She could have returned to Detroit. I heard her arguing on the phone with her mother, but she doesn't want to go."

I didn't say anything.

"What are you afraid of?"

"What do you mean?"

"Your lovely dead wife isn't going to come back and haunt you." He glanced up at me through his thick glasses. "Know what Braun told Louisa? She said Claire told her it was all right before she died. She knew, Claire did."

"I don't know, Carmen. What am I afraid of?"

"You're not going to insult Claire's memory by living your life."

I took a swallow of grappa. "You know how old Braun is?"

Carmen smiled. "I should be so lucky. It's getting warm—I saw her wearing a dress the other day. She has better legs than Cyd Charisse. You didn't notice?" He took the stool, which was now held together by four clamps—looking like some crazy science experiment—and set it on the floor next to the worktable. Then he splashed a little more grappa in our coffee mugs. "*Senti*. When you make a sacrifice you learn who you are. It's the best thing that can ever happen to you. You live for others, you live for God, and you find yourself. She already loves Mary, and the baby adores her. It will take time, but you must be patient. You have much to hope for." When he looked up at me again, his eyes were moist. "You're what, thirty-six, thirty-seven? My father, he waited till his mother was dead before he married my mother; nineteen years younger than him she was, and they were happily married for over forty years. Seven children, all of them strong."

I stared into my coffee mug of grappa.

"She put on a dress. Now take her someplace nice for dinner. We can watch the baby for an evening."

24.

did take her to dinner and we did marry the following year. In 1959 we had a son, Adino, whom we usually called Tony. By that time we had moved four hours west to Marquette, the largest town in the Upper Peninsula. I opened a shop that sold household furnishings and carpet. We bought a house on the East Side, the peninsula that juts into Lake Superior. We tried to have another child, but Braun miscarried. Mary had become strong and healthy, and Tony was an absolutely fearless boy.

Over the years I kept in touch with James Giannopoulos. Each spring I attended a sales convention in Detroit and would see him then, often having a meal at Tony's Grill. The food wasn't the same after Paolo went in on a restaurant with his cousin in Ann Arbor, but I never let on. Tony and Ginger eventually sold the bar and moved to Hawaii, where they opened a place called Mr. T's Bistro. Giannopoulos made sure my past remained buried—Vogel was, evidently, still alive and at large.

The children consumed our lives. Mary studied the piano and Tony played hockey. For years, compositions such as Mendelssohn's "Fingal's Cave" resounded from the baby grand in the living room, and we spent countless hours watching hockey games. From the time the children were small, there were photographs of

Claire throughout the house. Mary's eyes were dark, her hair fine and black, like her mother's, while Tony had Braun's fairness. As the children grew to understand that they had different mothers, they developed an unusual bond—siblings, but friends, too. By the time they were in high school, my health began to deteriorate. It started with my lungs, which had never been good since the shooting. But I began to have circulatory problems, and one summer I spent months on my back with a severe case of sciatica in my right leg. The children thought I was becoming forgetful, but Braun knew that wasn't really the case; I was becoming more distracted and, it seemed, a bit hard of hearing.

.   .   .

One morning in the spring of 1973, I noticed an article in the *Detroit Free Press* about a suspected war criminal being apprehended in Harrisburg, Pennsylvania. Horst Albrecht had worked for years as a clerk in the state capitol until he was arrested by the INS. Albrecht claimed to have emigrated from Austria at the conclusion of the Second World War, but the government believed he was actually Heinrich Vogel, who was wanted for the murder of Father Lou Brosnic and Hans Krantz. There was a photograph in the paper—an old one, of Vogel in military uniform, looking severe and erect—and it was accompanied by a photograph of an elderly man wearing sunglasses and walking with a white cane. I had no doubt that they had captured Vogel.

The Albrecht/Vogel story came and went in the press over the course of several months. I cut the articles out of the newspapers and magazines and kept them in a scrapbook. Vogel's blindness, not to mention his frailness, brought out an element of sympathy in some articles, and it was noted how he had been instrumental in making Braille an operational language in Pennsylvania state government. The German, Romanian, and Israeli governments all wanted him extradited to stand trial. I wondered why there was no mention of his son Anton.

Mary received a scholarship to study music at Michigan State. Tony could barely think beyond hockey, and at sixteen he got an offer to play for one of the junior teams in Canada. Braun was against this at first—it would mean that he would live with a family in Ontario, attend school there, and travel throughout the province—but I suggested that we let him go. A shot at the NHL was his dream and you can't tell a kid not to dream. He'd probably be back after a couple of seasons. To not let him try would create a deep resentment.

So Tony moved down to Brantford, Ontario, leaving just the two of us living in the house on Marquette's East Side. It was too quiet. No piano, no hockey pucks rattling off the garage door for hours on end. But after a few months I realized that, as much as I missed Mary and Tony, I accepted that they wouldn't be there to witness their father's decline. My breathing became increasingly difficult. My circulation was so poor that I was constantly cold, wrapped in blankets in my recliner in the den. I had pretty much turned the daily operation of the store over to my business partner, a man named Lloyd Wiegand, who colored his hair and wore too many rings on his fingers. I was constantly looking for something in the news about the Vogel case. For years I filled scrapbooks, which lined a shelf in my study—one of those cases that went on forever, and got nowhere.

■   ■   ■

If our lives were a trolley hurtling through the city night, through time itself, it now seemed to be traveling at what my kids called warp speed. So: April 1985, Giannopoulos called from Punta Gorda, Florida. He wanted to visit us in Marquette, and he arrived several days later dressed in the light clothing meant for a Florida climate. Since retiring he'd taken up golf. He was tanned and relaxed, and barely resembled the man in the dark suit and crisp white shirt and tie that I had known in Detroit. Braun made a pot of coffee and we sat in the living room.

"I thought I'd never leave Detroit," he said, glancing out the window at the snow in the backyard. "But you'd be surprised how easy it is to not miss winter." His eyes floated toward me. "Ever think of moving south?"

"Where's Vogel now?" I asked.

"He's free. But we are building a solid case against him."

"We?" I said. "I thought you were retired."

"I am, but I was asked to come up and talk to you. These things take years."

"Some of us might all be dead before it's over."

"That's a distinct possibility," Giannopoulos said. "Vogel's health hasn't been good." It seemed to me that he almost said "too," meaning that Vogel's health was no better than mine, but prudently he stared down at the oriental rug beneath his shoes. "Nice," he said. "You're beyond lampshades now." It was the closest thing to a joke I'd ever heard from him. He got up and went to the baby grand piano and studied the photographs of Claire, Mary, and Tony, their wedding pictures, their children. "Three grandchildren?"

"And one on the way," Braun said.

"You've a beautiful family. You're a fortunate man, Frank."

I heard from Giannopoulos periodically while Vogel fought extradition in the courts. Finally, in 1987, the United States government requested that I testify at a hearing in Washington, D.C. The following spring, after more appeals and legal maneuvering, Vogel was extradited to Germany, and I was asked to testify at his trial in Berlin. When I said my assumed American identity could cause me problems, Giannopoulos said that when I testified in court, I would be Francesco Giuseppe Verdi, former officer in the Italian army and prisoner of war. He guaranteed there would be no difficulties later for Frank Green. When I still balked, Giannopoulos said he'd accompany me to Germany.

"You don't need to do this," Braun said, as we walked our dog Gordie along the beach in McCarty's Cove, which was downhill from our house. This had become my primary form of exercise, walking Gordie.

"My health isn't going to improve, whether I go or not."

"What happened, happened decades ago. It haunts you. It haunts me, too. I just don't want it to kill us."

"I wonder about Anton, where he's been all these years. He must still be in communication with his father." She didn't say anything, and I knew I was closing in on something she'd always avoided discussing. "He is your half brother."

"My half brother I've never met. Never. I was too small, and there was the war. My mother rarely mentioned him. He was her child, but when they split up Vogel took him away from her. He was raised by some relatives who bred him for the Nazi movement. My mother considered him dead—though nothing could be more painful to a mother, of course."

"That day on Belle Isle," I said. "Anton wasn't what I expected. I thought he'd be a younger version of Vogel. He looked like his father, but there was something else there, more complexity. Doubt, perhaps. But he'd done these things. He'd done as he was told. It tormented him. I wonder if it still does."

"Sympathy for the executioner. Maybe you are getting old, Frank."

"I was thinking that people change."

"Do they?" She watched Gordie as he waded into the lake. It was a fall evening and the pastel clouds on the horizon were reflected on the water. We were holding hands—we often did when we walked, though it was in part because my balance wasn't very good anymore, particularly on the beach. "Have you changed, Francesco?"

"You tell me."

"Hiding inside this middle-aged woman there's still the Detroit girl," she said. "You know, that brat with too much makeup who was angry at everyone, everything. No matter how much or how often you change your identity, you'll always be that Italian officer."

"There are only a few people who know who I really am. But you know all my secrets."

She squeezed my hand. "And even though I've never met him, I know that Anton, whatever he is, whatever he becomes, will always be his father's instrument. My mother knew this. You ask how can a man use his son in this way, but the war taught her that anything is possible. Her own son killed my father. She suffered unspeakable grief." She looked at me then, this younger woman who had helped me build my life yet again. "You've lived with this so long, Frank—don't let it be the thing that kills you."

"I am an old man—and I can live with that. I died once already, so I know something about the alternative. But if I don't do this, if I don't go to Berlin and try to see this through, I don't know if I can live with *that*."

We stopped walking. Braun didn't say anything more—she didn't have to—but she did turn and put her arms about my neck and press her forehead against my cheek. "Giannopoulos said he would go to Berlin with me," I said. "He's protected us all these years, and I owe it to him to help finish this thing." When she tightened her arms around my neck, I said, "He's right. I am a fortunate man."

25.

Giannopoulos and I flew to Berlin in November. There was freezing rain and sleet, the worst imaginable weather. We had a full day to rest from the trip. The television in my hotel room had channels in perhaps a dozen different languages, several in Arabic. In the evening I found a football match between Juventus and Fiorentina, broadcast in Italian, but there were so many fires and smoke bombs ignited in the stands that the two teams roaming the pitch were no more distinct than warriors doing battle in some impregnable fog that seemed a remnant of the Dark Ages. It might have been the cold, damp weather, and the long flights, but my legs were sore and I was having difficulty breathing.

Thursday morning we took a cab to a courthouse. The building, like so many in Berlin, was impressively modern, the sign of a people determined to rebuild their country. Inside, we were greeted by several American lawyers and officials from the U.S. Embassy, and then we were taken to a small, windowless room to wait until we were called into the court.

A young woman from the embassy, who was a translator, sat with us. Her name was Ms. Campagna, but she asked me in Italian to call her Valeria. She was in her early thirties, about Mary's age, and she had deep brown eyes that looked right into mine when she spoke. I guessed that she came from Alto Adige—some of her phrasing almost sounded German—and she nodded, her auburn hair moving about her head. "I'm from Sarantino, a village between Bolzano and the Austrian border." Then all the joy in her face disappeared. "There may be some surprises, Francesco."

"At my age, it seems I have run out of surprises. What could be left?"

This brought a shy, reluctant smile from her. Here I was, an old wheezing geezer in cold, raw Berlin, and I was flirting with this pretty *Italiana*. It was the language. I was a different man, speaking my native tongue. Giannopoulos watched us from across the table; he'd never seen me speak Italian before, and he was seeing me for the first time.

"They will ask you questions," she said. "Keep your answers short. Everything in court must be translated, so there will be a delay which some find unnatural, disconcerting. Please just stick to the question. Don't elaborate, unless you are asked to do so."

"I understand."

"He has very good lawyers."

"Ex-Nazis."

"Worse," she said.

I didn't fathom her meaning, but then I said, "Their children?"

"Yes," she said.

"So," I said, somewhat pleased, "there may be surprises." On the table were bottles of water; I opened one and drank most of it without stopping. "Tell me," I said in English. "Will he be there in the courtroom?"

"Yes. And you—"

Giannopoulos did something across the table that caused her to pause. We looked at him, but he was only rubbing his forehead.

"What?" I asked him.

They stared at me, both reluctant to speak first, and then, to their relief, there was a knock on the door.

"It's time," Giannopoulos said.

■　　■　　■

The courtroom was cavernous: enormous slabs of concrete vaulting high overhead, making a person feel infinitesimal, clearly intended to represent our relationship to justice. I had expected more people to be present. Vogel's case had received international attention, but there were only the judges, three of them, in red gowns and caps; legal staff seated at two long tables facing the bench; and in the back a packed gallery, most of whom Valerie told me were journalists. There was heavy security—standing around the perimeter of the courtroom, almost seeming to blend into the concrete walls, were statuesque men and women in uniform, their expressions neutral, their eyes always staring dead ahead. They were armed.

Vogel was folded into a wheelchair next to his counselors. This didn't surprise me. He wore wrap-around sunglasses. His head was lifted slightly on his gaunt neck so that he appeared to be concentrating on a point on the wall above the judges' bench—his posture suggesting that he, and only he, could see a higher mode of justice. Once, just as the judges began to settle in their chairs, he turned his head in my direction, and it seemed he was looking right at me.

Everyone wore cordless headphones, for the translation of the proceedings. Valeria was right: it was cumbersome, disconcerting, and exotically unnatural. Lawyers spoke softly into microphones as though they did not wish to give offense and for long periods entire documents were read aloud. There was the odd sense that no one appeared to be paying attention—everyone seemed to be sorting through paperwork or conferring with a colleague—and yet this muted activity created not a hush, but a hum that seemed to confirm the serious business at hand, and I came to feel that such behavior was inappropriate, even disrespectful, much like whispering during Mass. Thankfully, Valeria, who was seated to my left, never attempted to speak to me, though occasionally she wrote a note in Italian on the yellow legal pad on the table before us. At one point I took her pen and wrote: *You have lovely penmanship—and lovelier hands.* To which she wrote back: *Don't worry. It will be fine.*

Vogel's lawyers were a man and a woman, both in their fifties. When the woman first got up to address the court, Valeria wrote: *Her father was SS.*

At one point one of the lawyers at our table, whose name was Pomeroy, leaned toward me and in a Southern drawl asked if I was ready, and when I nodded he patted my hand, though he didn't seem convinced. I didn't understand why an American attorney had been selected for this trial in Germany, but then Pomeroy stood up, and when he addressed the three judges on the bench he spoke what to my ear was flawless German. The proceedings started out slowly as all parties discussed what I can only call technicalities. But then the translations became of interest as Pomeroy itemized charges against Vogel. An obese man,

Pomeroy had that light sort of weight about his middle that is caused by certain diseases, so that his well-tailored black suit appeared to float about his broad hips as he moved back and forth in front of the judges' bench. He described Vogel's activities in Romania during the early stages of the war, which had been dealt with during previous days of the trial. His summary brought to mind the day I had walked the beach in Grosse Pointe Farms with Braun's mother, Elena. After Elena had died of cancer of the esophagus about a decade earlier, Braun said that the last thing she whispered was "Finally." Pomeroy mentioned numerous dates and places in Romania where Vogel was alleged to have overseen torture and mass murders. Occasionally, Vogel's defense, always the woman whose name was Ingrid Bok, interjected a comment, though she rarely objected—this was old business, and at one point, sounding disdainfully bored, she said to the judges, "Herr Pomeroy should consult his calendar. Romania was yesterday. Today we are concerned with the State of Michigan, where my client is guilty of ruthlessly slaughtering trees with an axe."

Pomeroy's laugh was self-deprecating and brief, and when he turned his attention to Camp Au Train everything seemed to slow down for me. He mentioned places and the names of prisoners that I knew, and after I finished the bottle of water on the table in front of me, Valeria gave me her bottle. I was afraid of what was coming, and when it did—when my name, Francesco Verdi, was called—I could barely breathe.

"Are you all right?" Valeria whispered in Italian, her hand on my sleeve.

I wasn't sure I could stand up, let alone speak.

Pomeroy came to the table and leaned down, looking concerned. "What is it?"

"His breathing," Valeria said to him. "He's short of breath."

"I'm all right," I managed, and slowly I rose from my seat and walked to the witness stand. I was sworn in, in German, but I could hear the translation in Italian in my headphones.

Pomeroy began by asking me a series of questions regarding my past, where I was born, where I was raised, what my family had done before the war. Then he moved on to my service in the Italian army, and soon we were up to the point where I had been captured in Africa and shipped to the prisoner-of-war camp in Michigan's Upper Peninsula, where I worked as a woodcutter. The fact that I had changed my name seemed of little consequence; just as Vogel had changed his name to Horst Albrecht, changing my name from Francesco Verdi to Frank

Green was treated as a curiosity of life in the New World. Pomeroy's questions were straightforward, many of them requiring merely a yes. But I could barely project my voice. To answer I had to lean forward and speak into the small, thin microphone that protruded from the railing in front of me.

With ease, Pomeroy shifted the questions to Vogel's leadership in the camp. And it was here that Vogel's attorney, Ingrid Bok, objected repeatedly. At times she was overruled; other times her objection was sustained, in which case Pomeroy would simply rephrase the question. But I realized that she was somehow forcing him to shift his strategy. I wanted to tell him he was asking me the wrong questions. He kept skirting things, unable or unwilling to ask me to describe how Vogel had treated the men in Camp Au Train.

Several times I glanced at Valeria; her face was utterly neutral, but I had the sense that she felt things weren't going as planned, either. In the gallery, Giannopoulos sat with his arms folded, looking determinedly noncommittal. He reminded me of certain parents at their kids' hockey games—the kind who don't stand up and shout and cheer, but sit quietly and observe the game, seeing every nuance of the play, and somehow knowing that to get excited would be pointless because it wouldn't influence their child's performance or the outcome of the game. Pomeroy, for his part, seemed content to display his oratory powers and occasionally run his fingers through his silver hair, which was quite full at the sides and in back. And Vogel—when I looked at him, sitting in his wheelchair, his hands folded on the blanket covering his lap—he pointed his face and sunglasses directly at me and didn't move a muscle.

Finally, Pomeroy asked me to describe what kind of leader Vogel had been at Camp Au Train. It was a question that required more than a yes or a no. I explained how Vogel ruled the camp according to the strictest Nazi principles, and that men who did not conform were judged, sentenced, and punished. I said that Vogel and his men threatened other prisoners, and in some cases they threatened to send word back to Germany that their families should be harassed. I said that this resulted in one prisoner committing suicide, another had ingested crushed glass that had been put in his food—something that could not be done without Vogel's express approval—and as I was about to mention Adino, Ingrid Bok stood up and objected. She spoke rapidly in German for several minutes. Previously, her objections had been calm, measured responses, but now she was on the verge of outrage. From the Italian translation I learned that she was telling the court that all these allegations were uncorroborated evidence at worst, or at best, the imaginings of an old man whose memory had been clouded by the passage of time. There followed a period where all of the attorneys were ordered to approach the bench, and for a considerable period of time they whispered with the judges. When the huddle broke up, the lawyers returned to their respective tables and put their headphones on again; no one looked satisfied.

When Pomeroy said reluctantly, "No further questions," I hoped my testimony was finished and was gathering the strength to get out of my chair, but then Fraulein Bok rose to her feet and approached the witness stand. Clearly, she had been a handsome young woman, perhaps even beautiful, but middle age had made her hard. I thought of the word calcification, which my doctors had told me was what was happening to my lungs. What had once been feminine in Ingrid Bok seemed to have turned to stone. She seemed intentionally monolithic. Her calves were massive and she wore a gray tweed suit, very subdued, very professional, which was cut in a fashion that seemed designed to conceal the fact that she had hips and breasts. The shoulders of her jacket were padded, and her hair, which I gather had once been blond, was white—pulled back in a bun so tight that it made her face seem taut, the nose, forehead, and cheekbones prominent. Her large blue eyes floated in their own solution, causing me to wonder if she had some medical condition that made them secrete constantly. Yet as she neared the witness stand, I realized that her stare was fierce, demanding, and utterly devoid of forgiveness. Her eyes confirmed my deepest fear: I was the one on trial here.

"Mr. Verdi," she began, "you were an officer in the Italian army during World War II, and you were sent to the prisoner-of-war camp in Au Train, Michigan."

This had already been established, so I hesitated, wondering if there was something I was missing, some trick to the way she had asked the question. But finally I said, "Yes."

"How long were you there?"

"I arrived soon after the camp was opened in May 1944, and—"

"You were released from the camp at the end of the war?"

I glanced at Pomeroy and Valeria, who stared back at me. "No," I said.

"Please clarify, Mr. Verdi. If you weren't released—certainly you aren't still there."

"I escaped."

"You escaped? When?"

"Late December, just before New Year's."

"And how did you manage to escape?"

"We were cutting down trees and I disappeared into the woods."

"This seems an indictment of the security measures instituted by the Americans."

"Perhaps. But the woods there are vast; the distances, they are greater than here in Europe. Others who attempted to escape sometimes returned voluntarily when they realized they could not survive in such an environment. Others simply didn't know how to get out of the woods and were easily captured."

"So you were successful in your escape. You got out of the camp and you got out of the woods. Alone?" Before I could answer, she returned to her table, picked up a piece of paper, and faced me again. "Didn't you escape with a Russian prisoner named Dimitri Sabaneyev?"

"Yes."

"Together."

"Briefly. Once we got away from the work detail, we went our separate ways."

"But, Mr. Verdi, how exactly did you get away from the work detail undetected?"

"I told you we ran away. It wasn't difficult in such dense woods."

Confused, she looked down at the sheet of paper in her hand. "You and Sabaneyev planned your escape?"

"Yes, of course."

"Why 'of course'?"

"Because otherwise we would be killed."

"Killed?" She walked slowly toward the witness stand. "And how did you know this?"

"Kommandant Vogel had ordered that I be placed on trial for treason and I was found guilty. The punishment for treason is death."

"Treason? In a prisoner-of-war camp."

"Yes."

"You were charged for what?"

"For saving a child, carrying an American baby out of a burning house. In Vogel's opinion that baby might grow up, become a soldier, and fight against the Third Reich." There was murmuring from the gallery, which halted as soon as one of the judges raised his hand. "And also I believe my handling of the camp's football squad was a treasonable offense."

Fraulein Bok seemed reluctant to ask, but unable to resist. "How so?"

"Along with being a midfielder, I acted as the team's coach and I selected the players with the most skill, so I didn't play many Germans."

There were a few snickers. The judge cleared his throat and told the gallery that anyone who made any more such disturbances would be removed from the courtroom.

When the room was silent, Fraulein Bok stood at the railing across from me and asked, "You attended this 'trial'?"

"No."

"So how do you know about these charges?"

"All the prisoners understood the situation. Vogel's thoughts on such matters were clear. The New Year was approaching and he wanted to make an impression on the entire camp. I would be an example."

"But you didn't wish to defend yourself?"

"I knew the outcome, and Sabaneyev and I escaped the next morning."

"So, you knew the outcome though you didn't attend this trial." Before I could respond, she asked, "Did you ever see or have contact with Sabaneyev again?"

"No."

"Do you know what happened to him?"

"I heard he was captured and sent back to the camp, where he was beaten to death."

"By whom?"

"Nazi POWs, upon Vogel's order."

"Did you witness this beating?"

"No."

"You know the verdict in a trial you didn't attend, and you know the fate of Dimitri Sabaneyev." She paused a moment, biting her lower lip in thought. "Thus far, Mr. Verdi, nothing you've told us is based on fact."

"I know what happened in Camp Au Train. I know how Vogel ran it."

"It may interest you to know that Dimitri Sabaneyev died a little more than two years ago." Carefully, she folded the sheet of paper in half, sharpening the crease by running it between her forefinger and her long thumbnail. "He died in Holland, where he had been living for years after the end of the war."

"I didn't know that."

"Apparently. Before he died, he talked about his experience at Camp Au Train—the interview was recorded and we wish to enter the transcript as evidence for the defense."

There followed several minutes where court officials proceeded to formally accept this evidence to the court. I sat, staring mostly at Valeria, who looked back at me trying to project a calm disposition, which might pass through the air and enter my body like some phantom spirit. I had reached the age where, when I sat perfectly still, I could feel and hear my heart beating. I did this several times a day, as a means of proving to myself that I was still alive. Sitting in the witness stand, I was so still, so calm that I could feel my heartbeat, and I was relieved that it wasn't racing, as I assumed it had been when I first took the stand. But all of this was making me weary. I closed my eyes, and for several minutes the sounds of the courtroom seemed to come to me from a great distance.

Then I heard Fraulein Bok's voice up close, and my eyes opened. She was standing before me, her hands gripping the railing between us. Her voice made me feel like I was a child, a boy who was lying in bed and was going to be late for school.

"Yes?" I said, looking from her to the judges.

"Are you all right, Mr. Verdi?" the judge seated in the middle asked. All three men on the bench were at least as old as I was, and the one in the middle looked almost sympathetic. "Do you wish to continue?"

"No." There was some murmuring in the gallery; then I said, "But I'm here, so go on."

I waited for the translation, and then the judge nodded his head. I suspected from his expression that he felt the same way.

When I turned back to Fraulein Bok, her expression made it clear that she believed she was staring at the most worthless specimen of a human being she had ever seen. "Do you remember a prisoner named Otto Werner?"

"Yes," I said.

"The day you and Sabaneyev escaped, Werner was working with you in the forest?"

"Yes," I said. "Werner informed me of the verdict at Vogel's trial the night before."

"Is that a fact?"

"Yes," I said.

"Did he escape with you?"

"Werner?" I looked toward Pomeroy, who was gazing down at papers on the desk. "No, he didn't escape with us."

"Why is that, Mr. Verdi?"

"We didn't invite him." There was just one snicker from the gallery, followed by a taut, overbearing silence—a silence in which I felt I could feel and hear the heartbeat of everyone in that courtroom.

"When was the last time you saw Otto Werner?"

"In the woods."

"In the woods," she said. "Did he bid you farewell?"

"Not that I recall."

"Did he say anything about your escaping?"

"Not that I recall."

"Might that be because he was dead?"

"I don't know," I said, "was he?"

"He was brutally beaten with a stick, his skull crushed."

I merely stared back at her.

"You killed him," she said.

"No, I didn't." I inhaled as much air as I could manage. "And I don't know that he died in the woods."

"Mr. Verdi, before Dimitri Sabaneyev died he said that you struck Werner on the head with a heavy stick, and when you ran into the woods, he realized that he had no choice but to run, too."

"That's not how it happened."

"It's all in the tapes. It's what Sabaneyev said shortly before he died."

"But that's not how it happened."

"If you didn't kill Werner, who did?"

I merely stared at her.

"Answer the question," one of the judges said.

"You want me to accuse a dead man?" I asked, still looking at Ingrid Bok.

"Who killed Otto Werner?" she asked, raising her voice just slightly.

"Dimitri struck him with a stick. Once. It was enough for us to get away into the woods without Werner alerting the guards. I don't know for a fact that he was dead."

"Mr. Verdi," Fraulein Bok began in exasperation, but Pomeroy stood up and spoke at length, raising an objection. Though he was fluent in German, he was speaking in English. I didn't know why—perhaps because it might have some effect on the judges' decision. Though I come from a country full of different accents and dialects, because I have always lived in Michigan since arriving in the United States, I find most Southern accents to be overly dramatic and false, to the point where I have on occasion suspected that at night people from places like Arkansas and Georgia go home and in private remove their Southern accents as they would a change of clothes and speak English like my friends and neighbors in the northern Midwest. Pomeroy seemed to speak with a determination to prove me wrong, that his Southern accent was as genuine as the day he was born. (This was a phrase he used, one of many such colloquialisms I understood without knowing its origin. He said to the judges that despite my poor health I had traveled all the way to Germany to provide testimony that was as forthright and honest as the day I was born.) He was very convincing. The essence of his argument was that I wasn't on trial, Vogel was, and with the exception of a tape of a purported dead man's voice, there was no evidence regarding how Otto Werner died, other than when he was returned to the camp there was a record of the fact that a doctor had determined that he was dead. There was no record as to whether the contusion on the back of his head was the result of a blow from a stick, a stone, or perhaps the result of a fall; and there certainly was no evidence, Pomeroy concluded with an impressive flourish, as to whether Werner's death was intentional, accidental, or even self-inflicted.

Pomeroy's remarks were followed by another gathering of lawyers before the bench, and again I found that by closing my eyes I could push the whole thing away, making their voices faint and distant. I was very tired.

This time the judges decided to call a recess, for which I was most thankful, although I assumed that meant that I would have to sit on the witness stand yet another day. They said that we would reconvene the next morning at ten o'clock, and we all stood—except for Vogel—as the three judges in their red robes and hats filed down from the bench and left the courtroom.

I walked back to the table where Pomeroy and Valeria were gathering up papers. There was much murmuring and shuffling of feet as the people in the gallery left the courtroom. Valeria handed me a bottle of water, giving me a faint smile. "*Bravo*," she whispered.

At the other table, Vogel was being wheeled toward the aisle that separated our two tables, but he raised his hand and the woman pushing his chair stopped. He angled his head up until it seemed that his eyes, concealed behind his sunglasses, were directed toward me. I didn't move; no one moved. Vogel didn't speak. He sat this way for what seemed a very long time, though it was probably no more than half a minute; then he lowered his hand, his wheelchair was turned, and he was pushed down the aisle and out of the courtroom.

■   ■   ■

We made our way to the lobby, where Pomeroy paused to speak with a group of journalists. Valeria suggested that I get some rest, so she and Giannopoulos accompanied me in a taxi back to the hotel. Before they left me in my room, she went to the desk and wrote on a notepad, *We can't really talk here. Room may be bugged.*

Alone, I lay on my back in the bed, staring at the walls, the light fixture in the ceiling, the framed paintings on the wall, the telephone, wondering if they concealed electronic listening devices, or perhaps even cameras, but soon my curiosity was dissolved by fatigue and the realization that an old man lying silent and still in a hotel bed doesn't provide much for eavesdroppers or voyeurs. I slept fitfully for a couple of hours, perhaps because I didn't feel alone.

That evening Valeria and Giannopoulos took me to a restaurant that was known for its Wiener schnitzel à la Holstein. They had reserved a booth that had a curtain, which could be drawn to allow privacy. After the waiter took our order, I picked up the salt shaker and inspected it closely, and then did the same with my fork. "I don't think they're bugged," I said, looking across the table at Giannopoulos. "Where's Pomeroy?"

Valeria, who was seated beside me, said, "He said he might be late."

"He was right about one thing." I kept my eyes on Giannopoulos. "My health is not great and I have traveled a long way. I've done this against my wife's better judgment. For what?" I waited, but Giannopoulos only stared back at me. "I came over here to let the daughter of an SS officer put *me* on trial. I thought they beat Sabaneyev to death. If anyone was going to survive, it would be that Russian. But I didn't touch Otto Werner." When Valeria tried to speak, I raised my hand and continued, without looking away from Giannopoulos. "Fraulein Bok has more balls than Pomeroy—how did your people come up with him?" When Giannopoulos still didn't respond, I said, "She's not just neutralized every fucking thing I've said, she's made me guilty." I slapped the table. "*I'm* not the war criminal here."

Giannopoulos leaned toward me, about to speak, but the curtain was suddenly opened and the waiter delivered our dinners, three plates of Wiener schnitzel à la Holstein, with späetzle and Brussels sprouts. After the waiter left, drawing the curtain closed, Giannopoulos tried to speak again, but I said, "*Basta.*

We eat. No talk. Too dangerous." I cut into my breaded veal, and though it was excellent, I was so angry I could barely taste it.

We ate our dinner in silence; Pomeroy arrived while we were having our coffee.

Once he was seated, I said, "The Wiener schnitzel à la Holstein is excellent, but the egg is bugged."

Pomeroy only nodded. I was the oldest person at the table and I was being treated like a recalcitrant child. He ordered a glass of wine, and after the waiter left, I said, "This is a German trial. Why an American lawyer?"

He seemed to expect this question. "I'm a German citizen, born here while my father was stationed here. My mother was German and I have dual citizenship. Like you, Frank, I've always felt divided between two countries."

"Now you know how I feel?"

"I understand why you're upset," he said.

"Understand? Spoken like a true lawyer. What I don't understand, Herr Pomeroy, is how you didn't know Sabaneyev was still alive."

"He changed his name," Pomeroy offered.

"Since when has that been an effective means of hiding? You found me. You found Vogel, eventually."

"It's unfortunate," Pomeroy said. "Frank, we've reconsidered our strategy."

"You have one?"

"You don't have to testify," he said.

"Fine, then get me on a plane home tomorrow."

Pomeroy was different than he had been in the courtroom. Now he was dismissive, acting like he had someplace else to go. "There's been a postponement. The trial will resume Monday."

"I came all the way over here for this? Why didn't you ask about my being shot? They nearly killed me on Belle Isle in Detroit. There's plenty of evidence — witnesses, a police report, hospital records."

"There's nothing that places Vogel at the scene. Besides, you said his son shot you."

"Don't you get it?" I said. "That's the way Vogel works. He never does the deed. Ask Giannopoulos about the fake priest named Brosnic. Or Hitler's former chef, Hans Krantz. Flayed alive. You want to talk about feelings? Do you *understand* the commitment someone has to have to take an order to skin someone alive? Vogel never does these things himself, he just gives the order, and he has such power that it's done." Pomeroy merely folded his arms. "Get me on a plane," I said. "Tomorrow."

After Pomeroy's wine was delivered and the waiter left us, he said, "We need you to stay for Monday's session." He took a sip of his wine and seemed unimpressed. "You may not have to testify, but we'd like you to be here. Just in case."

"Just in case of what?"

"In case we need you."

I gazed across the table, from Pomeroy to Giannopoulos. "What's going on?" When they didn't respond, I turned to Valeria and said, "*Che cosa?*"

Her eyes were contrite; she might have been my daughter and had broken some established rule, and then she looked at Pomeroy.

He unbuttoned his suit coat and settled himself in the booth. "Frank, if at the end of Monday you still want to go home, okay, we'll make the arrangements and you fly out Tuesday morning. Fair enough?"

"So I spend the entire weekend here in Berlin?"

"All the Wiener schnitzel you can eat," Pomeroy said.

I considered getting up, pushing back the curtain, and walking out. But it would be an empty, dramatic gesture. "Your strategy changed, how?"

Pomeroy raised his hand to his face and with a stubby forefinger tugged at the loose skin beneath his eye. "You're upset over today and I don't blame you. But I also don't think you want to leave things the way they are in that courtroom. Am I right?"

"I've been following this case in the news for years," I said. "You've tried to nail Vogel before and failed. What are the odds you'll get him this time?"

Pomeroy shrugged. "We don't get him this time, we try again." He placed his elbows on the table in an effort to look more optimistic. "Monday I think will be different. If not, home you go Tuesday." He glanced at Giannopoulos. "With the gratitude of your government."

"My government?" I said. "*My* government?"

"Absolutely." Giannopoulos nodded. "Go home and we never bother you again."

I picked up the salt shaker and held it in front of my mouth. "You hear that? James, you're on record now."

26.

Saturday afternoon Valeria was waiting outside my hotel room when I returned from the swimming pool. She carried a folded umbrella and was wearing a raincoat, jeans, and boots that went almost to her knees.

"You look more relaxed," I said. "I've always loved European women's love of boots."

"You look quite relaxed yourself," she said as I unlocked the door with my key card.

"The bathrobe is compliments of the hotel," I whispered. "I'm considering stealing it."

"Bored?"

"Why would you say that? I've gone swimming twice. I've talked to my wife on the phone twice. I watched one football match. If you're interested, Inter beat Lazio, two-nil."

"I thought you'd like to get out for a bit."

"Give me half a minute," I said, stepping into the bathroom. She went into the room and sat in the chair by the window, while I left the door slightly ajar as I dressed. I was about to ask where are we were going, but then realized she wouldn't give me a straight answer.

Her gray Audi seemed to move silently through the streets of Berlin, while Mozart's *Requiem* played from speakers all around us. "I'm surprised you're not playing Verdi," I said. "How did you know I love Mozart, too?" She only smiled, without taking her eyes off the road. "Your car isn't bugged?"

"I don't think so."

"Just us?" Still she wouldn't look at me. "Where are we going?"

"You had a tough day yesterday, so I want to take you someplace I think you'll like. Besides, I wanted you all to myself for a while."

"Giannopoulos will be jealous."

"He'll join us later."

"Pomeroy?"

She shook her head.

"I'm feeling better already." And she laughed.

When we were on the autobahn leaving the city, I said, "Did you know that I'm a distant relative of Giuseppe Verdi? And that when I was a boy, there was a fleeting moment when I had dreams of being the second great Verdi composer? But I proved to be a ham-fisted pianist and I had no gift for composition. In my teens I wasn't a bad midfielder, though. That was several lives ago. Then there was a war, and I was captured, brought to America, and it has gone on and on until right now, sitting in this car." I stared at her, but she wouldn't take her eyes off the road. "You can't tell me everything. I understand that."

She looked at me then, her eyes apologetic, even sad.

■　　■　　■

Soon we were driving through rolling farmland. Valeria shifted expertly through the curves in the narrow road, putting the car through a healthy and necessary exercise. After an hour we entered hill country, and the road climbed to a castle overlooking a vast plain. We toured the castle, reading about battles and sieges, some of which dated back to the twelfth century. Valeria talked about her family, how they had been Austrian until after World War I, when the borders were redrawn and Alto-Adige became part of Italy. She talked about the divided sense of loyalty in her family, how her grandfather fought for the partisans, while some of his brothers fought in Mussolini's army. The castle was magnificently eroded by time, and when we encountered steep cobblestoned paths, she would take my arm as if she was the one in need of assistance.

In the early evening, we drove into the village below the castle. Valeria knew of a *trattoria* there, run by a family from Tolentino that had emigrated north generations earlier, and I realized that this was the true purpose of our road trip. Giannopoulos was waiting for us at a table in back. Dinner lasted more than three hours, ending with Varnelli *mistrà*, a liqueur that is difficult to find outside the Le Marche region.

When we were finished, Valeria went to get the car, which was parked on a side street across the plaza. Giannopoulos was staring at his glass of *mistrà*. "It's popular in the region I come from," I said. "This is why Valeria brought me all the way out here, for this *digestivo*." Giannopoulos continued to stare at his glass. "If you can't take it straight," I said, "pour it in your coffee."

He did so, and then sipped his coffee. "At first I thought it would be like ouzo, but . . . it's better in the coffee. An acquired taste, eh?"

"The taste of home, yes." I watched him and he kept his eyes on his coffee cup, in case it might suddenly move. "You were busy earlier," I said.

He nodded.

"Something to do with the trial."

He shrugged.

"Pomeroy's change of strategy."

He took in a long breath, and then released it slowly. "We'll see if it works. You probably won't be needed to testify Monday and we'll get you on a plane Tuesday."

"Think they'll get Vogel this time?"

Giannopoulos picked up his cup and took a sip, and then another. "Yes, it's much better with the coffee," he said.

It was difficult leaving the restaurant, because I had to say goodbye to the entire family: the father and his son who cooked, the mother who had waited on us, and several girls who were daughters, nieces, and one who was married to the son and was pregnant with their first child. Hugs, kisses on both cheeks, all family for life now that we had dined at their table.

Outside it was snowing. Valeria's car was nowhere in the plaza waiting for us.

"That's strange," Giannopoulos said.

I pointed across the plaza toward the side street where she had parked. "How did you get here?" I asked.

"Taxi."

We crossed the plaza and entered the street. There were two young men standing by Valeria's car, and when they saw us they ran farther down the street.

It was too dark to see them clearly, other than that they both wore leather jackets and had wool caps pulled down tight on their skulls.

At first, I couldn't see Valeria, but then I realized that the driver's side door was open. We hurried around the back of the car and found her lying on the sidewalk. The snow was spattered with black strands of blood. Her face and clothes were covered with blood and she was breathing heavily through her mouth.

Above us an apartment window swung open and an old man said something in German, to which Valeria replied. She began to move, to get up off the sidewalk, and we helped her until she was sitting sideways in the driver's seat. "He called an ambulance," she said.

Leaning over, she vomited on the curb and her lovely boots. In the distance, we could hear the siren.

.   .   .

There was a small hospital in the next village. Valeria had a broken nose and a fractured cheekbone. Though Giannopoulos got us accommodations at an inn across the street, we both stayed in her hospital room until early morning, watching her sleep. A doctor, a woman who spoke heavily accented English, told us that there were no internal injuries. She helped translate when two police officers questioned us in the hallway. We could give no reason for the attack. The doctor said it might have been an attempted rape and that it was fortunate that we arrived when we did.

When we were alone in the hallway, I said to Giannopoulos, "It was a warning."

He didn't bother to reply.

Finally, we went across to our room at the inn, and as I lay in my bed, Giannopoulos was in the bathroom talking on his cell phone. I was certain he was talking to Pomeroy. I was just falling asleep when he came out of the bathroom.

"They're sending someone out from the embassy."

"It's a little late."

"Agreed. They probably won't go after you, because then Pomeroy could put you on the stand again, and wouldn't that be pretty. Still, to be safe they're sending two men to keep an eye on you, and to bring her back to Berlin when she's ready."

He sat on the other bed and stared straight ahead. His expression reminded me of when we were young men, sitting in a booth at Tony's Grill in Detroit—how he was so difficult to read at first, how he was utterly noncommittal yet driven. Still, there was something about him that I wanted to trust.

"What?" I said.

"When the guys arrive from the embassy, I need to go right back into Berlin. You stay here with her."

I slept for less than two hours. I don't know if Giannopoulos even lay down on his bed. When I woke up he was sitting in the reclining chair, staring out the window. As I got out of bed, he said, "They're here. One's down in the lobby and the other is outside her room. I'll drive their car to Berlin. They'll take you and Valeria in her car. I'll see you when you get back."

As he got up out of the chair, I said, "Years ago you asked me about an agent in northern Michigan."

He was backed by winter light, gray buildings, gray sky. "The one that disappeared."

"Yes, Roy Ferris. I don't know why, but being here in Berlin makes me want to tell you this. He was a rapist and we got caught in the middle of a long-running family feud. He shot Claire as she was running away in a cornfield."

"So what happened to him?"

"He's pig shit. That's all I'm telling you. He's pig shit."

Giannopoulos went to the door, but paused with his hand on the knob. "I'm sorry I brought you into this, Frank. I really am."

"I'm not."

He glanced over his shoulder at me as he opened the door. "Maybe after tomorrow it will have been worth it."

■   ■   ■

By that evening Valeria looked better. She was more alert and she was able to eat a little soup. She spoke with the two men from the embassy, Randolph and Gidge—they spoke rapidly in German, but I understood that she was demanding that they take her back to Berlin immediately. When the doctor visited that night there was a long discussion, everyone sounding angry and disgusted, but when the doctor finally stormed out of the room, Valeria attempted a smile, though clearly it was painful. "She will release me tomorrow morning," Valeria whispered to me, "because I can be such a pain in the ass."

Randolph and Gidge didn't appreciate the fact that she and I spoke Italian together, but we pretty much ignored them, and finally they went out into the hallway and sat on a bench there. Much of the time Valeria was on her cell phone, I presumed with people at the embassy, and once I was certain she was speaking in German to Pomeroy. Around ten o'clock she sent me back to my room at the inn—Randolph tagging along—where I collapsed into bed.

■   ■   ■

In the morning, Valeria was released from the hospital and we were driven back to Berlin. I had been wearing the same clothes since Saturday; though there was dried blood on Valeria's jeans, somehow she had obtained a clean blouse. "That doctor was so eager to get rid of me," she said, attempting a smile, "she was kind enough to give me one of her blouses."

The trial resumed at ten o'clock, and we arrived at the courthouse with only minutes to spare. We entered the courtroom and sat in the gallery directly behind Pomeroy's table. He spoke to Valeria for a moment, making a fuss about her injuries, primarily for the benefit of journalists who were gathering behind us. He looked at me and said, "I hope you're not too disappointed that we didn't send you home right away."

"I'm in no hurry to leave," I said. "If it will help, put me back on the stand."

Pomeroy seemed distracted, and I realized that he was one of those men who often thought three steps ahead of the moment. "We'll see," he said.

Vogel and his lawyers hadn't arrived yet and Pomeroy was clearly concerned; once he returned to his table to sort through papers with his assistant, he kept looking around toward the doors to the lobby.

Next to me on the bench, Valeria sat rigid yet weary. "Are you all right?" I asked. She only took my hand and kept staring toward the bench, though the judges hadn't yet arrived. Her face was terribly swollen, the skin beneath her eyes discolored, and black stitches were visible at one corner of her distended mouth.

When the doors at the back of the courtroom opened, the gallery stirred and we looked around—harsh sunlight reflected off the marble floor in the lobby, making it difficult to see as Vogel's wheelchair rolled slowly down the aisle. There was so much light behind him, he was just a dark silhouetted figure, seemingly larger than the frail old man I recalled from a few days earlier. The journalists in the gallery were reacting to something—I knew not what—and several stood up to take photographs.

Two guards swung the large double doors closed, cutting off the glare from the lobby. Valeria was staring at me now, and she gave my hand a squeeze before letting go, and then she took my arm, helping me as I struggled to get to my feet. I moved past her into the aisle and shuffled toward the wheelchair, causing the gallery suddenly to become silent.

"*Ciao, amico mio,*" he said, now an old man who seemed pinned by his own weight into the wheelchair. Yet the eyes were still the same, boyish and teasing.

"Adino?" I whispered.

I am not a man who cries easily, and certainly not in public, but somehow I was on my knees embracing Adino's thick shoulders, and we both wept while there was much jostling in the gallery as journalists tried to get a better view. "No one told me," I said. His warm jowl was pressed against my cheek, and he replied, "I told them I wouldn't come unless it would be a surprise—I wanted to see if you still had a strong heart." He laughed. "If not, then I could at least say farewell."

After perhaps a minute, hands took me by both arms—it was Giannopoulos—and I was helped to my feet, while Adino's wheelchair was rolled down the aisle to Pomeroy's table. Giannopoulos and I returned to the bench, and I sat between him and Valeria. She gave me a handkerchief, and it took me several minutes to calm myself.

When the doors to the lobby opened again, the gallery swelled with the sounds of murmuring and more jostling, and we stood up like everyone else. It was difficult to see at first, but slowly Vogel was wheeled down the aisle on a hospital gurney. There was something majestic about this entrance as he was accompanied by a medical staff of three, two men and a woman. The young woman, blonde and wearing a snug nurse's uniform, pushed a stainless steel cart upon which sat an electronic monitoring system that was connected to Vogel by wires. His head was propped up on pillows, and below the large sunglasses, his face was as grim as it had been during the last session in court.

Pomeroy turned to me and whispered, "This is an even better photo op than the tearful reunion between you two *paisans*."

"Had I known there was going to be a competition, Herr Pomeroy, I would have shown up in a coffin."

It took considerable time to get Vogel's gurney in place, and everyone in the courtroom settled. Finally, the judges came from a side door and took their seats on the bench, and this was followed by at least a half hour of haggling between the lawyers—to the point where it seemed that the session might not ever really begin. Eventually, though, Adino's name was called and he was wheeled up to where he was positioned in front of the witness stand.

He testified for nearly two hours, confirming everything I had said about Gerhardt and Ruup and Vogel's midnight tribunals. Medical records were introduced, all confirming that his Achilles tendons had been severed while he was a prisoner at Camp Au Train. Pomeroy led him through a series of questions that allowed him to describe in detail the night that he had been held down by several German soldiers while Vogel ordered that the tendons be cut. At this point Adino's voice broke, and he had to pause to control his sobs as he explained that my crime of treason was saving an infant from a house fire.

During cross-examination, Fraulein Bok was unable to undermine Adino's testimony. I came to realize that this had been Pomeroy's strategy, to put me on the stand first, knowing that Fraulein Bok would raise doubts about my testimony, all to be neutralized by Adino's appearance in court. He had not escaped the prison camp, and there were no questions about whether he was involved in the death of another prisoner. Upon Vogel's orders, Adino had been horrendously maimed, and then he was sent home; decades later, the result of those inflicted wounds were still evident in the courtroom, and Fraulein Bok could do nothing with this large, simple, honest man who for decades had been confined to a wheelchair.

Seemingly on cue, Vogel's medical staff became frantically active around his gurney, and soon the judges called for a recess so that he might be taken to the hospital.

■   ■   ■

We had lunch together before Adino was to fly back to Naples—the following day he was to attend a granddaughter's christening. He and I emptied our wallets, showing each other photographs of children, grandchildren, pets, a store showroom in Marquette, a butcher shop in Naples, each photo offered as further proof that what we had endured in Camp Au Train decades earlier had been rewarded. Adino could not eat much, a little soup, but he did have a glass of wine. He had learned a little English from his daughters when they were in school, and when we'd put our wallets away he asked Pomeroy, "The court will decide Vogel to be the guilty?"

Pomeroy seemed pleased with how Adino's testimony had gone, but he shrugged. "There's no knowing. It has taken years to get this far. It may take longer. But that stunt—rushing him out of the courtroom due to a medical 'emergency'—it's a sign that they fear things won't go their way."

After Valeria translated this for Adino, he shifted in his wheelchair and placed his hand on my wrist. In Italian, he said, "Did you see him there on that bed with all those wires? Do you wonder if he has suffered enough, that further punishment is no longer necessary?"

"I don't know, Adino." I glanced at Valeria's swollen face. Her eyes were welling up. "If you're asking if we've all suffered enough, I just don't know."

Adino looked down the table toward Pomeroy and Giannopoulos, and then said in English, "We have all suffered enough." He smiled then and whispered in Italian. When Pomeroy and Giannopoulos looked at me, I interpreted for them. "But I would have come here if it killed me."

Adino held out his glass and I poured him some more wine.

27.

returned home exhausted.

After Mary had her second child, a boy, Braun and I spent much of July down in East Lansing trying to help out. In August, Tony and his family drove in from Minneapolis for a visit. Labor Day morning I was eating a hardboiled egg at our kitchen sink when I collapsed from a heart attack. They put a stent in one blocked artery and I barely left the house for the next three months. In December we received a Christmas card from Giannopoulos. Inside the card he had placed a folded newspaper clipping from the *International Herald Tribune* about Heinrich Vogel, alias Horst Albrecht, receiving a life sentence in Germany.

After New Year's I began to feel stronger. For the most part I'd managed to keep my days remarkably uneventful and uniform. I just tried to keep my life pared down, wanting clarity and simplicity, not complication. Every afternoon, regardless of the weather, I walked our dog Gordie down to the beach. Sometimes on warm days Braun would accompany us as far as McCarty's Cove, where she would sit on one of the park benches overlooking the beach and read. Rarely was she interested in the walk up to Presque Isle. By spring I could maintain a steady pace from the cove to Presque Isle and back, about five miles. That year I sold my share of the store to Lloyd Wiegand.

. ■ ■

One afternoon in April, I was sitting at the kitchen counter while leftover lasagna heated in the oven. Braun was out doing errands. I was sorting through the mail—bills and advertisement fliers—when the phone rang.

When I answered, Giannopoulos said, "Frank, it's me."

"Where are you?"

"Florida."

I could tell from his voice that something was wrong. "What is it?"

"Klaus Stemple. I just learned that he's dead," Giannopoulos said. "I've kept up with him over the years, just as I have with you. After he left Detroit, he lived in Mexico for a number of years, but about ten years ago he moved to Tucson."

"And?"

"His daughter Juanita called me. She said he had been at his cabin up in the mountains somewhere outside Tucson and went missing for a day or so. The police finally found him. He'd been attacked by some animal—a mountain lion or something like that. He was really torn up. But when the police looked in his cabin they found signs of a struggle. Seems he'd been beaten first, then dragged outside. This girl, Juanita, called me from Mexico City, where her mother was from—Stemple had told her to go back there because she wasn't safe in Tucson."

"Anton Vogel."

"Over the years we've lost track of him," Giannopoulos said. "Once or twice there was some sign that he was in South America. During his father's trial, he may have gone to Europe, flying through Amsterdam."

"His father set him loose."

"I think so. I never told you—I'm not supposed to—but Stemple also came to Washington to testify against Vogel, but not to Germany."

"Any idea where Anton is now?"

"None."

"We'll never really be sure who killed JFK or what happened to Glenn Miller, and we can't keep track of Anton Vogel."

"Frank, I would get out of there."

"And go where? I don't have relatives in Mexico City, if even that's safe."

"There's no knowing how many passports he has—there's no sure way of finding him."

"Well, guess where he's headed. I was bait in Detroit. I'm still bait up here."

"You want to call the police?"

"Get serious."

"I can have an agent sent up there."

"It's a long way."

"Tell me what I can do."

Out the window, I could see the lake at the end of the street, raked by a gusting north wind. "I'll let you know," I said. "Thanks for the call."

. . .

I would meet people during my daily walk on the beach. There were the regulars: people who walked their dogs, and people who were drawn to the beach in any weather because they needed to be close to the lake. I came to look forward to seeing them, and we would talk as we strode along the sand—talk about anything: our families, sports, anything but politics. There is nothing more therapeutic than walking a beach, preferably with the wind at your back.

At McCarty's Cove, there is a stand of woods just above the beach. Gordie, who was always running ahead of me, loved to wander up into the woods, sniff around, and then sprint back down the beach to greet me. One afternoon, several days after Giannopoulos's call, I heard him barking. He'd gone out of sight up one of the paths. I went to the edge of the woods and called him, but he only kept barking. I looked back toward McCarty's Cove, where I could see, about a quarter mile away, Braun sitting on her bench, reading.

Gordie suddenly yelped and then I heard nothing. I went into the woods and followed the path. When I came to a small clearing, I found Gordie lying on the pine needle ground. He slowly got to his feet, and when he tried to walk he favored his right foreleg. I looked him over but couldn't determine what had happened. There were no bite marks, no blood, so I didn't think he'd gotten into a scrap with another dog. I looked around but saw no one.

I was having difficulty breathing. Slowly, I walked him back down to the beach. The bench in the cove was empty. Sometimes, if she were cold, Braun would go back to the house before Gordie and I returned. It took a long time to get him home. As we went along the beach, I kept looking back toward the woods where I had found him. When we finally got to the house I was relieved to find Braun at the stove making hot chocolate.

"I felt chilled suddenly," she said, without looking away from the stove.

"Wonder if you're coming down with something," I said as I took off my coat.

"No. Just the change of the season."

As I had, Braun looked Gordie over carefully. He seemed all right, though tired, and he curled up on his blanket by the back door. She returned to the stove and I sat at the kitchen table. There was only the sound of the whisk, which she swirled in the bottom of the sauce pan, a light metal-upon-metal sound that for some reason I have always loved.

"Why don't you go away for a bit?" I said. The whisk continued its slow work. "Someplace warm." Braun's arm stopped moving but she didn't look away from the stove. "Maybe San Diego? Your cousin's always asking you out. You haven't seen Marta in what?"

"Three years." The whisk resumed its slow, circular revolutions. "I went out at Christmas." She turned off the stove. "Want a cup?"

"Sure."

She poured the hot chocolate into two mugs, added some whipped cream, and sat across from me at the table. I gazed out the window at the backyard, where patches of snow still lay beneath the trees. She was watching me now. "You'd go with me, to San Diego?"

"I'll stay put." I could feel the heat coming up from the mug of hot chocolate. "I'll look after Gordie here."

"You don't really care for Roger."

I shrugged. "We don't have much to talk about, and I don't play golf. But you and Marta—you should see each other more."

All the years together, we'd been honest with each other, but now I was lying. Not outright, but I wasn't telling her the real reason I thought she should leave Marquette. It was a lie nonetheless. She picked up her mug and blew on the steam rising from the whipped cream. "I'll give it some thought."

■   ■   ■

Seldom did Braun decide things immediately anymore. Now in her fifties, she'd curbed her youthful impetuosity, but after several days she decided to go to San Diego, not because she wanted to, really, but because she couldn't find any good reason not to go. She would be gone twelve days, and if she had any regrets about the trip, they evaporated soon after she arrived in the California sunshine.

Roger, it turned out, was away on business, and Marta was teaching Braun how to make fish tacos and mix the perfect margarita. After telling me this on the phone—while drinking her second perfect margarita—I sat at the kitchen table and finished cleaning my Colt Python, which I'd bought years ago.

I didn't have a plan. I was more concerned with the possibility that Anton Vogel wouldn't show up before Braun returned from San Diego. Giannopoulos had called again, twice. Both times he'd asked if I wanted him to send someone up to Marquette. I declined. We didn't know for certain that Anton would come here, I said, and if he did, we had no idea when he would do so. After I explained that I was alone at home for a dozen days, there was silence on the line, until he said, "Frank, you're too old to be bait."

I didn't change my daily routine. Gordie and I walked the beach several times a day. Sometimes I felt up to cooking for myself, but other nights I'd go out to eat. It seemed strange to sit alone in a booth and order dinner for one—even stranger with the weight of a revolver beneath my jacket.

About a week after Braun had left, I brought Chinese food in just before the Tigers game started. I sat in the living room, eating off of a tray, with the television sound low, when I heard a noise outside. There was a deck off the back of the house, and it was not uncommon, particularly after the long winters, for a branch to snap off one of the pines that loomed over the yard and land on the deck, wood knocking on wood.

But it could also have been footsteps.

Gordie began growling at the back door.

I went into the kitchen and took my Colt from its holster, which hung on the hook next to my spring jacket. After shutting off the kitchen light, I stood at the back door. Gordie quieted down and we remained there, listening. Finally, I eased aside the curtain over the door window, switched on the outside light, but saw nothing unusual in the yard. I opened the door, then the storm door, and we stepped out onto the deck. It was cold, and there was a gusting east wind off the lake. I could hear the waves pounding the beach on the other side of Lakeshore Boulevard. Slowly, Gordie walked out into the yard and stood still. Looking to my left, I saw that one of the wooden deck chairs had been knocked over. I folded it up, leaned it against the wall, and then took one more look around the yard before calling Gordie and going back into the house.

The Tigers had just scored. I sat down in the living room and watched the replay, Trammell's line drive into the left-field bleachers.

■   ■   ■

The next day I was coming out of the post office when I noticed a car parked down Washington Street, almost to the *Mining Journal* building on the corner. I'm not sure why it caught my attention. The afternoon was chilly and damp, spitting sleet, and I could see vapor pouring out of the exhaust pipe. Nothing unusual there: in the U.P. people often leave their vehicles running while parked, particularly in cold weather. But there was someone—a man—sitting behind the wheel. I used to be able to identify almost every car on the road, but now they're imported from Japan and Korea and Mexico, and they look pretty much alike. It was blue, a blue sedan. The man, though, caught my attention. From such a distance, I couldn't determine any distinguishing features; couldn't tell his age. He wore a wool hat with a narrow brim—something you might see in Scotland or Ireland, but seldom in northern Michigan. There was nothing really remarkable about him except that he didn't move while I stared in his direction. He remained absolutely still, making himself harder to see.

I walked in the other direction, crossed at the corner of Third and Washington, and got into my built-in-the-USA Jeep Wrangler. I drove through the intersection, and then past the blue sedan. The man was still sitting behind the wheel. I didn't turn my head to get a good look at him. I only had the sense that he was middle-aged. And that he still didn't move.

I continued on down Washington Street, heading west, away from Lake Superior. After a few blocks, I turned right and went up the hill to Hewitt, which would take me into the East Side. When I looked in the rearview mirror I saw the blue Ford behind me, about half a block distant.

I decided not to go home.

■   ■   ■

I drove out of town, going south, and the blue sedan remained a few cars behind me. I took Route 28 east along the shore of Lake Superior, and after about thirty miles turned south at Au Train Bay. Once or twice a year I made the drive out there, always on my own. This time there was no question; the blue sedan cruised behind me, and in the rearview mirror I could tell that it was Anton. His face was severe, gaunt, and bunched up, like a fist. Like his father's face.

We rounded Au Train Lake and climbed into the hills to the east. I was returning to these woods again. I had driven through here in a U.S. Army jeep with a white star in a circle on the hood, and now I was in a Jeep Wrangler. I was driven out of these woods by Vogel's death sentence, but truly, I'd never really left, and now I was being chased into the hills by his son Anton.

When I turned off the paved road, the blue sedan followed me up the dirt lane that became a two-track with tall, dead grass in the middle. The first sign of the camp was a series of weathered posts that ran off into the trees. Farther on, there were the remnants of a guard tower. Other than that, what had been Camp Au Train had been reclaimed by the forest.

When I stopped, the blue sedan pulled up behind me. I sat there, looking at the rearview mirror. Anton didn't move. As I got out of my Jeep, I reached inside my jacket and pulled the Colt from its holster. I walked toward the sedan, holding the gun at my side where he could see it. Slowly, he got out of the car and closed the door. He faced me, his hands empty.

"It's remarkable," I said, "how much you have come to resemble your father, when he was here at Camp Au Train."

His eyes scanned the woods about us. "So this is it." There was something about his voice; it was devoid of any accent, which was no surprise, but there was an uncertainty, perhaps even curiosity that was baffling. "This is all that's left?"

"And me."

He looked at the gun in my hand. "I am not armed."

"No gun? No knife?"

"No weapon."

"What did you plan to use, your bare hands? Is that what you used in Arizona?"

He shook his head.

"Then what is my punishment to be? I'm sure your father told you; he gave you specific orders. If you don't stab my heart and hands or flay me alive, what?"

"No."

"What then?" He only looked at me. "I'm not putting this away."

"I understand," he said. "I wouldn't, if I were you."

He looked about at the woods again. "He said that this was the most difficult command he'd ever had, because of the inactivity. Discipline was difficult to maintain when soldiers weren't able to fight. He said it was essential to remind them that there was an enemy."

"So he created one," I said. "But I wasn't the enemy. The others—Agostino, and Germans named Gerhardt and Ruup—they weren't either. We were all just men, living here in the woods, removed from a war that our side was bound to lose. He was unable to accept that."

"No, my father never accepted defeat."

"The war was over for us, and we were all doing our best to survive," I said. "So, what are you going to do?"

"I would like a walk. I would like to see what's left of this place."

■   ■   ■

As we walked, I remained a couple of steps behind him, to his left. This, I had never imagined. He seemed willing to allow me to take control. I was the one with a gun. I told him when to stop, when to turn as I pointed out where things had been: our barracks, the mess hall, the latrine. For the most part it was all just woods again. Our feet shuffled through a thick layer of soggy leaves that gave off a rich smell that I have always associated with my time in the camp. Upon careful inspection, there were certain signs. I pointed out a straight ridge in the dingy snow, which was the foundation of one of the barracks. We found another guard tower, this one having toppled into a tree so that the boards were entangled in the branches.

We came to an open area where there were smaller trees and bushes. "This was the football pitch," I said. "We cleared and leveled it with rakes and shovels. It was our field."

As we looked out at the overgrown pitch, Anton said, "Mind if I have a cigarette?" He held his arms out from his sides, turning his empty palms toward me.

"All right."

He reached inside his coat and took out a pack of cigarettes and a book of matches. After lighting a cigarette, he offered me the pack.

"I quit," I said. "My lungs are bad enough since Detroit. I don't remember it too well. All of a sudden I was shot and lying on the ground, drowning in my own blood. What did I do?"

Anton put the pack and matches away. "Nothing. But I knew what you planned to do. We both knew why you were there," he said, taking a deep drag on his cigarette and exhaling. "We thought you were dead."

"I was dead. In the hospital, my heart stopped and the doctors revived me."

He nodded. "My father always believed you were different from the others."

"How so?"

"I'm not sure. I guess he thought, more than the others, you were brave."

"No, Adino was brave."

"Father admired you, but you were wrong. Too independent to follow orders. And what you did—running away—made his job in the camp almost impossible." He glanced at me. "You don't know what happened after you escaped from here?"

"No."

"They rioted," he said. "The men revolted against my father's command. It was . . ."

"A revolution."

"They shipped some men to other camps, and soon after that the war ended. And this place. My father has been bitter all these years." Anton studied the field. "But no one remembers now. Except you."

"And for that he wants me punished."

Anton began walking across what had once been the soccer pitch. I followed, and we worked our way through the smaller trees, around dense patches of brush; some of them now produced good blueberries in the summer. He walked with his hands clasped behind his back, his head lowered so that he could stare at the ground before his feet—the posture of contemplation; the posture of a prisoner, of one who is not free. My right hand, which held the gun, was cold, so I stuck it in the outer pocket of my jacket.

"He had his orders," he said.

"After the war, they were all he had."

"And I had mine."

"You were his son, an obedient son. I met your mother, years ago. She was devastated when you were taken from her." When he glanced at me, I said, "You do know who my second wife is?"

"Yes. My half sister."

"This is largely due to the way you were raised. You were bred for this. That's not the same as belief, is it?" When he didn't respond, I said, "So now. Doubts?"

"There's a phrase they use here in the newspapers when describing some murders. They say it was perpetrated by a 'ruthless killer.' They're saying that the murderer—my father always insisted on the word executioner—has no thoughts, no emotions. One just performs the act. Not even instinctual, like an animal bred to protect or kill to survive. More like one of these robots you read about now, these machines that are programmed to perform specific functions."

"So you discovered that you weren't like that. When?"

"A while ago."

"Your father—"

"He was upset, at first. It was his work. With him, it was a question of honor. He couldn't perform his duties without me. I was a disgrace—at first."

We had reached the south end of the pitch and were facing a distinct line of taller trees, many of them pines, with stands of white birch among them. There was a rock at this end of the field, just as before, and I sat on it.

"During halftime we'd retreat to this end of the pitch, and I'd often sit here while we discussed strategy. I hated being here, but I've always been thankful for those games. You have no idea what they meant to us." I looked at Anton, who was gazing down the field. "You said 'at first.' Something changed? You changed, and then your father?"

"He became increasingly philosophical with the years. First there was just work, but then there was greater consideration of the significance of it. There's another term you hear in America: that someone is *conflicted*. My father became conflicted. I became conflicted."

"I find that hard to believe, about your father. Doubt is good, but it's not enough."

"He had doubts." Though Anton spoke quietly, he might have been speaking to that stretch of open land, or even to imaginary people who occupied it. "One does not simply get up one morning and abandon one's beliefs. There is great torment. My father and I discussed this often. But we remained obedient. We wanted to be honorable. Perhaps you understand this: it was a question of honor. My father concluded that if anyone would, it would be you."

"So you continued to carry out your orders." He didn't answer, which I took as confirmation. "The latest being Klaus Stemple, down in Arizona."

"My father died six months ago. While he was in prison we could exchange coded letters through an intermediary. He and I discussed what I should do and decided that I must carry out my work—his work. Until now. And here we disagreed."

The revolver was still in my hand and for a moment I considered taking it out of my pocket. But I was quite certain by then that Anton wasn't armed. If I was wrong, I could still fire the gun through the jacket. My anxiety wasn't out of fear of him, what he might do; it was because there was something else going on here, something entirely unexpected—coupled with the fact that I was back in the Au

Train woods—and all of this made me feel weak and frail. I had been so young and strong here, clearing the forest every day, playing football, and eventually feeling such overwhelming desire for Chiara. And now I was an old man.

"How?" I asked. "How did you and your father disagree?"

"The day before he died, he got a message out from his prison cell. He sent word that I should contact you, tell you that you were free, that your conviction and sentence had been commuted. And he encouraged me, no he *ordered* me—I was still the obedient son—to leave America for good. We have been very adept at changing identities, as you have, and he said I should return to Europe and start a new life. He was never fond of America, always missed Europe."

"You would be pursued by the authorities. And possibly by the Nazis."

"Over the years, arrangements have been made, documents procured, funds put aside, which would enable us to 'disappear.' He wanted me to disappear. I should be in Eastern Europe now."

"Which is where your father's career started, in Romania, at the beginning of the war. But you aren't there. You're here. You came of your own volition."

Anton, as he had been in the car, was very still, very economical with his movements—a consummate, practiced stillness that seemed potentially threatening. "I guess you could say that my decision to come up here is a sign of my own liberation." There was, for a moment, the faintest smile. "The irony is that my intention was to ask you to take me out here, to the camp."

"I simply didn't know where else to go."

"No." His eyes became bright, almost happy. "Somehow, instinctively, you knew, you understood what was necessary. You led me back here, to this place I'd heard about my entire life. You knew that I wanted to see it, to witness it myself. Really, my father spoke of it so often that I feel as though I've been here before."

"You remind me so much of him. And now that we are . . . here?"

"I can die."

I couldn't look at him, so I stared at the trees beyond the far end of the pitch. "No."

"It's the only way. Don't you see?"

I got up off the rock. "No."

"You have that gun. You have given thought to this, what you might have to do."

"That was before I met you, before we talked. That was a matter of survival."

"It isn't any different now."

"Now, it would be murder."

"You'd be doing me an honor."

"We have very different notions of honor." I began walking back across the field, using my arms to push branches aside, walking so fast that I was having difficulty breathing. I could hear Anton behind me, crashing through the brush behind me.

■　　■　　■

It began to snow. Big spring flakes, heavy enough that I could hear them pelting the leaves on the ground. When Anton caught up he walked beside me, to my left. We might have been two old friends strolling through the woods.

"I am not a murderer," I said. "Or an executioner, if you prefer."

"You are a soldier. You have a responsibility."

"To what—all those people you killed?"

"Well, then to your friend, Adino."

When the cars were in sight I stopped, nearly out of breath. I placed one hand on the trunk of a maple for support. "I will take you to the police, if you want. That's what I should do."

"I am not a common criminal."

"True." I straightened up and began walking again, slowly. "You're much worse."

"That would not be acceptable. It would not be honorable," he said.

"Stop talking about honor. You've committed crimes."

"All right." He made a sarcastic snort. "But how will you turn me in? Shoot me?"

"I could put a bullet in your foot. Consider it compensation for what your father did to Adino. Your father said he believed in justice? So do I."

"You won't shoot me."

"You shot me, years ago."

"It's not the same, not now." He shook his head and held his hands out away from his sides. "Unarmed."

"Anywhere else, no," I said. "But out in these woods, everything's different."

"You'd really turn me in?"

"You shouldn't have come up here, Anton. No matter what your father told you, you can't understand this place."

"These woods, what don't I understand?"

"From the moment I arrived up here," I said, "there was something about the land, the nature of the forest, which made me feel invisible. I wasn't who I had been, who I thought I was meant to be, and this seemed like a slow, laborious death, until years later I came to realize that the only way to survive was to lose who I was, entirely. But survival isn't enough. You don't have one life, but many lives to live. With luck, you will live them all."

"We all have just one life."

"I said, you don't understand. All these years you and I, and your father, we've been forced to live different lives, different names, different occupations, so many residences—everything changed to conceal who and what we really were. Tell me this didn't happen to you often. A man looks at you and you feel he's seeing something—or perhaps someone—very different from who you really are."

"To live incognito," he said, nodding. "It's worse when a woman looks at you like that."

"Yes," I said. "I never felt this way before I was brought to the United States, years ago. Man or woman, there's a hard assessment in the eyes. Something about the set of the mouth that makes me begin to have doubts—doubts about myself, about who I am, who I am pretending to be, what I claim to have done or not done. This happened while I was here at Camp Au Train, and it was more frequent when I became Frank Green in Detroit. Since I returned to the Upper Peninsula, it's happened less as the years have gone by. To most people, I'm just an elderly man, with a younger wife and children, who runs a local business. But still occasionally someone will look at me in a way that suggests that I'm lying, as though everything I had said—everything I had ever claimed to have done—was a complete fabrication."

He stopped walking, so I did as well, and facing him I began to draw the gun out of my jacket. I felt helpless. My hand, my arm, they were separate from the rest of me. "And you had to fight the urge to tell them that you were guilty," Anton said.

"That's right," I said. "Perhaps you can begin to understand?"

Anton looked beyond me, his eyes perplexed—no, wary.

And then I heard it: footsteps rustling the leaves.

I looked around. I knew I shouldn't turn my back on Anton, but I couldn't help it. The snow was heavier now, heavy wet flakes falling straight down. There was a pointillist quality to the air, to the woods. Beyond the cars, something was moving among the trees, but I couldn't see what it was—all was browns and grays and blacks behind the veil of falling snow. A deer, I thought. And I had a sudden recollection of cleaning deer with Adino, digging machine-gun bullets out of their carcasses. The footsteps came closer and I saw movement beyond Anton's sedan. I pushed the revolver deep into my jacket pocket.

Then there was silence, except for the sound of snow on the leaves. I looked back at Anton just as his expression changed from alert curiosity to awe. His shoulders collapsed almost imperceptibly, making him smaller, and he was perfectly still.

I turned, and thirty yards down the path, a wolf emerged from the trees, moving toward us, its gait ponderous and steady. A wolf—it was far too big for a coyote. I couldn't tell whether it was aware of us, though I couldn't imagine that it wasn't. It paused next to the Ford and cautiously sniffed the rear tire, until its yellow eyes found me. I eased my forefinger around the trigger of the gun in my pocket. There was a lack of expression on the wolf's face, making it impossible to guess at how he was reacting to the sight of us—the cars, two men, things not of these woods. Those eyes possessed a sense of comprehension that I couldn't fathom. Perhaps this wolf had never seen human beings before, or at least at such close range. It seemed neither alarmed nor impressed.

Nor was the wolf afraid. It was indifferent. No longer concerned with the car, it shook itself, causing the snow lining its back to be flung out into the air, pelting the leaves. And then it began to walk, not toward us, but off the path at an angle, a sauntering yet heavy stride, and it never again looked in our direction. I was disappointed. I wanted to speak to the wolf, to ask it to wait, to stay a bit longer. Foolishly, I thought that if I did say something, it would understand. But I realized that even if it could understand me, I couldn't put my thoughts and feelings into words. The wolf left the path and disappeared into the trees. I listened to the diminishing sound of its paws, until I could only hear the snow rattling on dead leaves.

I had been holding my breath. I began to inhale desperately and my heart was racing so that it was punching against my ribcage. When I turned around, unsteadily, because along with my respiration my balance seemed to have been affected, Anton was no longer standing behind me. He was gone. Gone, running through the woods, as I had done years ago, desperate to escape. I'd never see him again, never know if he got out, if he made it to Eastern Europe, or wherever he would assume another identity, another life, and I wished him luck, whispering

Buona fortuna. I went to the sedan, opened the door, and found that he'd left the keys in the ignition. I put them in the coat pocket that wasn't weighed down with the gun.

As I walked back to my Jeep, the snow melting in my hair sent cold water down my face, and my skin felt washed clean. Looking about the forest, I knew the wolf was still there, would always be there, but that I'd never live to see it again. I was, for the first time, utterly free, surrounded by these woods, my prison, my salvation.